Advance Praise for
Jessica Harmon Has Stepped Away

"A rich, engrossing portrait of a mother and daughter fencing their way toward a truce."
—Kirkus Reviews

"The only thing better than a road trip novel is a literary, mother-daughter road trip with a side of romance. I loved this story of an aspiring writer and her larger-than-life poet mother, their toxic relationship and the unexpected journey that changes everything for both of them."
—Annabel Monaghan, bestselling author of *Summer Romance*

"In her latest, *Jessica Harmon Has Stepped Away*, Gentin explores the complicated intersection of family secrets across the past and present, and the ways in which mothers and daughters might deceive one another—and themselves. Told with heart, wit, nuance, and humor, this one will have you rooting for Jessica as she steps away, seeking bravely to find the truth, and the strength she'll need in order to face it."
—Allison Pataki, *New York Times* bestselling author of *Finding Margaret Fuller*

"*Jessica Harmon Has Stepped Away* is an honest and absorbing exploration of mothers and daughters. Spanning elite literary circles, long-held secrets, and eventual tragedy, Gentin brilliantly captures the pain and longing of familial abandonment, the path to acceptance, and the people we should know best, but never fully do. Poignant and unputdownable."
—Rochelle B. Weinstein, bestselling author of *This is Not How it Ends*

"*Jessica Harmon Has Stepped Away* is a smart, compelling, genre-blend—a mother-daughter road trip, a coming-of-age story, and a literary satire. Kudos to Reyna Marder Gentin!"
—Karen Dukess, author of *The Last Book Party* and *Welcome to Murder Week*

JESSICA HARMON HAS STEPPED AWAY

REYNA MARDER GENTIN

JESSICA HARMON HAS STEPPED AWAY
Copyright © 2025 by Reyna Marder Gentin
SC ISBN: 9781645386209
JESSICA HARMON HAS STEPPED AWAY
By Reyna Marder Gentin

Cover design by Dana Breunig
Interior design by Dionna Hayden

Published by Ten16 Press, an imprint of Orange Hat Publishing

For information, please contact:
www.orangehatpublishing.com
Wauwatosa, WI

This book is a work of fiction. Names, characters, places and incidents
are the product of the author's imagination or are used fictitiously.

*For my mother, who loved her daughters fiercely
and with a full heart.*

"But behind all your stories is your mother's story, for hers is where yours begins."

–Mitch Albom, *For One More Day*

CHAPTER ONE

I draped myself over the side of the unmade bed and slid my hands across the cool hardwood floor, feeling for my bra.

When I looked up, Tyler was leaning against the doorjamb. Beaming at me.

I sprang up and pulled the duvet over myself. "What's with that face?"

He raised his hands in mock surrender and let his grin go full on. "I apologize for being happy to see my beautiful girlfriend in the morning."

Tyler's smile was so disarming it could charm the pants off the most curmudgeonly, yours truly included, and he knew it. Despite myself, I felt my grouchiness come down a notch. Still, the fact that I was at his place at seven in the morning on a Tuesday, and topless at that, violated my rule: staying over on the weekend was fine, but not on a weekday. Yet here I was again, and it happened more often than I cared to admit. Rules are meant to be broken—especially absurd, self-imposed ones—but I was annoyed with myself.

My lame excuse for crashing at Tyler's place was that he lived in Greenwich Village, a twenty-one-minute walk to my office in Union Square and way closer than my place in Astoria. Sometimes it was too tempting to stay with him and avoid an hour on the subway during the morning rush. But we both knew it wasn't about the commute.

We'd been together for nearly a year, and Tyler was the

most decent, generous guy I'd ever been with—the kind who'd move his whole schedule around to sit in the waiting room at the ophthalmologist's office for an hour while I had my eyes dilated to make sure I was okay and then escort me home. He had seemingly endless patience for what he fondly called my neuroses (more of my idiosyncratic rules) and a sense of humor that smoothed over my rough patches. I could name at least ten of my single girlfriends who would have leapt at the chance to be with Tyler. But sleeping at his apartment in the middle of the week sent the wrong message about where the relationship was going. As much as a part of me wanted to let myself fall head over heels and start stockpiling bridal magazines, I was wound too tight for that. I'd been straight with Tyler from the start about my ability to commit—I couldn't—but I knew he held out hope.

"You can smile all you want, you lunatic, but now I have to go to work in the same clothes I wore yesterday and hear about it from Clark all day. Why didn't you at least wake me up early so I could go home and change?"

Tyler plopped down on the bed. He wrapped his arms around my waist and pulled me close. "And miss this tantrum? Not on your life. And you should wear that same shirt every day. It brings out the color of your eyes." His body gave off a scent that was tingly and comforting like hot apple cider on a cool September day, like the one that stretched out before me, and I leaned into him.

"This shirt is red."

"So it is. You know, Jessica," he whispered in my ear, "it wouldn't be a huge statement if you left a spare set of clothes here."

It was the sort of comment Tyler had made a bunch of

times over the past several months. One day he'd gone further and flat out asked me to move in. And his offer hadn't followed on the heels of a night of unrestrained passion either. To the contrary, he asked me to live with him after several hours patiently helping me sort out my renewal lease with my super-shifty landlord.

"Why don't we rip up this contract and you, your knock-off Tiffany lamp, and your Ficus tree can move in with me?" He hadn't been joking; those were my most adult possessions. I was still living like a student, camouflaging my Ikea futon with pillows from Target, my books in milk crates that my best friend Penny and I had dragged up the four flights of stairs together when we became roommates after high school. Now, Penny and I were both thirty, and she was married with two little kids, living on the Upper East Side. She'd happily ceded her claim to half of the crappy furnishings to me, and I was camped out in our one-bedroom rental in Queens. With the occasional sleepover at Tyler's.

I pulled away. "You know I can't do that." The thought of intentionally leaving underwear at Tyler's apartment made me hyperventilate. Cohabitation was a non-starter.

I hurried away from Tyler's brownstone on Christopher Street toward W. 9th Street, past the stores starting to open, past the Stonewall Inn, barely registering the fresh morning air as the city came alive for another day. I liked to get to the office ahead of Larry, my boss, to settle in before he started pushing my buttons. I took the ramshackle elevator to the fifth floor, unlocked the door, and made my way to what passed for the

3

kitchen. Throwing my dollar into the top drawer, I popped a Green Mountain Nantucket Blend pod into the Keurig just as Clark sidled into the room, frantically patting his pants and shirt pockets.

"It's unbelievable Larry makes us pay for our coffee," Clark said. "What a cheap bastard."

"Looks like you can't afford any today." This was an exchange we had easily as often as I inadvertently slept at Tyler's. I always ended up sponsoring Clark's caffeine consumption, but it seemed important to give him a little bit of a hard time about it. I watched my limited finances closely, but who walks around without a dollar to his name?

"I swear, if you spot me today, I won't hit you up again."

I did my best Larry imitation, drawing out the words, nasal and whiny and vintage Brooklyn. "You know what the boss says: it's pay to play."

Clark snorted, wagging his finger at me. "Pay to play with a *conscience*."

It was, indeed, the unofficial motto at Canyon Publishing, a semi-selective small press where aspiring writers who hadn't been picked up by a literary agent or a traditional house forked over good money to have their books produced and avoid whatever lingering stigma still attached to self-publishing. It was a perfectly legitimate business, and the quality of some of the work that Canyon chose to publish was on par with what came out of the big houses. Some authors won awards, and the books were reviewed by reputable magazines and bloggers. Larry edited the most promising manuscripts himself.

Most of the submissions were something else entirely, ranging from earnest but poorly written all the way to drivel.

The would-be writers were unknowns with a glimmer of talent or hacks who had a connection to Larry, or, sometimes, a mixture of both. The way Larry explained it, the fees from publishing the subpar books subsidized getting the worthwhile ones out into the world. And everyone was happy in the end.

What made Canyon different from other similar outfits was Larry's genuine commitment to ensuring that all the books he published, even the amateurish ones, were not embarrassing. Despite his tendency to speak in monosyllables, Larry was an intelligent guy with a passion for literature, and he could only sink so low. The old vanity press model relied on writers who wanted to see their books in print regardless of their quality, but the industry had changed. With self-publishing now so affordable and so painless, the people who turned to Canyon were willing to pay to give their books respectability.

Which is where Larry's motto, "pay to play with a conscience," and Clark and I, came in. Our job was to give the second-rate manuscripts the bare minimum of TLC so Larry could live with himself. We sharpened plots, polished settings, and tweaked character arcs. We eliminated clichés, threw in the occasional metaphor, and spiced up the language. We added commas and subtracted commas, rescued dangling participles, and repaired split infinitives. The work wasn't as collaborative or creative as real editing, and it was sometimes downright painful, but I tried to convince myself I was doing something good for these would-be writers. It was our assignment to shepherd the manuscripts through the editing process so that they stood the best chance of reaching the heart of some reader, somewhere, however hapless.

I stuck my nose into the milk carton and sniffed—only three days past the "use by" date, not too bad—and poured some into my coffee. As I turned to go back to my desk, Clark stepped in front of me, blocking the door.

"Whoa, there. Wearing the same clothes as yesterday, I see."

I shrugged. "Why mess with what's working?"

Clark raised his eyebrows up and down in a decent Groucho Marx imitation. "Don't try to pull that on me, sister. Someone slept over at Tyler's for some unpremeditated weekday nookie!" Under any definition, Clark's comment qualified as sexual harassment or at a minimum created a hostile work environment. Except we were friends, and I knew he was teasing. Besides, I appreciated his use of the term "nookie."

I shoved him out of the way, which was no easy task given our size differential. "You spend way too much time worrying about where I sleep. Move. My coffee's getting cold."

Clark leaned back against the counter. "Why don't you marry the poor guy already? He's crazy about you. Can I bring a guest to the wedding? Maybe Sven. And don't seat me too close to the band."

"Sven hasn't agreed to go on a second date with you. And who said I was inviting you to any wedding?"

"What? We spend eight hours a day sitting six inches apart in a stultifying dead-end job. How could you exclude me from your big day? Besides, you've got money—it'll be a classy affair. I'm thinking shrimp scampi to start, braised short ribs with leeks over couscous for the main, and something decadent and chocolatey to finish. And raspberries. And champagne." Clark closed his eyes and licked his lips.

"When was the last time you ate a decent meal? And we've talked about this. I can't marry Tyler. I'm not the marrying sort. Thank God he hasn't asked." I took another dollar from my wallet and handed Clark a coffee pod. He swapped it out for a different flavor, plunking it into the machine.

"Thanks. And tell me again why you can't get married? Oh my god. I figured it out. You're not human; you're a carnivorous plant. Like in that Broadway show—what was her name?"

"Why would you think I have money?"

Clark looked down and spoke to his size twelve loafers. "I just meant, you know, since your mother is Cynthia Harmon—"

Ah. Clark had connected the dots and revealed a dollar sign linking me and my famous mother. I understood his thought process, but he couldn't have been more off base.

My mother, Cynthia Harmon, hit the trifecta of talent, sex appeal, and money, and she exploited it all. Her wealth was inherited (her father had made a killing in the burgeoning auto industry in the 1930s) and allowed her to live well beyond the means of the very prominent poet and college professor she was. In 1979, at the age of twenty-seven, Cynthia won the prestigious Yale Series of Younger Poets Prize and the publication of her debut collection, *When It Rains*, gaining her entrée (that, and the aforementioned money and sex appeal) into the homes, studios, and occasionally the beds of a who's who list of writers, painters, musicians, and actors. A *New York Post* photo from 1986, a few years before I was born, featured a glamorous Cynthia, all legs in a white cashmere pantsuit, exiting the Whitney Museum on the arm of Philip Roth, twenty years her senior and in-between wives. A steady output of published poetry in the decades that followed earned Cynthia a devoted, if self-selecting, fan base. Now, close to seventy, my mother still moved effortlessly among a wide circle of intellectuals, academics, artists, and the well-to-do, ensuring she stayed in the limelight and in the know.

Clark was hardly the first to leap to the conclusion that if my mother was rich, I must be too. It was a laughable proposition. Cynthia didn't like to share. Although it was theoretically possible that at some point I, her only child, would inherit her wealth if she didn't endow a chair or a literary award to perpetuate her legacy, she had no plans to kick off any time soon. Anyway, I'd decided long ago to earn my own way or go broke trying.

I was so lost in thought that Clark's voice startled me. "What are you holding out for? Prince Charming must have plenty of other options."

"You sound like my mother." Except that wasn't true. That would require Cynthia to take a normal maternal interest in my personal life, which she rarely did, despite my efforts to keep her in the loop. Clark didn't need to know any of that. We weren't *that* good friends.

I left him in the kitchen pondering the state of my love life and my bank account and wandered over to my side of the cubicle. As I did every morning, I silently thanked Larry for my ergonomic chair, his one concession to the fact that I sat on my butt all day, Monday to Friday. At least I wouldn't be stooped over like an old woman.

I pulled up the manuscript I'd been editing. A cyberpunk thriller entitled *Morbid Automagic*, it was written by a precocious college student named Michael who called himself Meteor and who had literary delusions of grandeur plus a daddy who played golf with Larry. I read a few sentences and then typed "what does this mean?" in the margin in response to his casual use of the term "wonking turbocharger." I leaned into the computer monitor as though getting closer would make the story make more sense to me, but all it did was compromise the efficacy of my wonderful chair.

I was trying to parse another of Meteor's more opaque sentences when Clark reached his arm over the cheap plastic divider between our cubicles and waved his cell so close to my face I had to lean back to avoid being smacked in the nose.

"Were you planning on keeping this a secret, Jessica?"

I swatted his arm away. "Jesus, Clark. You almost decapitated me."

He walked around to my side of the cube, reading aloud from his phone in what I took to be his dramatic stage voice.

"We are thrilled to announce that the Bollingen Prize for Poetry at Yale University is awarded this year to Cynthia Harmon for her lifetime of achievement and her new volume of collected works, *Broken Wings*. Among the most prestigious prizes available to American writers, the Bollingen Prize for American Poetry has, for more than fifty years, been a force in shaping contemporary American letters. Early Bollingen Prize winners—Ezra Pound, Wallace Stevens, Marianne Moore, E.E. Cummings, to name a few—are today widely considered to be writers whose work defined a new American literature of the twentieth century. More recent winners—John Ashbery, Robert Creeley, Louise Glück, Anthony Hecht, John Hollander, Stanley Kunitz, W.S. Merwin, Gary Snyder, Mark Strand, and Richard Wilbur—represent an exciting stylistic diversity in American writing; the work of these poets will influence and characterize the future of American poetry in all its variety."

Clark paused before screeching, "Your mother won the Bollingen!!!"

There seemed to be no denying that. Nor was there any

point in admitting to Clark that Cynthia hadn't bothered to share with me that she'd been nominated for one of the country's top literary prizes. Or that this was the first I was hearing that she'd won.

"Do you follow my mother on Twitter?"

"We're in publishing, Jessica. I follow all the major literary awards, and you should too. I would've been following your mother if I'd known she might win one."

I was about to contest Clark's comment that we were "in publishing" when I heard the unmistakable squeak of Larry's rubber-soled shoes on the linoleum floor and shooed Clark back to his desk. I wondered what Wallace Stevens would make of Cynthia. I shook my head and attempted to re-engage with Meteor's work. I added a gentle suggestion on his word choice ("ravishing vs. ravaging, I can see why you'd get those confused,") but it was hard to concentrate with Clark loudly humming "Blackbird" on the other side of the divider.

Clark gushed. "I adore *Broken Wings* as a title for your mother's collection. It's so evocative. And so clever to use a lyric from a tune absolutely everyone knows. Your mother's a genius."

"An evil genius," I muttered, as I pulled up the press release from Yale on my computer.

I studied my mother's photo. To her credit, she'd finally had a new publicity shot taken instead of using the one from when she was in her forties. Someone must have told her she couldn't get away with it anymore. In this picture, she was clearly an older woman, but one with no intention of fading from view. Cynthia looked straight at the camera. Defiant. Triumphant. A hint of a smile, not on her lips, just in her eyes—as though she'd beaten you at some game you didn't know you'd been playing.

I tore myself away from her probing stare and moved on to the bio.

"Cynthia Harmon was born in St. Louis, Missouri, and moved to New York to attend Hunter College in 1970. Ms. Harmon earned a B.A. in English and stayed on at Hunter for her MFA. She has remained a faculty member at Hunter for her entire career, engaging in the greater life of the university and inspiring students and colleagues in her own department and across fields of literature from around the world. Her poetry, published widely over many decades, is now for the first time collected in one volume, Broken Wings. Her sensibility is confessional and deceptively accessible. Reading Harmon's work, one feels both an intimate connection to the poet and an awareness that much remains hidden. The duality teases and intrigues, but ultimately satisfies. Ms. Harmon has one daughter, Jessica Harmon."

I blanched at my name. An afterthought in Cynthia's lifetime of achievement. Clark must have been reading the press release too. "Hey, you're famous!"

I was grateful he couldn't see the look on my face.

Cynthia had been well known in poetry circles for years, but this prize would vault her to a different level, and it was certain other accolades would follow. That's how the industry worked; everyone wanted a piece of something someone influential had deemed exceptional. My head was spinning, and I couldn't sit there another minute with Clark's vicarious pride in my mother threatening to overflow his workstation.

I needed air.

I stole a last look at my mother, taking a little pleasure in the hint of a double chin I'd missed before, and closed out the Bollingen's website.

"I'm going to walk around the block."

"What do I tell Larry if he asks where you are?"

"Tell him I had cramps." I'd never met a man who could argue with cramps.

I breathed in the fumes of the taxi traffic on Lexington Avenue and dodged the onslaught of pedestrians speeding by on the sidewalk, allowing the city's frenzy to push the specter of my mother away. I was beginning to feel calmer when my cell phone rang. I figured it was Penny. She was the only person who called me during work hours; she said it was the prerogative of the best friend to call "whenever and wherever." I answered without looking at the caller ID.

"Hey. You won't believe what happened," I said, shouting over the undulating siren of a passing ambulance.

"I'm glad I caught you." Cynthia's raspy voice was unmistakable. Years of smoking had taken its toll before she quit under pressure from her health-conscious students. All my entreaties as a child had made no impression whatsoever.

"Congratulations," I blurted out.

Cynthia sounded disappointed. "Oh, you've heard."

I stopped walking and leaned my cheek against the wall of a bank building, the limestone cool against my skin. A guy in a FedEx uniform banged roughly into my shoulder as he hurried by, and I lurched forward, barely keeping my balance. I wanted to close my eyes, but I wasn't stupid—the last thing

I needed was for someone to steal my wallet. I thought about hanging up, an easy if temporary escape, but Cynthia's pull on me was too great.

"Were you surprised you won?" I asked.

"You sound surprised I won."

I rolled my eyes. There was no winning with Cynthia.

She plowed on, the time for niceties apparently over. "The Bollingen Committee has instituted a new requirement in conjunction with the award. The Committee believes that poetry is not popular with the masses. I'm supposed to fix that by traipsing all across the country for six weeks, from the beginning of October to mid-November, bringing the poet to the people—blah blah blah. I wanted to tell them that my poetry wasn't intended for the masses, but I thought that would sound ungrateful. I'd be more inclined if I thought the tour would sell books, but these days you're either Amanda Gorman or you need teenage girls with tattoos and body piercings dancing half-naked on Tic Tac to accomplish that."

I left that alone. My silence didn't deter my mother; it never had.

"Anyway, the whole thing is an absurd waste of time. I looked at the itinerary, and the events are mostly luncheons and dinners at private libraries, benefactors' homes, literary societies, and university functions. Hardly venues where I will interact with the common man or woman, whoever that is."

A woman in a snug charcoal gray suit leaned against my bank wall and checked the bottom of her ankle bootie. I took that as my cue to speak.

"Why are you telling me this?" My mother and I didn't keep tabs on each other's whereabouts. There were times when Cynthia would go off to Europe and I'd only know she'd left the country when she texted me to go to her apartment and water the plants or check on the cats.

Now it was Cynthia's turn to be quiet. When she spoke, she sounded smaller. "I was hoping you'd come with me."

I fought the urge to ask her to repeat herself.

"Why don't you take one of your grad students?" I suggested. "It'll be a great learning experience." I wasn't being snarky, not exactly. But we hadn't spent an entire weekend together in years, and now she was proposing that I spend a month and a half with her. Had she lost her mind?

"I thought it could be an opportunity for us to reconnect. Do you have much holding you here?"

It was such a big question, and my answers were so tenuous. I had a job, but not one I was passionate about. And I had a boyfriend, but not one I could give myself to without reservation. What did I have holding me that couldn't wait six weeks while I sorted out my relationship with my mother?

Then I felt the old anger percolating. Didn't Cynthia understand that if I had failed to launch, she was largely to blame?

Still, my mother had made an overture. She'd said she wanted us to spend time together.

"When do you need my answer?"

I ended the call and texted Clark.

Cramps really bad, practically hemorrhaging. Going home. See you tomorrow.

Then I headed uptown on the subway to Penny's apartment.

14

CHAPTER TWO

Sitting cross-legged on the rug in Penny's living room, we might as well have been back in middle school, strategizing how to study just long enough to pass our algebra test but still have time to go shopping for new jeans. Instead, here I was, an adult at least chronologically, praying Penny's kids would nap a little while longer so she and I could talk. I still found it hard to believe we weren't roommates anymore, much less that she'd married Carlos, had two kids in quick succession, and moved from Queens to Manhattan.

"So, your mother called you and gave you a week to decide if you would drop everything and run around the country promoting poetry, and you're actually considering it? Where's your self-respect, Jess?"

"I know, I know."

"What's her motive, do you think?"

"Who knows? There's always something she's not saying. But she's getting older. I guess she needs someone to drag her suitcases around, check her into the hotel, fend off her fans." I stretched out my legs, nearly toppling a tower of blocks.

Penny shook her head. "Then she should take one of her kiss-ass students. They love her. She's won every teaching prize Hunter gives out. She's been much more maternal to them than she's been to you."

"I suggested the same thing. But maybe there's something in it for me."

Penny grimaced. "Like what?"

"I don't know. Maybe this is my chance to understand what her deal is. What makes Cynthia tick."

"Who gives a fuck what makes Cynthia tick?" Penny clapped her hand over her mouth and peeked into the bedroom to make sure the kids were asleep. "I'm sorry, Jessica. I didn't mean that. It's just that your mother did a number on your self-esteem, and you want to go back for more. I guess I just think you're better off without her around too much."

"That's easy for you to say. You have parents who adore you," I said.

"I have parents who adore *you*."

I loved Mr. and Mrs. Chan, but your best friend's parents can only substitute so far. "It's not the same."

Penny reached over and squeezed my knee.

I tried to keep the sadness out of my voice. "So, I shouldn't think about going?"

When Penny didn't answer, I stood and wandered over to her bookcase, picking up a framed photo from the day of our high school graduation. In the picture, we posed in front of Tavern On The Green: Cynthia, me, my grandparents, Penny and her parents, standing in a row and smiling. Except for Cynthia, who looked straight at the camera as if daring frivolity to approach.

"Do you remember how hot it was that day?" Penny said.

"Sweltering. I can still picture Cynthia's face when right before we received our diplomas, that boy in our class—Dennis something—"

"O'Leary."

"Yeah—he poured a water bottle over my head and ruined

the expensive blowout Cynthia had finally agreed to pay for."

Penny nodded. "That would explain the drowned rat look in the photo."

"I guess so."

I sat on the couch, remembering the day. My hair had been the least of my problems.

The lunch had been awkward, to put it mildly. I'd spent a ton of time at Penny's house since we'd become best friends in the fourth grade, and her parents treated me like another daughter. At the beginning of the meal, Mrs. Chan presented Penny and me with identical blue boxes from Tiffany's. "Just a little something to mark this momentous occasion," she said, as we unwrapped the packages to find delicate silver bracelets, Penny's with a topaz charm, her birthstone, and mine with garnet. We both hugged Penny's parents, the easy affection apparently too much for Cynthia, who looked away.

My mother had always been cordial to Penny, but she hadn't gotten to know the Chans and couldn't be bothered to make small talk at the lunch. Worse, Cynthia was barely civil to her own parents, who had traveled from St. Louis for the graduation. If I hadn't been giving the valedictory address, I'm not sure Cynthia would have thought to invite my grandparents at all. When she'd moved East to go to college, Cynthia had sloughed off her parents and the Midwest like so many dead skin cells, the origins she'd had to leave behind to allow Cynthia Harmon, New York poet, intellectual, and upper-crust socialite to emerge. She'd kept them at arm's length ever since. My mother acted like I was a special treat my grandparents didn't deserve, time with me a privilege doled out sparingly and only when it suited Cynthia.

Before the dessert arrived, Penny and I excused ourselves

and raced down the hall to the ladies' lounge. We sat in front of the mirrors for a minute and tried all the miniature lotions and sprays in the vanity basket, pocketing the tampons for good measure. But Penny was anxious. "How much longer can you put off talking to your mother if we're going to move in July?"

We'd been clandestinely scheming to room together in a small one-bedroom rental near Penny's parents in Astoria. In the fall, Penny would be a freshman at Queens College; I was starting at Hunter, Cynthia's home field, at Cynthia's insistence. I'd be under her gaze if she chose to watch over me, although that seemed unlikely given her track record as a parent so far. I didn't protest. Hunter was an excellent school and, more importantly, as part of the City University system, it was tuition-free. I wouldn't be in Cynthia's debt. I'd turned to my grandparents for help with the rent money. They hadn't seemed surprised at my request or asked why I wanted to move out. I guess they knew my mother well enough.

When the lunch ended, Cynthia wasted no time hailing a cab and herding her parents toward it.

Nana pulled me to her. "Come give us a hug, Jessica." I didn't need much encouragement. I wrapped each of my grandparents in my arms, tears leaking unexpectedly down my face.

Pops ducked into the cab. "We'll be in touch about what we discussed." He'd spoken quietly, but Cynthia's selective hearing had always been her superpower.

"What was that about?" Cynthia asked as the cab pulled away from the curb.

"Nothing."

Cynthia raised her eyebrows but didn't ask any further questions. I followed her as she stepped away from the restaurant and took off her blue silk cardigan. I tried not to stare at her upper arms glistening and jiggling in the sun. She was fifty-five, not the oldest mom in the grade by a long shot with all the new fertility treatments in vogue, but certainly on the upper end. She was attractive and vain and had always kept herself in great shape. But no one, not even Cynthia, could stop time.

"Shall we walk in the park for a bit? I don't need to be back at the college for another hour. Unless you're too warm?"

"That would be great," I said, jumping on the offer before she could remember she had an appointment that couldn't be rescheduled. I was sweating in my dress and dying to change out of my heels, but I'd promised Penny I would talk to Cynthia about our plans.

Cynthia glanced back at the restaurant, grumbling. "That place is such a tourist trap. But I guess that's why your grandparents chose it." I didn't remind her it had been Penny's parents, who'd lived in Queens for twenty years, who had made the suggestion.

We walked in silence, Cynthia likely brooding over her overpriced meal, although my grandparents had picked up the check, and me gearing up to tell her I was making my escape. When she looked at her watch, I realized it was now or never.

"I'm moving out."

Cynthia slowed and then stopped. She took her glasses off, held them up toward the sun, peered through the lenses, and put them back on. She looked surprised that I was still there.

"I won't permit it." She turned off the path and sat on a

nearby bench, smoothing her dress out over her long legs and looking anywhere but in my direction. I sat next to her.

"What do you mean? I graduated from high school today. I get to make my own plans now."

"And what is this plan you've hatched? Or maybe this is a spur-of-the-moment decision?"

"I'm moving in with Penny. We'll both be in school. You went away to college at my age."

"Exactly." Cynthia's voice caught, and I thought for one thrilling second some emotion was welling up inside her, that she might turn to me and plead with me not to leave home. As much as I loved Penny, I would've nixed the whole thing on the spot if my mother had wanted me with her.

She cleared her throat, and I followed her eyes as she gazed a little distance away, where a woman was watching a young boy climb on some big gray rocks. Each time the child scrambled up a few feet toward the top, the woman stepped closer and held him by the waistband of his red shorts as he slid down the smooth surface back to the ground to start over.

"Shame she doesn't know," Cynthia said.

"Doesn't know what?"

"Not to get attached. You lose them, one way or another. They either get taken from you or they leave of their own accord. It's all the same in the end." Then she looked at her watch again, fleetingly rested her hand on my shoulder, and tore off across the park.

That was it. Cynthia had registered her disapproval. She wasn't going to explain or fight for me; it wasn't that important to her. I wasn't that important to her. I stormed back to the apartment, my feet screaming for mercy, and packed as many of my belongings as I could into two rolling duffels. Then I took a cab from the Upper West Side to Astoria.

That night, I wept with my head in Penny's mother's lap.

• • •

Penny came over and put her arm around my shoulders. "Look, Jessie, all I'm saying is you made a break for your sanity a long time ago. What do you gain by spending this kind of time with Cynthia now?"

I carefully put the photograph back on Penny's bookshelf. "I'm not sure, but maybe the only way for me to move forward is to stop running away."

CHAPTER THREE

The day after Cynthia invited me on her book tour, I could barely drag myself out of bed. Rationally, I knew Penny was right—I shouldn't seriously entertain the thought of going with her. It would be an enormous setback to spend that kind of time in her company, undoing years of attempting, however unsuccessfully, to loosen the unhealthy ties that bound us together.

But nothing in Cynthia's orbit was that simple.

When I got to my desk, Clark was sitting in my chair, waiting for me. I tried to play it casual, although I knew yesterday's disappearing act meant I was in for an interrogation.

I tried to preempt him. "Are you here to pay me back for the coffee? We're up to an even twenty bucks."

I threw my bag under my desk and scooped up the remains of yesterday's breakfast I'd abandoned in the aftermath of my mother's award announcement. The festering half-eaten fried egg on a croissant seemed a fitting metaphor for my dream to be a writer—something promising and essential that had been neglected and was no longer of use to anyone.

Clark didn't give me my money, but instead handed me the cup of water he'd been drinking. "Believe it or not, I was worried about you. You looked very queasy when you left yesterday. Larry may have bought the time of the month excuse, but I didn't. What's the deal?"

I took a sip and handed the cup back to him. "My mother is going on a cross-country tour sponsored by the Bollingen Committee to promote poetry with a capital P, and also her new book, and she wants me to go with her."

Clark jumped up from my chair, a big smile on his face like I'd announced I'd been the one to win an award. He gestured for me to sit. "That's incredible. Think of all the industry people you'll meet—writers and agents and publishers and patrons—you'll make a million valuable contacts without even trying. And your mom will get to show you off to all her adoring fans."

Clark was so clueless it was almost endearing. I thought about telling him how things really were, but why burst his bubble?

"Thanks for the water," I said, turning my back so he'd go away. It didn't work. Clark leaned against my desk, his long legs stretched out in front of him.

"Are you going to go with her? It's a great opportunity." Then, as the reality of the situation must have hit him, he let out a wounded plea. "Oh God, don't leave me here alone."

I was so caught up in the emotional ramifications of my mother's proposal I hadn't pondered the practicalities of my work situation.

"I'm not going anywhere. But hypothetically, do you think Larry would give me the time off? A leave of absence, I guess. I mean, unpaid, whatever, but I've been working here for five years. Doesn't that earn me any goodwill? He should be thrilled about the prospect of me running around with Cynthia Harmon, hobnobbing with the literati. It would be free advertising for Canyon Press." The more I rambled, the more

23

it became obvious my boss would veto the whole idea.

Clark lifted himself off my desk with a sigh. He looked like he wanted to hug me but thought better of it. "So, you don't think you'll be going? That's a big relief." When he got back to his side of the cube, he knocked three times on our common wall. I knocked back.

I pulled up Meteor's manuscript. I had six or seven like it backlogged on my plate, plenty to keep me mired in this amateur show for the foreseeable future. I closed my eyes and tried not to think about Cynthia.

A few minutes later, I stuck my head over the divider. "I'm going in!"

I must have startled Clark, who jumped up from his chair and bumped his head on the very low ceiling above.

"Hey! That hurt."

"Sorry. I didn't mean to make you do that. You're so tall it must happen all the time."

"Not really. What's got you so revved up, anyway, Harmon?"

"Listen. If I don't come back in ten minutes, send out a search party."

"Where are you going? You've got a crazed look in your eyes. Maybe you should sit and have some more water." He tried to hand me the cup again, but I shook my head.

I picked up the announcement of the prize that I'd printed out in case Larry hadn't seen it. "I'm going to talk to the boss. As much as I hate to admit it, I need this job. If taking the time off to go with Cynthia is a non-starter, I better find out now."

Clark rubbed the top of his head. "Want me to go with you?"

I smiled. He must've been the kid who offered to accompany the class clown to the principal's office in fourth grade.

"No, I'm good," I said.

Clark gave me two big thumbs up. "You are good, and don't forget it."

I walked down the short hallway, repeating "I'm good," to myself under my breath. I knocked on Larry's door.

"Come in." Larry was sitting at his desk in his shirt sleeves, his jacket thrown over the back of his chair, tie askew, piles of papers in disarray in front of him. He usually looked as though he was working furiously, but given that he'd delegated all the manuscripts that needed serious transformation to me and Clark, I thought it was probably an act. "What can I do for you, Harmon?"

"My mother—well, you know who she is—she won the Bollingen Lifetime Achievement Award, and she's going on a tour to promote the reading of poetry in American culture." He didn't ask me to sit. I handed him the printout.

Larry glanced at the sheet of paper and handed it back. "Well, winning the award is quite impressive. As for the victory tour, she'll be preaching to the converted, in my opinion. What does this have to do with you? Or more importantly, what does this have to do with me?"

I took the chair that hadn't been offered and tried to sound confident. "I'd like to take a leave of absence to go with her on the tour. It would be a unique opportunity for me . . . ." I paused, searching for something plausible to say, "to join the conversation on the importance of literature in today's media-dominated society. And it would be great exposure for Canyon Press. For you," I added, hastily.

"How long are we talking about?"

"Six weeks. I mean, I hadn't really thought about it, but I guess I wouldn't have to go for the whole time if you needed me to come back earlier—"

Larry waved his hand in front of his face, like he was dispelling a bad odor. "Actually, Jessica, if you go, don't come back. I was on the verge of firing you anyway."

"What're you talking about? Why?"

"You take too long transforming each hopeless manuscript into something you'd be proud to have written yourself. That's not your job. I thought you'd get the hang of it after a while—for Christ's sakes, it's been years—but it's only getting worse. I can hire two twenty-two-year-olds straight out of any reputable college for the same salary I pay you. You can stay if you want, but you'll need to up your productivity in a major way, and there's no time off to follow Mommy around on her tour. The books *you* work on here at Canyon Press are not winning any prizes, and you need to get that through your pretty little head."

Larry swiveled his chair around so his back was toward me. The conversation was over. I dragged myself out of his office and back down the hallway.

When I returned to my desk, Clark was back in my chair. He stayed seated but followed me with his eyes, the confused look on his face telegraphing that he didn't know whether to be happy or sad for me. To be honest, I wasn't sure either.

"What happened?" he said.

I pitched the printout into the trash basket next to my desk and rummaged through my drawers for two plastic supermarket bags I'd stowed away. I threw a couple of pairs of shoes into one, a cardigan, two steamy beach reads Penny had loaned me, and a plush stuffed animal frog one of my writers had given me as a token of appreciation into the other. On second thought, I reached into the bag and handed the frog to Clark.

"What happened? You weren't in there very long," Clark said.

"I told Larry about the prize and that I was considering going with Cynthia, and he said if I go, I shouldn't come back. That my turnaround time was too slow because I was editing the manuscripts."

Clark hugged the frog to his chest. "Okay. So you'll stay. I can show you how I handle the manuscripts—believe me, no one would ever call what I do editing." He held up his hand for a high-five, but I left him hanging.

"I told Larry to go fuck himself."

A few minutes later I was wandering toward Madison Square Park, plastic bags in hand, when my cell vibrated. I thought it might be Larry, calling to say it was all a big misunderstanding, that he'd gotten up on the wrong side of the bed and of course he needed me to stay at Canyon. How would the press function without me? He'd gladly give me the time off so I could go on the tour with my mother, perhaps sweeten the deal with a small raise.

More likely it was Clark, begging me not to leave him there alone.

It could be Tyler, although it was early for him—he usually called me during lunch hour. He was going to be shocked Larry had fired me, or I'd quit, whatever had happened back there. I hadn't broached the question of going on my mother's tour with Tyler, who'd met Cynthia only a handful of times, the last when he'd persuaded me to include her in his thirty-fifth birthday celebration. It hadn't gone well, although I couldn't for the life of me figure out what kind of mother could object to all-around great guy Tyler, a man who only wanted to take good care of her daughter. Cynthia had feigned a migraine about half an hour into the party, and I had to send her home in an Uber.

Of course, it was Penny. Since she'd left her job and was home full time with her kids, she had less time to talk to me on the phone but called more often. Our conversations consisted of her starting a sentence, turning away from the phone and screaming something at Avia or Kyle, then getting in a few more words with me before asking if she could call back. It was both lovable and infuriating. Some days, like today, I didn't pick up the first few times she called on the theory that by her fourth attempt, she might be free to talk.

I wasn't ready to tell anyone I was unemployed, including Penny. Maybe especially Penny, who would undoubtedly suggest it was a good thing I'd left a job that was so beneath me, even though I had no better prospects. I couldn't take that level of optimism. Besides, I'd been bluffing with Larry, feeling out the possibilities. I hadn't decided whether to go with Cynthia. I knew that's why Penny was calling—to see if I'd made up my mind, and tell me, again, in her opinion, it'd be madness to reengage with my mother.

I answered a millisecond before it went to voicemail, and Penny didn't miss a beat. "Why does it take you so long to pick up? I've been trying you for twenty minutes."

I looked at the screen and saw the missed calls. Six of them—worse than usual.

"What's up, Pen? I'm in the office, remember?" I hoped her kids were making enough noise that she wouldn't hear the street sounds around me.

"What's up is that I'm going to warn you about something, though I've been sworn to secrecy. But I know how much you hate surprises."

Penny wasn't kidding. She'd been there on my fifteenth birthday, the one and only time anyone tried to throw me a surprise party. Cynthia wasn't plugged in to who my friends were other than Penny, and she didn't bother to consult her about the guest list. Instead, my mother invited all the girls in the ninth-grade class at Hunter College High School—nearly a hundred of the most entitled, snooty, cliquey kids on the planet. They flooded into our apartment, not to celebrate with me—a lot of them couldn't have identified me in a line-up—but to party with each other. I was entirely irrelevant, an excuse. When I walked in and realized what was going on, I turned to leave. Rather than making a smooth getaway that might have been perceived by my classmates as cool, I tripped on a field hockey stick Marisa Epstein had left on the floor and went flying headfirst into a doorknob. I had a welt in the middle of my forehead for a week.

But today wasn't my birthday. A growing panic crept into my chest. "Who would want to surprise me?"

"He'll never talk to me again for ruining this. It's Tyler."

"Tyler?" Penny's silence filled my ears, and I covered my eyes with my hands, cell phone and all, as a vision of my sweet boyfriend down on one knee played out in my head.

When I put the phone back to my ear, Penny's kids were crying in the background. They'd woken up, and I knew I'd only have a few seconds of her attention to find out what she knew.

"Penny, I'm begging you to tell me it isn't what I'm thinking."

I could feel Penny rolling her eyes. "Even someone as deep in denial as you could figure this one out, Jess. Of course, Tyler is going to ask you to marry him. He's invited me and Carlos, and a few other friends—mostly his, you've neglected yours so badly you hardly have any left—and his parents, his sister, and Cynthia to dinner at your place to witness the event."

"How is he planning to fit all those people into my apartment?"

Penny shushed the kids, and I heard her turn on the television for them. "That's what you're worried about? The seating arrangements? Would you also like to approve the menu?"

I was stunned. "How could he think I would marry him?"

"Hmm. Well, let's consider the situation. You're thirty years old, the two of you have been together for a year, and Tyler is a well-adjusted, hot guy with a great job on Wall Street, money in the bank, and patience for your craziness. Oh yeah, and he worships the ground you walk on. Go figure."

I shook my head. "But he knows me, Penny! I can't leave a toothbrush in his apartment. How could he think I'd say yes?"

Penny groaned. "I'm not sure he did think you'd say yes. That's why he invited an audience. Maybe you'd be too embarrassed to say no?"

With a little coaxing, Penny spit out the rest of Tyler's plans so I could stop the process before disaster ensued.

On the subway out to Queens, I tried to come up with a way to turn down Tyler's impending proposal that would preserve the status quo ante. There was a lot that was right with us as a couple, so much we liked to do together. Cycling on obscure trails in city parks no one else had heard of. Inventing new cocktails, giving them clever names, and drinking them with friends or just the two of us. Spending long Sunday afternoons reading—me, novels shortlisted for the Booker Prize, and Tyler, three or four different newspapers—the act of reading together powerful foreplay for other less tame activities that followed. But what I appreciated most about Tyler was that he didn't push me. Until now.

Why had he pierced our happiness with the M-word? I'd spent my twenties dating men who wouldn't marry me— either because they belonged to someone else, were only looking to mess around, or were emotionally bankrupt in some other way. Those men were safe; they wouldn't realize *I* was the bad marriage prospect, the one who didn't deserve a happy ever after.

But I'd let down my guard with Tyler, and we were both about to pay the price.

I unlocked the door to my apartment and threw my keys onto the front table so I wouldn't give Tyler a fright. Bruno Mars was playing softly in the background, and Tyler had dimmed the lights, obscuring the ugliness of my cheap furniture. Small candles flickered all around, sending light splintering off a tray of champagne glasses waiting to be filled. The room smelled of roses and something savory warming in the oven I hardly ever turned on. I was tempted to ditch my whole reason for being there and pull Tyler down on the couch, tell him it was all good. But I knew it was impossible.

"Hey, Penny," he called out. "Thanks for coming early. You can put the ice in the freezer if you can find room—"

I didn't answer. Standing in the doorway, I could see Tyler had moved my furniture to the perimeter of the room to make space for four round tables, six folding chairs around each, covered with white tablecloths. Small vases with red roses were lined up on the kitchen counter ready to go. There were framed pictures of the two of us from a vacation we'd taken to Turks & Caicos at Christmas decorating the milk crates. It was perfect. I started to cry.

Tyler rushed across the room when he saw me, banging his knee on one of the tables as he reached for me and wrapped his arms around me.

"Why are you crying? And why are you home so early? I was going to have this all perfectly set up and surprise you when you got here. Penny was supposed to come and help, but instead, you showed up—" Tyler stopped as the realization of what had happened must have washed over him. "She ruined it."

I broke free of Tyler's embrace and headed across the room, sitting down heavily on the couch. Tyler disappeared into the bathroom and came back with a box of tissues.

"Don't be mad at Penny. This is wonderful, Ty. Who would have thought you could transform my place into somewhere beautiful? And it was so thoughtful to include the people we love in this moment. Even Cynthia might have been charmed. But it would've been horrible to have them all watching when

32

I said no. I can't get married. I just can't."

"What are you talking about? We love each other. There's no reason we can't be together."

For a moment I could picture our future as Tyler must have, having grown up in a functional family. His parents had recently celebrated their fortieth wedding anniversary, and his siblings visited on Sundays and sat around the dining room table, eating lavish home-cooked meals. Once when I was visiting, a game of charades broke out.

And then the vision shattered and was replaced by one from my childhood. Cynthia, perched coyly on the edge of the navy damask couch in our living room, me trying desperately to get her attention as she accepted the fawning advances of a bearded professor of nineteenth-century British lit, his hand resting lightly on her knee.

I'd learned nothing about loyalty or devotion or committed relationships from my absentee father and not much more from my larger-than-life mother. I wouldn't inflict my warped sense of loving or being loved on anyone, and certainly not on someone as deserving of happiness as Tyler.

"You're making a lucky escape," I said.

"That's bullshit, Jessica, and you know it. You use your childhood as an excuse so you don't have to grow up. It's a cop-out. But I love you, and frankly I'm willing to pull the weight for both of us until you get your act together."

I wanted nothing more in the world than to tell him I would try, that we could get married, that I'd become the undamaged person he believed I could be.

"I think you should go," I said.

Tyler stayed for another hour, a scowl replacing that one-hundred-watt smile that normally lit up his face. While I sat on the couch surrounded by a pile of used tissues and the now-flat ginger ale he'd brought me to settle my stomach, he dismantled what could have been our future. He called the guests and told them the dinner was off, polite as always but barely disguising his anger. He stacked the tables and chairs neatly against the wall, banging them against each other, and called the rental company to arrange an early pick-up. He folded the tablecloths, spilled the water out of the vases, and trashed the flowers in my kitchen garbage pail. Only the framed pictures remained.

"You can't take those memories away from me," Tyler said. "You'll have to live with that." He walked out without looking back, a bottle of champagne in each hand. I took some comfort that while I had hurt him, he hadn't shattered.

I called Penny. I couldn't speak when she answered the phone.

"Jess? You okay, Jess? Should I come over?"

A sound somewhere between a sob and a laugh erupted from deep within me. Everything was so fucked up. Cynthia was on top of the world, about to parade her lifetime of achievement across the country. And where was I, her only daughter? In one day, I'd flushed my career down the toilet and rejected the first man who had offered me a chance at real love. Although I took responsibility for digging myself into this hole, I also knew my mother's fingerprints were all over the shovel.

Now Cynthia stood at the edge of the pit, reaching out a hand to me. It could be a trick. But it could be a lifeline. And the window for figuring it out was closing.

CHAPTER FOUR

I spent the entire week before we were scheduled to leave on the tour fighting off nearly intolerable urges. The urge to call Cynthia and tell her I couldn't possibly go with her after all. The urge to call Larry and plead for my shitty job back. The urge to throw myself at Tyler and beg for his forgiveness.

I did none of these things. Instead, I locked myself in my apartment, ate bowl after bowl of ramen noodles, and watched episodes of *The Gilmore Girls* for the thousandth time. I ignored all but a few of Penny's texts, maintaining just enough contact so she wouldn't call the police to check if I was alive.

The untrained ear would have missed the hint of maternal warmth in Cynthia's "Oh!" when I told her I'd decided to go with her. But I'd had years of practice in listening for the drop of tenderness underneath her characteristically business-like manner. It wasn't a lot to hold onto, and it didn't make me look forward to the six weeks in her company that lay ahead, but it was something.

"The first stop is Yale, a reading and reception at Battell Chapel at 7:00 p.m. The Bollingen Committee has arranged for the car service to pick you up at your apartment in Queens at three o'clock. Then you'll come get me in Manhattan, and we'll go to New Haven. I'll have my luggage brought down to the lobby. No need for you to come upstairs. Tell Andreas to buzz me when you arrive."

I hadn't been to the apartment where I grew up since

Christmas, and until Cynthia made it clear I wasn't invited now, I hadn't realized how much I longed to go home, however briefly. Maybe this was better. Every time I visited, a little more of my presence was erased, which was certainly Cynthia's prerogative and to be expected, but it stung anyway. Nothing stays the same. The doorman had a name I didn't recognize. The rejected and rejecting daughter would be kept at a safe distance.

I threw out a suggestion about perhaps leaving the city earlier. "I've never been to Yale. I'd like to take a look around the campus."

Cynthia shut it down. "I was there years ago, before you were born. It's what you'd expect—Gothic towers, ivy, professors, and students who think the sun rises and sets by them. We'll be in New Haven by five 'o clock. You can take a walk before the event."

So that's how this was going to play out. My notion that I might get to see and enjoy some of the country's great universities and literary establishments was extinguished. I was left only with the prospect of time spent with Cynthia in modes of transport and eating rubber chicken dinners, alongside hours of readings and signings, surrounded by her fans in a mutual love fest I'd never myself experienced.

It didn't matter. I could forgo the sightseeing, and I certainly had no lingering thoughts of being an ambassador for Canyon Press or making professional connections in the industry. No. My mission during this time of enforced togetherness was personal. If I didn't gain some understanding of my mother and our tortured dynamic, I'd never pull myself out of the rut I'd fallen into.

On the day the tour was scheduled to begin, Penny's parents insisted on seeing me off. They walked the three blocks from their apartment to mine to wait with me for the car service to come.

"I'm only going away for a few weeks. There's really no need." But I understood. They were worried about me going with Cynthia, the same way they would have worried about me getting into a car with a stranger. I took the package of rice crackers and shrimp chips that Penny's mom had brought and gave them each a hug.

"I know you'll be in touch with Penny, but if you need us, you call," Mrs. Chan said. I thought I saw Dr. Chan wipe a tear away, but it might have been something in his eye.

When the car service arrived, the thought passed through my mind that the only sane thing to do would be to send the driver on to pick up my mother without me. I tried to picture Cynthia's face when she looked in the back seat and I wasn't there, but I didn't know if I'd see relief or disappointment. I wasn't sure what had possessed my mother to ask me to accompany her on the tour, but I knew what had made me say yes. The connection between us, so worn and destructive, was holding me back. It was a cord that needed to be strengthened or cut, and I hoped the time spent together would tell me which.

While I hesitated, Dr. Chan put my suitcase in the trunk and opened the rear passenger door.

I got in the car.

Cynthia was standing outside when we reached her apartment building, her suitcases arranged neatly by her feet and the doorman, presumably Andreas, nervously pacing the sidewalk. I was fifteen minutes late—Cynthia hadn't figured on traffic— and she was not a woman to be kept waiting. She was dressed in taupe slacks, a black cashmere sweater, and a tasteful gold brooch in the shape of a dolphin I recognized as a gift from a Faulkner scholar named Jed with whom she'd once vacationed and later dismissed. At sixty-seven, Cynthia looked far more chic than I. At least I had on my black suede boots, which would have gone nicely with her outfit.

The driver and I both hopped out of the car. I wished I had his purposeful task of putting my mother's bags in the trunk rather than the awkward one of greeting her. Stepping closer, I realized I hadn't seen her in person since she'd walked out of Tyler's thirty-fifth birthday party with her feigned migraine a month earlier. She reached out and squeezed my elbow.

"Let's get going," she said.

I opened the door to the back seat and slid across the bench, making room for her. Instead of joining me, Cynthia opened the front passenger door and moved some papers the driver had there onto the floor by her feet.

"I prefer to sit here. I get nauseated in the back."

That was the last thing Cynthia said to either of us until we arrived in New Haven an hour and a half later.

The driver pulled up in front of a swanky-looking hotel called "The Study" on Chapel Street, art museums on either side of the street, and the campus visible just beyond.

My mother shook her head. "This isn't it. We're staying at the Colony."

The hotel was new and modern, the building all glass and light wood, a fitting addition to New Haven's gentrified look. I was not inclined to switch. "Are you sure? This place looks nice."

She glared at me, but didn't respond. I checked the itinerary.

I passed her the page, pointing to where it clearly indicated we'd be spending the night at this address on Chapel Street. "No, this is right."

Cynthia opened the front passenger door and stepped onto the sidewalk. She looked up and down the street in both directions, her lips in a tight line and her eyes squinting as she focused on the facade of the hotel.

"This *is* the Colony. They've changed the name." With that, she picked up her purse, leaving the rest of her bags for the driver and the bellhop to sort out, and marched inside. Sure enough, on the wall there was a plaque commemorating the Colony Inn, which had been built in 1963 and closed its doors in 2006. I wanted to ask her how she knew and why it mattered. Had she stayed at the Colony before? Instead, I waved off the help and rolled my small duffle into the lobby.

I opened the door to my mother's hotel room, and the overwhelmingly sweet scent of two dozen long stem red roses in a vase on the credenza wafted over me.

"Wow! You must have a secret admirer." I was only half joking. When she was a younger woman, there was always at least one suitor, usually many more, pressing his attention and sometimes more on Cynthia. Penny had a Chinese expression she used to describe my mother—it translated to a "spicy little sister" or something along those lines.

"Don't be ridiculous. The flowers are from the Bollingen Committee. This tour is grueling and a big ask for a scant return. They feel guilty, hence the flowers. The least they could do." Cynthia plucked a card out of the center of the arrangement, glanced at it briefly, and put it into the pocket of her pants. "Yes, as I suspected."

"Well, they're beautiful. Good thing you're not allergic— they're super potent." I lifted the largest of my mother's suitcases onto the luggage rack and then unlocked the internal door to the adjoining room. The beige and blue décor was soothing, and the king-sized bed looked so comfortable, I had to hold myself back from lying down. I spoke loudly from my room so Cynthia would hear me.

"We have an hour and a half until we need to be at the reception. I know you want to rest and we have to get dressed, but let's walk over to the campus for a few minutes. We can check out the quad where the freshmen live. I've heard it's lovely."

"It's called the Old Campus. I told you; I've seen it before. You go on ahead without me. I'll order up some tea and read over my notes."

I walked back into her room. Cynthia stole a glance at the roses again, and I wondered what she was thinking. It was the first day. I wanted to get things off on the right foot.

"Why did you ask me to come on this trip if you're going to sit alone in the hotel room? Take a walk with me. I promise to get you back in plenty of time." Cynthia looked at me for an extra beat and picked up her purse.

On Chapel Street the sidewalks were teeming with students in jeans and sweatshirts, backpacks and messenger bags slung over their shoulders. They chatted in twos and threes, snippets of their conversations floating by on the breeze.

"Global History—all-nighter . . ."

"—party last weekend—"

". . . going to freak!"

The students didn't look arrogant or entitled as Cynthia had described. They looked young and vibrant and confident.

We reached Phelps Gate and turned into the quad. It was magnificent. Not flashy or overwhelming in the way I'd found Harvard when I'd once visited Cambridge, where the buildings exuded a self-conscious prestige that was utterly intimidating. This was different. The oldest part of the campus gave off an air of understated exuberance and the possibilities that lay ahead for brilliant or lucky kids with their whole lives before them. It was intoxicating.

"What do you think?" Cynthia asked.

"It's fantastic." A Frisbee came flying in my direction and landed at my feet. I reached down and handed it to a guy with braids wearing purple basketball shorts who came to retrieve it. He flashed me a smile that made me feel young and old at the same time.

I leaned with my back against the wooden fence that ran around the perimeter of the grassy area. Cynthia stood, her arms across her chest, shifting her weight from one foot to the other, as though she might make a break for the hotel at any moment.

"So many girls," she said.

"Women. And why wouldn't there be? Yale's been coed for decades."

"1969." She stared straight ahead, her gaze fixed on the students as they passed in front of us.

"How do you know that?"

Cynthia glanced at her watch and then at the tower on the other side of the quad as the carillon bells rang, announcing six o'clock. "I told you: I spent some time here. A lifetime ago. I remember things, little details."

Cynthia was like that. Tiny nuggets most people would discard, she stowed away in the recesses of her brain, to be pulled out and inserted into her poetry when the connection became clear to her. Phrases and pieces of conversations, her own intimate ones and those of strangers overheard in public places. Lines from novels, song lyrics. She had a writer's mind; I recognized it. I had one too, or I did before I starved it to death.

"When did you spend time at Yale?"

Two impossibly good-looking guys walked by on the path in front of us, leaning into each other and laughing about something as they turned into one of the dorms.

Cynthia smiled, always appreciative of a display of sexual energy. "Do you think they're a couple, or just hormones let loose for the weekend?" I felt a stab of loneliness.

It didn't surprise me that my mother had evaded my question. She didn't like to talk about the past. But she'd opened the door, and I pushed my way in a little further.

"Did you ever wish you'd had the freedom to travel more? Maybe live in a different place, feel the buzz of somewhere new?"

Cynthia barely paused before answering. "No. You and I are the same. We're too pragmatic to believe that changing one's location can change one's fortune. Besides, I've been in New York City all my life. It's the whole world in one place.

There's no reason to live elsewhere."

So much was off in Cynthia's response—starting with "you and I are the same"— that I didn't know where to begin.

"*I've* spent my whole life in New York City. You spent the first eighteen years, your entire childhood, in St. Louis." I pictured my grandparents' stately brick colonial home set back from the street and the lush front lawn. They were formal people, but gracious and kind. Cynthia, an only child like me, had lived a privileged and sheltered youth, with private schools and horseback riding lessons and garden parties with platters of canapés and fruity cocktails. I knew this from my grandparents, not from my mother, who said almost nothing about her younger days.

By the look on my mother's face, you would have thought my grandparents had held her hostage in St. Louis. "That doesn't count. I meant my whole sentient life, not the years when I was being dragged around by the nose by my parents, told what to do and whom to talk to and what to think."

I felt offended on my grandparents' behalf, but I pressed on. "I wasn't suggesting you would go back to St. Louis. I meant maybe there was a time when you wanted to see the world. Felt there were more possibilities. Like before you had me."

"You didn't stop me from doing anything I wanted to do."

As if to prove her own point, Cynthia gave a little wave and then strode off in the direction of the hotel.

I watched the cute guy and his friends throw the Frisbee around and wondered what the hell I was doing there.

The rays of the setting sun rippled through the stained-glass windows of Battell Chapel, a suitably severe venue for the first stop of my mother's tour. I wrapped my cardigan around my shoulders against the chill and sat in a pew close to the back of the starkly beautiful room that had lifted up and beaten down New Haven's faithful for more than two hundred years. Tonight, the church would be the backdrop for a different sort of worship—the adoration of Cynthia Harmon. Given how the place was filling up, it appeared her devoted followers were ready to be inspired.

I surveyed the room and spotted my mother already sitting on the dais, greeting people with a kind smile she seldom bestowed on me and autographing copies of *Broken Wings*. According to the schedule I'd been given, I was supposed to facilitate the book signing at the end of the evening after Cynthia had finished reading, making sure her fans stayed at a respectful distance, presenting one copy for signing, etc. But Cynthia looked comfortable with the change in protocol. She was a pro, after all.

I'd seen my mother give readings at Hunter many times when I was in college. I'd go with a friend, eat the English department's oatmeal cookies, and sit in the back pretending it was cool that Cynthia barely acknowledged me. When she had gigs at other local universities, sometimes I'd sneak in, uninvited. I wondered if a daughter's yearning would be visible to the audience, a ribbon of longing stretched out to her mother, never quite reaching its mark.

Cynthia was on her game at these events, but tonight there was something different, something more. She looked lovely and much younger than her age in a close-fitting cobalt blue silk dress and heels that accentuated her toned calves. She was more dressed up than her usual outfit—straight skirt and turtleneck—alluring but decidedly professorial. I wondered if she'd made a special effort because Yale University sponsored the prize or because this was the first stop on the tour. Perhaps there was another reason.

"Isn't she amazing?" I'd been so engrossed in watching my mother's every move that I hadn't noticed the young woman take the seat next to me, a copy of *Broken Wings* clasped to her chest. Her long brown hair was pulled back into a loose ponytail and her round wire-framed glasses accentuated the expression of wonder on her face. "I'm hoping she'll sign my book. I'm freaking out! Where's your copy?"

"I might buy one after the reading. I'm not familiar with her work," I deadpanned. "What is it you like about her poetry?"

The young woman gazed up at the ceiling, as if receiving her insights from the magnificence of the vaulted space above. She turned back to me, transformed. No longer simply a college student attending a poetry reading on a Tuesday night, but now a Cynthia acolyte, spreading the Word. Maybe it was the chapel, but the purity of her admiration gave me the heebie-jeebies.

"Cynthia's poetry bridges the existential gap between souls. She expresses the eternal truth that while as individuals we can only perceive our fundamental aloneness, in reality we're part of a larger cosmic whole. Cynthia dispels the notion of the primacy of the self, a concept that has been so destructive to civilized society throughout time."

I guess I should have expected that kind of answer from a Yalie. I suppressed an eyeroll. I was tempted to say: *Cynthia Harmon is the most self-obsessed person ever to walk the halls of academia or the streets of the Upper West Side. It is always about her, yet she manages to convince her readers otherwise. She is a great poet and an even greater con artist.*

I smiled sweetly. "That's wonderful."

The sound of applause pulled me back to the chapel as Professor so-and-so, distinguished lecturer in Contemporary American Poetry, introduced my mother and called her to the podium.

Cynthia rose from her chair and took her time walking to the center of the dais. When she reached the lectern, she pressed the length of her body against it, placing her elbows on either side of the microphone. Then she leaned in, took three deep breaths, chest rising and falling, and closed her eyes. It was a routine I'd seen before, her method of creating a palpable intimacy with her audience. It worked every time. The student next to me was squirming in her seat.

When the applause died down, Cynthia proceeded to thank the Bollingen Committee, Yale, various people involved in organizing the tour, her publisher, her publicist, etc. For a second, I thought she might thank me, but she didn't, and I was glad she hadn't blown my cover. When she finished her preliminaries, the room thrummed in anticipation of the reading. Even I held my breath, waiting for Cynthia's first words.

Those first words were all I heard. I was swept up in the poet's performance rather than her poems, which were some of her most well-known crowd-pleasers I'd heard and read countless times before. It wasn't the written language that captivated me, although her words were raw and compelling. No, it was Cynthia's body language that mesmerized.

There was no denying my mother was magnetic. Her appeal

wasn't solely sexual, but it was irrefutably sexual. She exuded a sensuality that, even as she got older, made both men and women catch their breath and press a little closer. A buzzing at the base of the neck that signaled someone electrifying was in their midst. She achieved this reaction not with revealing clothing or salacious language, but with a penetrating glance, a slight tilt of her hips, or the momentary brush of her fingertip on her breast—so fleeting you thought you'd imagined it, except your mouth is dry and you can barely swallow.

I'd watched this same performance on a smaller scale growing up, as Cynthia hypnotized the hangers-on who showed up at our apartment on Central Park West at all hours. Grad students and professors and writers invited or merely not excluded, but all under her spell. Cynthia made a person want more—more beauty, more poetry, more life. More Cynthia.

With a nod of her head, at exactly the forty-five-minute mark, Cynthia stopped reading.

As though the Q & A was a spontaneous addition, rather than carefully choreographed into the evening, the professor who had introduced her smiled widely at Cynthia and asked, "Would you mind taking some questions from the audience, Ms. Harmon?"

Cynthia purred into the microphone. "Why, of course, I'd so enjoy that."

I had a vision of myself rising from my pew and pelting Cynthia with everything I planned to ask her during our time together on the tour, the audience sitting in stunned silence. Instead, three super earnest-looking students, dressed in conforming lit-major black, took the microphone in turn.

"I wondered if you could speak about your unusual choice of syntax and meter in the poem, 'Climbing A Hill'?"

47

"Am I right in sensing a certain resonance between your poetry and the writings of Gloria Steinem?"

"Sorry—this is a two-part question. Can you share something about your writing process with us, and how has it changed over the years?"

Cynthia answered each inquiry, without smirk or sigh, managing to convey that the question and the questioner had tapped into some deeper truth only she could reveal. She was masterful.

The young woman sitting next to me was transfixed. "Wow, that was sick. I'm getting in line to have my copy signed. Want to come?" I noticed a small tattoo of a blackbird near her collarbone, the image on the cover of Cynthia's book.

"Did you get that tattoo for this event?"

She smiled as she took off for the front of the room, speaking over her shoulder. "Oh, yeah. It isn't permanent. It's the kind you can wash off. I thought Ms. Harmon might like it."

I followed her at a distance. The signing was already in full swing. From the middle of the room, I tried to catch Cynthia's eye, but she was totally engaged.

The line now stretched out toward the door, and I wondered how my mother would possibly sign all these books by 8:30 when the program was slated to end. I contemplated going back to the hotel—really, what was I doing anyway?—when I saw an elderly man near the end of the line. He had to have been at least eighty, a stark contrast from the bevy of young students who filled the chapel. His appearance and demeanor telegraphed professor. The fringe of white hair on an otherwise bald head, a bit of a paunch underneath a navy V-neck sweater, a camel hair blazer, loafers that needed polishing. He too had brought a copy of Cynthia's book, and he was waiting patiently as the line advanced slowly toward her, exchanging a word or two with the students on either side of him. Occasionally, he took a step out of the line, as if to leave, but then he'd rejoin. He seemed both hesitant and determined in his mission, and I couldn't take my eyes off him.

As the crowd dwindled, Cynthia rose from her place at the signing table, pointing at her watch. It was 8:35, but there were only six people left on the line, including the old man, who had now been standing patiently for over half an hour.

I watched as one of the evening's organizers leaned in close to Cynthia, speaking quietly near her ear. Although I couldn't hear what the woman said, Cynthia's response was loud and clear.

"No, I can't. I won't. You're supposed to protect my time. Please apologize to them." I'd come closer to the table and was standing by my mother's side. Cynthia turned toward me. "Jessica, please get our coats." The urgency in her voice seemed unwarranted. What was another five minutes?

I lifted my chin toward the man and spoke so only my mother would hear. "I'm sure he's a faculty member. At least sign his book? Isn't that the collegial thing to do?" I took a few steps toward him when I felt my mother's hand on my back, forcibly turning me in the other direction.

"This is my show, Jessica. Please do as I say." She marched toward the coat room, took her jacket off the hanger, and handed me mine. I was so stunned, I followed her out into the New Haven night, not having said a word to those remaining in line.

We walked briskly out of the Old Campus and back onto

Chapel Street. "What was that about?"

"It wasn't *about* anything. Don't be so dramatic. When you reach a certain level of renown, the public will eat you alive if you allow it. I refuse to suffer that fate. I engage with the audience to refuel myself—their admiration is my elixir. But when I've gotten what I need, I call it a night. Self-preservation, Jessica. You should learn the skill."

I felt heat rising to my face and struggled to keep my voice modulated. "So that's why you couldn't sign that old man's book? Because you didn't need his admiration? Can you hear yourself?"

"Don't get histrionic. It's been a long day. We're both tired. Let's get some rest."

We reached the hotel. The doorman held the door open for us. "Welcome back, ladies." Cynthia ignored him and walked toward the elevator, turning around when she realized I wasn't following. "Are you coming?"

I shook my head. "It's not even 9:00. I'm not ready to go to bed yet. You go. I'll hang out in the lobby for a little while."

"Suit yourself." Cynthia pushed the button for the elevator and waited. She looked diminished, and I almost relented and went with her, but I couldn't. When she disappeared into the elevator, I looked for the entrance to the hotel bar.

CHAPTER FIVE

The Heirloom Lounge was quiet, save for a lifeless cover of Elton John's "Goodbye Yellow Brick Road" playing softly over the sound system. I surveyed the clientele. A middle-aged guy with a scruffy beard and heavy eyelids sat alone at the far end of the room, communing with a pint of beer. At a small round table near the entrance, a pair of students who looked like they'd wandered out of a J. Crew catalog were getting cozy over a plate of French fries.

I sat at the bar.

"What can I get for you?" The bartender was young with a deep voice and a small scar above his eyebrow that cried out to be touched. Or maybe I was feeling lonely.

"Jack and Coke, please."

He mixed my drink and placed it on a napkin he slid in front of me. "Bourbon drinker. Wasn't expecting that."

"Sometimes the situation calls for it." I pulled out my cell and perused my texts. A couple from Penny that would wait. Nothing from Tyler. He wasn't a man to beg. I didn't regret breaking up with him, but I missed him.

I looked up and the bartender was studying me, a question lurking before he spoke it aloud. "Are you staying here in the hotel?"

I leaned forward just enough to keep his attention. "Couldn't think of anywhere better."

He lowered his voice to a gravelly whisper. "I can probably get you upgraded to a king suite with a hot tub."

"I'm sharing a room with my sixty-seven-year-old mother. She tends to take up a lot of space. And the hot tub would be great for her arthritis."

The bartender gave me a quick nod. "Touché," he said. "Let me know if I can get you anything else."

My mother's performance at the reading and her prima donna shenanigans afterward at the signing had left a sour taste in my mouth that alcohol couldn't erase, but it didn't stop me from trying. The burn of the whiskey as it slid down my throat reminded me of a Sunday afternoon during college, sipping Jack-laced Swiss Miss with Penny in the apartment we shared while I was at Hunter and she was at Queens. The spiked hot chocolate was the same color as the ratty tweed sofa we'd bought for thirty dollars off some guys on Queens Boulevard the day we moved in. Penny's mom was deathly afraid the couch would bring a bedbug infestation we'd never eradicate. I wasn't familiar with bedbugs. I figured they were too afraid of Cynthia to make an appearance in the white-glove building on Central Park West where I'd grown up.

Penny was still my closest friend, but as we neared college graduation, our paths had diverged. She'd taken a practical route, studied social work, and was starting on an MSW in the fall. Despite the screaming voice in my head telling me to run in the other direction, I had pursued creative writing.

That day, we were discussing our futures. Penny had firm opinions. "You shouldn't take any job unless you're sure it's the right thing to do—that you're not closing doors."

I took a long sip of my drink. "Easy for you to say. You have skills and a plan. You'll be able to get a decent job in a couple of years. I've got nothing."

I wasn't lazy. I'd worked all sorts of jobs during my college years, with weird hours, in weird places, for weird people. Nothing much to put on a resume, and nothing "in my field," apart from the summer I worked in an artsy indie bookstore in the Village where I'd had to bite my tongue whenever anyone so much as leafed through a book of Cynthia Harmon's poetry. Most of my gigs were waitressing in places where the food was suspect and the clientele more so. My shortest stint was as a sales associate at a Gap Kids. The manager, a big hairy guy named Dante with an arresting overbite, said I wasn't folding the sweaters right. I lasted three weeks, and on the day I quit I refolded the entire inventory of boys' sweaters, size extra-small through extra-large, inside out.

In the meantime, my grandparents subsidized my share of the rent, and Cynthia sent me a check each month to assuage her guilt that I'd moved out and our relationship was so strained. I used her payoffs to buy textbooks and get my laptop repaired. I never spent Cynthia's money on a new sweater or concert tickets or anything I'd enjoy.

I'd recently been offered an entry-level position as a copy editor at a fourth-tier publishing house. I wasn't nearly the snob my mother was, but even I had to admit that Oaktree Press spewed out fiction for a female demographic that, to be kind, was either severely intellectually challenged or lacking in imagination. Maybe mixed in were average women who desperately needed a break from their regular lives. The romance novels Oaktree churned out were appalling. They had no plots and no character development, and nothing that approximated real love. Even the sex scenes, which were plentiful and explicit beyond the telling, were dull and sad.

The job paid minimum wage and afforded the privilege of putting on my resume something marginally relevant to my chosen career.

I knew the possibility of me taking the Oaktree job pissed Penny off. "You may not have a lot of marketable skills, but you have talent. Are you going to waste it fixing spelling errors in *Peggy Porks Pittsburgh*?"

"Maybe I'll change it to *Penny Porks Pittsburgh*. What do you think of that?" I kicked her leg, spilling hot chocolate down the front of my shirt in the process. "Damn."

Penny got up and threw me the roll of paper towels from the kitchen. "Blot, don't wipe," she said. Then she returned to the couch and the subject of my future.

"Look, Jess, I don't know anything about good writing or what aspiring authors do for a day job. No one wants to live like this forever," she said, looking around our apartment. "But not too many of our peers are winning writing competitions and having their short stories published in prestigious literary journals like you are. I bet you're going to get a departmental prize at graduation. I think you should at least consider applying for an MFA. Or, if the idea of more school right now makes you want to hurl, then be impoverished and sit in a rundown, romantic café in some foreign country for a year and smoke cloves and write a novel. You know what I mean?"

Of course, I knew what she meant. I'd grown up with noted poet and bon vivant Cynthia Harmon, who spent vast amounts of time and her parents' money catering to her own needs, stimulating her senses with fine wine and finer men, and, in due course, producing wonderful poetry. It was an enviable lifestyle, and it was theoretically possible it could be mine as well.

As if reading my mind, Penny scooted closer to me and rested her head on my shoulder.

"You do know who you have to talk to about this, right?"

"Oh, no."

"Oh, yes."

She tossed my cell over. Penny knew. Even after everything that had gone on between us, my mother's opinion was the one that counted. "Call her. Do it now, so you don't back out."

Cynthia picked up on the fourth ring. She accepted my coffee proposal without hesitation or enthusiasm.

"Do you want to meet me at home?" she asked.

The word was so loaded. I'd long ago abandoned a Hallmark card version of "home"— a fire crackling in the hearth, the smell of apple pie floating in the air, my mother and I laughing or crying together depending on the occasion. That wasn't the home I'd experienced.

And I could count on two hands the times I'd been in the actual apartment where I'd grown up since the day I packed my bags to move in with Penny four years earlier, mostly when my grandparents were visiting from St. Louis. This didn't seem like the opportune time for a return visit. I politely declined, and we agreed to meet at "Java Girl," a student hangout near Cynthia's office at Hunter where I'd waitressed a couple of years earlier. Public space, my turf.

An hour later, I was on the N train to Manhattan. Dressed in Penny's clean shirt and my own faux-suede mini skirt, out of season but stylish and short, it was an outfit designed to flaunt my twenty-two-year-old legs in front of my fifty-nine-year-old mother. I tucked a notepad and a pen into my backpack as though I was about to conduct a formal interview for the school newspaper rather than grab a cup of coffee with the woman who gave birth to me.

When I arrived, Cynthia was already seated in a booth near the door, her back to the front window. I stood outside on the sidewalk, studying her. She hadn't waited for me to order—I could see her blowing on her coffee to cool it down. A student's assignment lay on the table in front of her, a pen poised in her hand. It had been a few weeks since I'd run into her on campus, and the tight feeling in my chest was either heartburn or heartache—it was hard to tell. I pinched my leg, hard, to make myself go inside.

When I reached the table, Cynthia stood, opened her arms, and pulled me into a kind of half-hug, the fronts of our bodies barely touching. Thankfully, it lasted only a few seconds. As she stepped away, Lois, my old boss at the café and a giant oak of a woman, raced over and embraced me so fully and forcefully that she lifted me a couple of inches off the ground. Then she put me down, nodded at my mother, and went back to work.

"Do you know that woman?" Cynthia knocked her hand into her cup, spilling some coffee onto the table.

"I'll have a cappuccino and a banana chocolate chip muffin, please," I said to the waitress. "We can share," I added, looking my mother in the eye. Worried she hadn't picked up on my subtle overture, I quickly explained why I had asked to meet. "I was hoping to talk to you about my plans after graduation. Maybe get some advice."

Cynthia's shoulders visibly relaxed, and she settled herself back into her seat. She was comfortable in this role, often generous with her time and willing to help with her connections. Mentoring was her labor of love, for the students who came to official office hours, and for the ones I used to find sprawled on our living room sofas in clumps of three and four, late at night, listening to my mother recite Whitman while she helped them brainstorm their senior theses or their personal essays for their MFA applications. If I could fit into that mold, I'd be graced with my mother's attention.

Cynthia took a small piece of the muffin between her thumb and finger, holding it mid-air but never lifting it to her mouth. "What are you considering?"

I explained I was thinking about accepting the copy-editing job at the publishing house because it was a foot in the door and might be a stepping stone to something more respectable.

"But what I want to do is write."

I'd been writing all through college, of course, and my professors in the English department and the friends I'd worked with on the literary magazine knew I had a passion. But lots of student pursuits, even the most earnest ones, fade after graduation. I believed I was different. I had words and stories in my soul bursting to come out. My declaration to my mother of my deepest desire, not just to write but to *be* a writer, sounded naked and forlorn as it floated in the booth between us. How dare I? I was no Cynthia Harmon.

I waited for Cynthia to say something encouraging, something comforting. To gather my frightened dream in her arms.

Instead she asked, "Which genre are you thinking of pursuing?"

For a minute, I thought she was joking. That she'd break into a laugh, and I'd quip, "Oh, Cynthia, you're too much."

When I realized she was serious, I stared down at my hands

where they rested in my lap to keep my eyes from filling with tears and tried to parse out her question. I wrote fiction. Surely, she knew that. Granted, I hadn't waltzed into her office and handed her my short stories to read, waiting patiently for her to mark them up with insightful questions that would bring out their deeper meaning. We didn't interact that way, and of course, I hadn't studied with her formally. But we'd walked the halls of the same department for four years. We were in each other's spheres. I studied with her colleagues, and my classmates were her students. When she published a poem in a faculty magazine or in a literary journal, I read it. When she won a grant or a prize, I was aware of it. Had she been oblivious to my accomplishments?

When I didn't respond, Cynthia scowled. "I know you write both fiction and nonfiction. I've read some of your memoir pieces."

Then it made sense. In my sophomore year, I'd written a series of three essays which were published in *The Olivetree Review*, the college's undergraduate literary and arts journal of which I later became an editor. The first was about the cognitive dissonance of growing up with a world-renowned mother but never having met my father. The second was about the summers I spent with my grandparents in St. Louis where I was banished (mostly happily) so my mother could "write in peace." The third was about trying to live as an ordinary child in a home that doubled as a literary salon. All the essays were tightly written, factually accurate, and left the emotional truths to the imagination of the reader. In other words, they were revealing and concealing at the same time. Cynthia's hallmark.

"You read the memoir pieces because you were worried

about what I'd said about you."

"I was curious."

"What did you think?"

"I think writing memoir is immensely therapeutic."

"Maybe you should try it," I said. We sat, drinking our coffee, in silence. Then I remembered I'd come for advice, not to argue.

I folded my hands on the table in front of me, willing them not to shake. "I write fiction. Have you read any of my stories?"

Cynthia didn't answer immediately but instead made a show of putting away her student's paper and the pen and popping her cell phone into her purse. I wondered whether she was getting ready to devote herself entirely to our conversation or preparing to leave.

"Jessica, you're an intelligent woman and you've always been an excellent student. But I would hate to see a daughter of mine become a writer or a professor. It's a terrible life."

"How can you say that? You've led a charmed existence."

"Academia is a dirty business. The politics, the power struggles, the sexual manipulation. My success came at a cost. You don't know the half of what I've lost."

I leaned forward, my elbows landing hard on the table and spilling what little remained of Cynthia's coffee. "Then tell me."

I must have raised my voice more than I thought because Lois looked over and then purposefully circled back past our table.

"Give a holler if you need me," she said, staring down at Cynthia before she walked away.

My mother had already recovered from our exchange, the calm exterior back in place.

She looked around the coffee shop and threw a particularly disdainful glance at Lois. "There's too much to explain. This isn't the time or place. For now, you'll have to accept that my advice would be to take the editing job. It will be solid work experience, without the drama."

I didn't need her to tell me twice. She didn't think I had what it took. I'd never be as good as Cynthia Harmon, so better not to enter the arena. With that no-confidence vote floating between us, I tossed seven dollars on the table—everything I had in my wallet—and got up from the booth.

"Jessica, you asked me what I thought about your fiction. You're a competent writer." She paused. "Talent?" Cynthia answered her own question with a shrug.

I turned and walked out of the café.

On the way to the subway, I texted the publisher at Oaktree and accepted the job.

• • •

"You sure were far away there," the cute bartender said. "Another drink?"

"I thought you'd never ask."

I was still thinking about my mother and my aborted writing career when a statuesque Black woman came in wearing a striking white wool cape and a taupe beret. She sat at the bar a couple of seats away from me, placing a handbag large enough to hold a five-course dinner for two on the bar, along with a copy of *Broken Wings*. She ordered a glass of Chardonnay.

I didn't need the visual of Cynthia's book to place this woman. I'd noticed her right away sitting in the front row. She hadn't applauded wildly like the amped-up students, but had instead regarded Cynthia with quiet respect, nodding at the end of each poem. "What did you think of the reading tonight?" I asked.

"I enjoyed it very much. I do some work for the selection Committee, and I'm helping with logistics for the tour, but I came tonight as a private citizen to hear Cynthia read. I hoped I might run into her here this evening."

"Stalker? Or do you know her?" I was only half kidding.

She reached for a bowl of mixed nuts further down the bar, placed it in between us, and took a sip of her wine. I wondered whether she was stalling before answering my question or simply enjoying herself.

"I do know her. May I join you? My name is Monica Banks, by the way."

"Please," I said, removing my jacket from the next barstool. "Although I warn you, I've started drinking without you."

Monica smiled. "You're Cynthia's daughter, aren't you? Jessica. You look like her."

"No, I don't. But yes, she's my mother. Do you teach at Hunter? I don't recognize you."

She shook her head, picking out four or five almonds from the bowl. "I work for the Bollingen Committee now—here's my card in case you need anything during the tour."

I stuck it in my wallet. "Seems unlikely."

"You never know. Anyway, I met Cynthia at a conference in Seattle in 2004, right after I began teaching fiction in the creative writing program at Brown. Diversity hiring was gathering steam, and I was a bit of a novelty in the department. We became friendly—Cynthia helped me navigate some sticky situations."

I signaled the bartender. "No ice," I said. The first two drinks had loosened my tongue; the next was to help me forget this conversation when it was over.

"Am I remembering correctly that your mother told me you are a writer?" Monica's tone was chatty, almost chummy, but I didn't fall for it.

"Seattle was the conference where Cynthia was encouraged to leave early."

Monica looked down at her drink. "I don't know anything about that."

"Yes, you do, if you were there. Besides, everyone in those circles knew. It's the kind of gossip college English departments live for."

Monica looked down into her glass, swirling her wine. "I don't generally go in for gossip."

"Well, other people were not as restrained. Besides, maybe it was true? I'm sure you've heard the story. Cynthia drank too much at the closing reception and supposedly lured one of her grad students into a corner. She tried to pinch his ass, and then, when he reported her to the conference organizers, she insinuated he'd made a pass at *her*. He ended up leaving the PhD program because none of the professors were willing to supervise his thesis out of solidarity with Cynthia, and my mother got tenure the next year." I motioned to the bartender. "Another Jack. No Coke."

"You sure?" he asked. My glare sent him reaching for the bottle.

Monica tapped the rim of her glass and changed the subject. "She talks about you often."

"I don't believe that."

Monica fished around in her handbag and pulled out a lipstick. "Believe what you want."

I finished off my drink and contemplated a chaser, but I was out of practice and I didn't want to stagger into our room or, for better or worse, go off with the young bartender. I was about to get up when Monica put her hand on my arm.

"Listen—"

"No, you listen. I'm glad Cynthia has come through for you. But I'm the only family she has, and her history with me leaves a lot to be desired. Tonight was a four-drink night. I'm hoping by the end of this tour I don't know all the hotel bartenders between here and California."

I plunked down thirty dollars on the bar. "Sorry I can't leave you a better tip, but thanks for the offer earlier. You were the highlight of my night."

CHAPTER SIX

We spent the remainder of the first week and part of the second appearing at events in Hartford, Providence, and all over the greater-Boston area, crisscrossing the universities, libraries, and private homes of the well-read and well-heeled. When it was time to move on from the Northeast, I was grateful for the travel day and glad to board the plane to Chicago.

Cynthia slid into the window seat and pressed her head against the pulled-down shade as though trying to meld herself into the body of the plane. She turned her body to the side and drew her legs in toward her chest, impossibly scrunching them in on themselves like a terribly uncomfortable grasshopper.

I reached up and adjusted the air-conditioning so it blew directly on me. "One more day in that car and I would have lost it. Thank goodness the Committee paid for business class so the honoree won't arrive with stiff knees and a killer backache. Although the way you're sitting—"

My mother let out a low groan. "I paid for business class, not the Committee. If I'm going to be airsick, I want to vomit on my own kind."

I wondered if this was an act. At least twice a year when I was growing up, my mother had gone jet-setting around Europe. I would sit on her bed and watch her pack her Louis Vuitton suitcases, and she'd let me help pick out which strappy sandals to take. Then she'd kiss me on the top of my head and leave me with Vera, the housekeeper. When I was little, I would cry. When I got older, I wouldn't give her the satisfaction.

How could someone so widely traveled be a poor flier? "Do you want me to put your handbag in the overhead compartment?"

She closed her eyes and shook her head, managing to fold herself further into the seat. I ignored her contortions and tried to make conversation to distract her.

"Do you know anyone in Chicago?" I asked.

"I know people in every university town; it comes with being part of the academic community. My former students take posts all over, and colleagues get turned down for tenure and end up in other locales. But I try not to visit anyone living anywhere requiring me to be thirty thousand feet in the air." She unfurled herself enough to pull the emergency card out of the seat pocket in front of her. She studied it more carefully than I had ever seen anybody do before.

I tried to remember the last time we'd flown together. As often as Cynthia traveled, she rarely took me along except to visit my grandparents in St. Louis. "Are you afraid to fly?"

"Please, Jessica. We gain nothing by putting labels on my emotions. Make yourself useful and get me a Bloody Mary. The beauty of business class is that you can start drinking before take-off."

"Is this fear of flying a new thing?" I asked.

"It's an old thing that is becoming more debilitating."

"Maybe you should take something? I have Klonopin in my backpack if you want." I wasn't afraid to fly—I barely had the opportunity, what with my finances—but I often had trouble sleeping.

"I did already. I've got exactly half an hour of terror ahead of me until the Valium kicks in."

I pressed the call button for the flight attendant and ordered Cynthia's drink, munching my mini pretzels in silence, the salt stinging my lips. Our conversations had remained mainly logistical, and my hopes of achieving some deeper understanding of her or our screwed-up dynamic were fading. At this rate, I'd go back to New York with nothing to show for having subjected myself to the journey.

When she swooped in with a question out of nowhere, I figured it was the pills talking.

"Do you want to discuss what happened?"

"You mean yesterday? At the luncheon?" My mind raced back to the last event, hosted by a Harvard scholar of Whitman at the Boston Athenaeum. It had all gone smoothly until the Q & A, when someone asked Cynthia about professors who had influenced her when she was a college student. The question should have been a softball, but it seemed to rattle her. She stood silently and looked at me so beseechingly that I said the first thing I could think of to bring the program to a close, that it was time for dessert. The look of relief that had passed over Cynthia's face had puzzled me, but then I forgot about it.

"No, not that." She turned her head back to the window. A moment passed before she spoke again, and her voice sounded thicker, more subdued. "I was wondering what happened with that man you were seeing. Skylar."

I'd told Cynthia I'd broken things off with Tyler but hadn't gone into detail. The feelings were too raw to have them dissected. Besides, my mother's track record with men suggested she didn't have much to offer me by way of advice. On the other hand, I was touched that she had asked.

"Tyler, not Skyler. It wasn't going to work out."

We sat without speaking while the plane took off. I pulled the in-flight magazine out of the pocket in front of me and skimmed an article about Brooke Shields and her charity fighting childhood food insecurity in Africa. I was pondering what it must be like for Brooke to pretend she didn't care that her looks were fading because underneath was her true philanthropic calling—when the pilot's voice came over the public address system to announce that we might experience some turbulence.

Cynthia handed me her empty drink glass and put her head on her tray table. "Oh, God."

Twenty minutes later, the plane began a series of minor dips and rolls. "I don't think that's a good idea. You might get banged around," I said. Cynthia sat upright, grabbed my hand, and squeezed, digging her long, manicured nails into my palm. She muttered something—a prayer or an obscenity, or maybe both, I couldn't tell. Then she opened her eyes wide and spoke louder and with more urgency. "If this is the end, there are things I need to tell you."

I smiled and shook my head. "Like where you've hidden the bodies? Relax. It's just some rough air. The pilot said we'll be out of this stretch in a little bit." But I was sure Cynthia had secrets, and if she believed the plane was going down, maybe it was a good time for an inquiry of my own.

"Do you remember when I started asking questions about my father?"

"No." Cynthia squeezed harder as an overhead luggage compartment several rows ahead of us rattled, threatening to open.

'Well, I do. On the first day of kindergarten, my teacher, Mrs. Keneally, made us each draw a picture of our family on a big piece of oak tag."

"Very original assignment. When I think of all the tuition I paid to that school—"

"Hunter is a public school. You didn't pay any tuition. Focus, okay? Otherwise, I'm not going to let you hold my hand."

"Okay, go on."

"I can see it all like it was yesterday. Akhil drew four stick figures with a brown crayon, the mom with a slash of red I thought was blood but was supposed to be a sari. Ashley's picture had a big green patch in the middle and one parent on one side and one on the other—they were divorced and lived on opposite sides of Central Park, and she alternated weeks. Rory lived with his two dads, Per and Tony—which seemed cutting edge in 1994 when I was five years old."

"I suppose we're getting to your picture now, and it will evidence severe trauma for which, twenty-five years later, I'm supposed to make amends." As if to punish Cynthia for good grammar in a time of mortal danger, the pilot took to the airwaves again and let the passengers know the turbulence would continue.

"My picture revealed more by what was missing. I drew the two of us, standing apart. My hand was reaching out toward you, but your hand was at your side, your eyes looking straight ahead. At five years old, it hit me that I only had *you*, and that connection seemed tenuous."

"Even back then there were single mothers, Jessica."

"That's not what I mean. The point is that I don't know

why, but I'd never wondered all that much about my father until that moment. I'd accepted he wasn't around."

Another dip, another death grip squeeze of my hand.

"I guess you weren't as precocious as I thought."

"Don't make jokes. When I asked you about my father, you told me his name was Vincent Galway, that he was a visiting professor at Columbia, and that you'd only been together for a short while. That he was killed in a freak accident while you were pregnant. There was no elaboration, no 'he was a very good man' or 'I thought we'd have a life together' or 'it's such a shame you never got to know him.'"

"I told you what you needed to know, in case you had to draw more pictures in the future."

I closed my eyes hard to keep the tears in check. "But you didn't tell me what I needed to know; that's the point. You left it to my imagination. That was cruel."

The plane bumped and rolled. Babies were crying and flight attendants instructed passengers to stay in their seats. I wondered how many other nervous fliers were talking about their pasts, trying to sort out old pain during moments of present fear. I felt Cynthia's fingers loosen, although she was still holding my hand. Her head had fallen back against the headrest, and her eyes were closed. It looked like the Valium had kicked in.

My memories were thick around me, and as usual, I was alone to face them. I wished I'd had a drink and taken a sleeping pill, knocked myself out like Cynthia for the rest of the trip. Instead, I followed my thoughts, sober and sobering.

The boys in grade school liked to speculate on all the gory ways this mystery father of mine had met his end, while the girls indulged in romantic fantasies about Cynthia's lost love. None of it seemed all that relevant to me. Lonely and shy, I was happy for the attention my dead father brought me.

Then in fourth grade, Penny transferred into Hunter and changed everything. Hunter only allowed students to start in kindergarten or seventh grade. We figured she must be a genius. It turned out her father, Dr. Chan, was the principal's optometrist.

On Penny's first day at school, she marched up to me at recess, where I was playing boxball by myself. She caught the red rubber ball and hit it into my square, waiting for me to return the volley before she introduced herself. "I'm Penny. I'm new. You can remember my name because I'm a shiny new Penny."

"Okay," I said. We hit the ball back and forth. Penny looked scrubbed and presentable in a way I hardly ever did, even with the expensive clothes Cynthia bought for me. Penny's pin-straight black hair was pulled back into a careful braid, and she wore brown leather shoes that looked way more grown-up than my scuffed white Keds.

She must have noticed me looking. "These are penny loafers. See the penny stuck in the slot near the middle of the shoe? It's another great way for the kids to remember my name, since I'm new." Penny's novelty was beginning to wear off. I was about to walk away when she took another tack.

"Dylan says your father died in a freak accident."

"Yeah."

"What happened to him?"

"I don't know."

Penny threw the rubber ball aside and stepped closer to

me, placing her hand on my shoulder. "It's time for you to find out, don't you think? You're not a baby anymore."

When I got home from school that afternoon, I found Cynthia sitting in her favorite reading chair in the living room, a glass of red wine in her hand, and her worn volume of Emily Dickinson open in front of her. Our housekeeper, Vera, met me at the door and took my backpack from me. Vera was a woman of no fixed age but past her prime, with a surname I couldn't pronounce and a fondness for Eastern European cooking I didn't share. She guarded Cynthia's time ferociously and enjoyed polishing the silver and ironing the tablecloths, but not cleaning the bathrooms or mopping the floors. My mother hired a second woman, Feliz, who picked up the slack on the weekends, with Vera none the wiser.

"There's a snack in the kitchen," she said. When I started in the direction of my mother instead, Vera hissed, "Don't bother her. She's working."

I ignored Vera and sat on the ottoman near my mother's chair. Cynthia put down her book. She opened her mouth to say something, but I interrupted.

"I'm not a baby anymore. You should tell me about my father and the freak accident." Once I'd spoken the magical words—tell me about my father—I felt a powerful need to understand the truth, a longing that hadn't presented itself before that moment.

"You haven't been a baby for some time, Jessica, but you've shown no interest in this subject."

I felt heat rising to my face. I wasn't curious enough. I'd disappointed Cynthia, again. I forced myself to make eye contact and said, "Tell me now."

Cynthia lifted her glass and took a long drink before placing it carefully back on the coaster. She gazed out the window to her left, the treetops in Central Park filling the panes of glass, the leaves beginning to change color. I wondered whether she was seeing the freak accident in her imagination or thinking about something unrelated. I had to pee, but I waited quietly, afraid if I moved, she'd never tell me.

"He was walking down Central Park West early in the morning. It was an exceptionally cold day, but he liked to take a stroll before he taught to clear his mind. They were doing maintenance on the San Remo, and a piece of scaffolding fell. It hit Vincent right on the head, crushing his skull. He didn't stand a chance." Cynthia finished off the wine in her glass and reached out to stroke my face, but her hand was cold and I recoiled. "I'm sorry. It's not a pretty picture, Jessica, but real life rarely is. Now at least you know."

I ran past her into the bathroom, where I peed first and cried second. I'm not sure what brought the tears. I didn't have any more feelings for the mystery father than I had before. But the thought of his brains spilled out on the sidewalk was worse than anything the boys in my class had dreamt up.

When I came out of the bathroom, my snack was waiting—carrots and celery with ranch dip and a glass of chocolate milk. Vera was sitting at the table, leafing through a copy of Vogue that I was sure she'd swiped from the counter downstairs where the letter carrier left items that didn't fit in the mailboxes.

I pulled the scrap of paper from my pocket where Penny had written her phone number and picked up the cordless phone. I pressed the buttons slowly so I'd get it right.

Penny answered, and I told her what I'd learned. She cried, too.

. . .

When the Valium wore off an hour later and Cynthia stirred, I was ready.

"When we got a little older, ten or eleven, Penny and I made it our duty to find out more about Galway's death." I watched Cynthia carefully to see if she'd react, but she looked at me impassively.

"We snuck off to the library and figured out how to search the microfiche, but we found nothing about a man dying on the sidewalk in front of the San Remo. And we spoke to each of the doormen on the block—especially the old ones who had been working in the buildings for a million years—but no one remembered any tragic death from falling scaffolding in the late 1980s."

Cynthia pressed the call button and ordered another Bloody Mary. "I'm not surprised. People back then minded their own business. Now there'd be fifty strangers gawking with cell phones and making it impossible for the ambulance to get to the body."

I didn't tell Cynthia that as an adult, I'd spent countless hours scouring the internet for any reference to a Vincent Galway who could possibly be the visiting professor and fleeting lover of Cynthia Harmon in the spring of 1988, enamored long enough to impregnate her before his tragic demise.

I was no longer sure he existed.

CHAPTER SEVEN

Chicago had been grueling, the conversation about my father still turbulent in the air between us. What made those days bearable was that we were constantly on the move, surrounded by other people. The Committee had booked community events at the University of Chicago, Northwestern, and Loyola, as well as a members-only dinner at the Poetry Foundation. Three days in the Windy City and my mother had definitely had the wind knocked out of her.

The transition to St. Louis wasn't looking much better. Cynthia had been distracted all day. Picking at her scrambled eggs, changing her shoes several times, then staring out the window in the lobby of the Hilton as we waited for a car service to take us to the venue.

"I thought you'd be excited about this stop on the tour," I said. I hadn't been back to the city since my grandparents passed away five years earlier, but from the brief walk I'd taken, the city seemed rejuvenated. I was looking forward to seeing the kind of turnout Cynthia would get. My mother was less sanguine.

"Why would you think I'd be happy to be here?"

I tried to keep the exasperation out of my voice. "Because you grew up here. It should be exciting to return to your hometown—local girl makes good, or whatever."

Cynthia picked at a piece of lint on her wool pants. "What

should be doesn't necessarily coincide with what is."

You said it, not me. I checked to make sure I had thrown a cardigan for each of us into my backpack. The weather was turning cool as the end of September neared. The tour was a third of the way over. I'd had more concentrated time with Cynthia than at any point in my adult life, and I was nowhere closer to the answers I needed. I wasn't sure I even knew the questions.

Cynthia perused the itinerary for the umpteenth time. "What exactly is this place where I'm appearing this afternoon? I haven't heard of it."

"It's called High Low. It opened recently. It's run by a private arts foundation. It has cafés, galleries, and performance spaces. It's trendy. Hip." I thought the youthfulness would appeal to Cynthia, but she seemed dubious.

"I assumed the event would be on the Washington University campus. The Committee was right. No one cares about literature anymore. The liberal arts are dead. Everything is business, economics, computers." Cynthia rose and meandered off in the direction of the ladies' room.

"Don't get lost—we need to leave soon."

In the car, I tried again. "Do you have memories of growing up in St. Louis? You hardly ever talk about your childhood. It's like you didn't exist until you got to New York."

"Of course, I have memories, Jessica. I'm not demented. Just because I choose to keep my own counsel rather than overshare about my past doesn't mean I don't remember. Besides, my poetry is tremendously reflective. A careful reader who wanted to know would learn a lot about me."

Cynthia's jab was so off the mark that it didn't sting. I'd

read every line of every poem she'd ever published. Searching for her.

I paid the driver, careful to put the receipt into my wallet to submit to the Committee for reimbursement when the tour was over. This trip was costing me emotionally; no way would it cost me monetarily. Cynthia got out of the car and charged ahead, not bothering to wait for me. When I went into the building, she was already engaged in conversation.

I would've recognized him anywhere by the tilt of his head and the slope of his shoulders as he bent toward Cynthia, asking a question or sharing a thought in a soft but sure voice.

Raj Chakrabarty, the Mumbai-born golden boy of the Lit department at Hunter College. A grad student when I was a sophomore, he was brilliant, good-looking in a clean-cut, boy-next-door sort of way, and super confident. What impressed me the most when I met him back then was how easily he made conversation with students and professors alike, something I couldn't do even though I'd grown up around Cynthia and her crew. Or maybe *because* I'd grown up around Cynthia and her crew.

Raj was the first person to take my writing seriously, a far more potent turn-on than what any of the undergrad boys had to offer. We'd worked together on the literary magazine—he was the graduate editor; I was on staff. One night, after midnight, we were in the lit mag's student office, binge-reading manuscripts for the upcoming short story issue. A few showed promise, but most were mediocre. Some were dreadful. I hadn't submitted anything, too uncertain of myself with the specter of Cynthia in her office down the hall. But it was late, and I was tired, and I let slip to Raj that I'd written a story.

"You show me yours and I'll show you mine," Raj teased.

"Promise you'll be gentle."

I handed him the printed pages I'd been carrying around in my backpack since the beginning of the semester. Raj sat back in his chair, shoes kicked off, his red socks on the conference table in front of him. He read slowly, his lips moving slightly, showing no emotion. I couldn't stand to watch him, so I paced the hallway outside the room, ducking into the women's bathroom to splash my face.

I'd abandoned the standard sage advice to "write what you know" and penned a gothic romance set in Panama, 1989, the year I was born. The story was about an American soldier who is hopelessly in love with a young indigenous woman but inexplicably stands by silently as she starves herself to death in protest against the American invasion. I was aiming for dark and passionate, but I was worried I might've achieved only culturally insensitive and creepy.

Raj's verdict was mixed, honest but kind. "The story needs work, Jessica. I don't think it's ready for this issue. But the voice is authentic and compelling. That's what matters."

I smiled. "I guess I could use some more mentoring."

"Sounds like I'm the right guy for the job."

The evening ended in a memorable make-out session on the couch in the Lit mag office, Raj blockading the door with several cardboard boxes loaded down with past issues of the journal. He was skillful and self-assured, and I let myself get lost in the moment.

I could have attributed Raj's generous evaluation of my writing to ulterior motives, but I respected his talent and his opinion. His confidence in my potential gave me the conviction to tell my stories, a conviction Cynthia soon decimated.

And now here he was, ten years later, charming Cynthia. My mother enjoyed speaking with a handsome man, and Raj was certainly that. He'd grown into his looks since I'd last seen him. The raw material had been there, for sure, but now his body had a solidity and his facial features a precision that bespoke a mature sexiness. Seeing Raj banter with Cynthia, even though I knew his flirtatiousness was purely a courtesy, was almost more than I could stand.

"Raj!" I called out. "What an unbelievable coincidence!" I stopped short so he could look me over, praying he'd recognize me after all this time. When his eyes lit up and he reached out for a hug, I stepped into his arms, enjoying the moment all the more for the shocked expression on my mother's face.

"You two know each other, I presume?" Something in Cynthia's tone made me hesitate, but Raj jumped in.

"We do. We were at Hunter together in the English department."

Cynthia looked steadily at Raj, her eyebrows raised. "If you studied English at Hunter, why don't I know you?"

"I focused on fiction, Professor Harmon. I didn't take any of your poetry seminars, but you were a legend in the department when I was there. You still are. I saw you speak and read several times. And had I thought more about it, I might have anticipated Jessica would be on the tour with you."

I threw a sidelong glance at Cynthia. "Oh, I don't think anyone could have anticipated that. So, what are you doing here, Raj? You're not from St. Louis originally; I'd have remembered. My grandparents lived here. I spent my summers at their house when I was a kid."

"No, I'm from Brooklyn. After I finished my master's at

Hunter, I came out here to do a PhD at Wash U. I'm ABD but working on a novel that I hope will fulfill the requirements. Eventually."

Cynthia did a slow three-sixty, and I could tell from the look on her face she thought the place resembled a men's locker room in a cheap gym more than a perfectly presentable, hip, performance space. "And what brings you here, to the Up Down?"

Raj smiled. "High Low. I found academia was a little staid for me—at this stage of my career, I need to be more in the mix. No offense, of course."

"None taken," Cynthia said. I swallowed a giggle.

"I work for the Kranzberg Arts Foundation—they operate several venues serving different arts communities all across St. Louis. This is the newest location, and the best, in my opinion. I organize the exhibits, concerts, theatrical productions, and readings like yours, Professor Harmon. It's a great job—I get to interact with creatives across the spectrum—and it leaves me time to write." Raj had been speaking to both of us, but his energy was aimed at me. Cynthia must have felt it, and she turned away.

"Can I show you around, Professor Harmon? There's a provocative exhibit in the gallery if you'd like to have a look."

"Please stop calling me Professor Harmon. It makes me feel old and makes you sound like a child. Can you direct me to the room where I'll be reading? I'd like to check out the acoustics and the configuration of the seating."

"Of course. I'll take you there right away." Raj stepped forward and offered his arm to Cynthia.

She scowled at him. "Not necessary. I prefer to have some

time alone in the space. A simple pointing of your finger will do." Raj obliged, and Cynthia strode off toward the auditorium.

"Wow. That didn't go very well," Raj said.

"My mother doesn't hesitate to express her needs. Don't worry. It has nothing to do with you. I'd love a tour of the gallery."

"Part of my job is to make sure the artists like me. But as long as the daughter is still on my side, it's all good. Come right this way, Mademoiselle," Raj said, bowing from the waist and gesturing toward an adjacent hallway.

We walked into the gallery, a cavernous room easily twice the size of my apartment, all white walls, exposed pipes, and concrete floors. The current exhibit featured photographs by a local St. Louis artist—black and white shots of internal organs at very close range. I tried to keep my face neutral and murmured and nodded as Raj pointed out his favorites. "This is a lung." "Check out the liver." "I think this is an appendix, but it could be a gallbladder?" I nodded until Raj stopped in the middle of the room and gestured toward the walls. "Disgusting, no?"

When we stopped laughing, we sat on a small bench outside the gallery entrance. Cynthia was out of sight, and Raj smelled like peppermint tea. I felt relaxed for the first time since we'd left New York.

"So, what are you writing?" Raj asked.

"I've been working as an editor since I graduated from Hunter. Two different shops; nothing worth talking about. Then this tour came up, so I figured it was a way to see the country a little bit." I hoped I sounded less pathetic than I felt.

"Must be great. I love your mom's poetry. She's a

96

fascinating woman."

"She's unique, I'll give you that." I wanted to stop talking about Cynthia, to keep Raj to myself for a little while longer. "Are you really working on your dissertation?"

"You know how writers talk about manuscripts they stick in the proverbial drawer? I used to think that was crazy, like how could anyone get that far on a novel and then not figure out how to make it work. Now I have two of those myself. And I'm working on something new. We'll see where it goes."

"I'm sure it will be fantastic. And the ones you shelved probably are wonderful, too." I was gushing, but being close to Raj after all these years was exciting.

Raj brushed off my comments, but I could tell he was pleased by the "aw shucks" smile on his face. "Hey, I just had an idea. What if you read something of yours tonight, alongside your mother? A cameo appearance. The audience would love it."

I stared down at my black suede boots. "I'm not writing anymore."

I could feel Raj studying me, but I refused to make eye contact. "I don't believe that. You're a writer. That's who you are. I still remember when we were working on the magazine, and you organized that all-night student reading in the Lang Recital Hall. You opened and closed the program with two of your short stories that began the same way but had divergent endings. You were on fire."

I shook my head. Raj was right, I hadn't stopped writing. But my words hadn't seen the light of day since college.

I stood and walked over to the window. The sky was heavy with clouds. "I haven't published anything since you knew me."

Raj ambled over to where I was standing and put his hand lightly on my back. "No worries. You can read from a work-in-progress. Or read from the story that won that prize when you were a senior—"

I turned to face him. "How do you know about that? You weren't even at Hunter anymore."

"You were a rising star. I kept my eye on you." Raj smiled at me, and for a second, I forgot my rising star had crashed and burned. His idea that I should read was a total non-starter. Cynthia would never allow me to share the spotlight with her.

"I couldn't read that. I was twenty-one years old. It's juvenile."

"I doubt anything you've written is juvenile. Youthful maybe, but there's nothing wrong with that. Except maybe your Panamanian murder-by-hunger-strike story. That might've been juvenile."

It was my turn to smile, amazed that Raj remembered. My mood deflated when he returned to his official duties. "Come on, let's go see what *Cynthia* is up to." The exaggerated way he said her name made her seem less fierce, and I followed him toward the auditorium.

"Maybe we could go get a drink instead?" I was only half-kidding.

"Hold that thought."

My mother was sitting in the front row, legs crossed and arms folded across her chest, staring straight ahead at the stage.

"What do you think of the room, Prof—I mean, Cynthia?" Raj was smooth, his tone deferential.

"It's adequate. Hopefully, the seating capacity won't greatly exceed the turnout. A half-filled house is demoralizing."

"I'm sure all your appearances have been standing room only. We've had nice advance registration, and there are usually more people who buy tickets at the door. You're a big draw."

Cynthia waved her hand above her head, playfully swatting Raj's words away.

He was undeterred. "And Jessica tells me you grew up in St. Louis. Will you have family or friends from the area coming?" Raj sat a few seats away from Cynthia, leaving me standing off to the side. It was the sort of male attention my mother usually gobbled up, so I was surprised at her gruff response.

"No."

Raj looked over at me, his eyes questioning. I shrugged.

We were all quiet for a moment. The lights in the auditorium glinted off Raj's blue-black hair, and I had an insane desire to touch him. Instead, I watched as he leaned in toward my mother, as if they were the only two in the room. "Cynthia, I wanted to run something by you. I had an idea I think could enhance this afternoon's program."

I took a step toward him, as if I could physically stop him from continuing. "No, Raj—don't."

But he kept going. "I thought it would be fantastic if Jessica joined you on stage toward the end of the presentation and read a short passage from her own work. The audience would be delighted to see you pass the baton to the next generation."

Cynthia addressed Raj but looked directly at me. "I'm not quite ready to pass on yet, Raj."

"It wasn't my idea," I said. Though in the ten minutes since Raj's plan had been hatched, I'd pictured myself at the podium. Reading my story that had held such promise. And maybe for one brief moment outshining the great Cynthia Harmon.

Raj backpedaled as fast as he could. "That didn't come out right. What I meant was it could be exciting to explore the mother-daughter element, especially since you work in different genres and have such unique voices. It would add a layer of complexity to the presentation. And it would be fun, heartwarming." Raj sounded desperate, and I felt sorry for us both.

Cynthia did not give an inch. "Frankly, it would be inappropriate. These people have paid to hear me read. Having Jessica on stage would be nepotism of the worst kind. It would be like subbing in the understudy when the lead is perfectly able to perform."

Raj shook his head slowly. "Well, you clearly have strong views on this, Professor Harmon. I didn't mean to upset you before the event."

I jumped in to save Raj from himself. "Don't worry. You can't rattle my mother that easily. She has nerves of steel."

Cynthia looked up at the ceiling. "If you mean that I'm a professional, Jessica, yes, I am. I'm strong, and not ashamed of it. It's the only way a woman can survive."

I thrust my hands in my pockets to stop them from trembling. "Strong or harsh? I would have preferred some tenderness along the way."

Raj pulled out his phone and played around with something on the screen as he spoke. "I apologize if I unintentionally stepped into a minefield here. I feel like this is probably a bigger conversation for another day."

But I was just getting going. "I'm not sorry. It's great to see my mother show some emotion. She's usually so focused on herself, she can't be bothered with anyone or anything else. Are you catching what got her riled up here?"

"Please, Jessica, that's enough," Cynthia said.

"My mother would rather have me hail her a taxi or order her oatmeal at the hotel than have people hear my work and maybe think it's good. She always has to be the star."

"Jessica, really. You're embarrassing yourself."

Raj looked from Cynthia to me. "I'm going to leave you two. The doors open in thirty minutes." He walked out of the room, touching my shoulder lightly as he passed.

Cynthia stood and walked toward me, fists clenched at her sides. We were inches apart, only a column of fury separating us. She spoke quietly, but there was venom in her words.

"That was mortifying. Imagine! Airing your complaints about me in front of a total stranger."

"That's what's bothering you? Not that you hurt my feelings by rejecting Raj's idea without a moment's thought? You are unbelievable."

Cynthia looked in the direction where Raj had left the auditorium and then turned back toward me. "What's bothering me is that you are acting like a petulant child. One might have hoped that someone who has been blessed with so much in life might exhibit some gratitude."

I took a few steps away from her, afraid that otherwise I might slap her. "This is so fucked up. You really don't understand that you take up so much space you don't leave any room for me to breathe, much less succeed. Maybe if you acted like a normal mother sometimes I wouldn't be reduced to screaming for your attention."

"What is that supposed to mean?"

"What's it supposed to mean? Think hard, Cynthia. When was the last time you took an interest in anything about me, really talked to me about what would make me happy or whether you could help me? Do you even know where I was working before I quit my job to come on this damn tour with you?"

Cynthia pulled a small mirror out of her purse and checked her make-up. "You're getting overwrought, Jessica, and it's unbecoming. I understand you're disappointed you won't be reading tonight. I'm sure you wanted to impress your friend."

I stamped my foot on the ground. "This isn't about me getting up on that stupid stage with you!"

Cynthia crossed her arms over her chest and leaned toward me, unruffled and her tone even. "Then what is it about? What is the terrible grievance you are carrying around? Go ahead, unburden yourself."

She'd given me the green light, and I didn't hold back. "My whole life, it's been all about you, the acclaimed poet and intellect, Cynthia Harmon. Your poetry, your accomplishments, your colleagues, your lovers. You made me feel like I constantly disappointed you. You made me feel like you resented my existence. You can have all the adoring fans in the world. But I know what kind of person you are."

My words seemed to puncture something in Cynthia. She sat down heavily on the edge of the stage, suddenly showing her age.

"You've got it all wrong, Jessica. Your whole life, I've been protecting you from the truth." She turned her face away from me.

I should have let it go, given the old woman a pass, but I couldn't. "I don't think you'd even recognize the truth anymore. Penny always tells me there's an explanation for the way you are. But I think she's wrong. I can't imagine what horror could have produced you."

Cynthia recoiled from the attack, but when she looked at me, her gaze was steady and piercing. "Thirty minutes before a public reading is not the best time for us to talk. There's a lot you don't understand."

We were back to square one. She'd never tell me what she was hiding. She wasn't capable of that level of honesty. "You know what? I'm tired of your secrets and your lies. I'm tired of being Cynthia Harmon's daughter."

I turned my back on her and strode out of the auditorium. I had no doubt she'd compose herself before the audience arrived, but she'd have to go on without me.

CHAPTER EIGHT

I found Raj in the reception area, quietly instructing a petite woman with pink hair to let the ticket holders in promptly at 5 p.m.

When I spoke, the words stuck in my throat. "Sorry to interrupt, but I'm going to catch a cab back to the hotel now. I wanted to say goodbye."

Raj took my elbow and led me gently away from the exit toward a table where iced tea and pastries had been carefully set out. "Please, don't leave, Jessica. I'm so sorry about what happened. I started this whole mess. You tried to warn me not to suggest you join Cynthia on stage, and I was so caught up in what a great idea I thought it was that I ignored you."

"It's okay. It's not your fault. Honestly, this blow-up was a long time coming. If it hadn't happened here, it would have happened soon somewhere else. Maybe it's the reason I came on this tour to begin with."

Raj took my trembling hands in his. "Look, I know you're upset; you have every right to be. Even though I didn't understand what was going on in there, I could tell it was horrible. We've barely had a chance to catch up. Stay. Please."

My resolve wavered. But Raj's sweet pleas were no match for what I was in for if I stayed with Cynthia. I couldn't do it to myself. Even I had my limits.

I pulled my hands away and looked at my watch. "If I go

now, I can make a flight that won't land in New York at some insanely late hour. It was great to see you. And I'm sorry you had to witness that. The best thing I can do at this point is to put some physical distance between me and my mother." I pulled my cardigan out of my backpack and put it on, handing Cynthia's sweater to Raj. "Please, give this to her."

Raj took the sweater from me, but he had a faraway look in his eyes. I felt a wistfulness about him that made me think he knew a thing or two about anger or regret. Then he reached into his pocket and pulled out a large set of keys, holding one out from the rest. "My office is on the second floor, the door right in front of you at the top of the stairs. Hang out a while. See how you feel. We could get a bite to eat after the reading."

The adrenaline had retreated, leaving a deep weariness in its place, and I took the keys from his hand. I was still determined to get out of St. Louis as quickly as possible. But maybe Raj was right, and I needed a little time to regroup.

"I can't promise you I'll wait around until after the event."

"Fair enough."

"And don't worry that things got heated right before showtime. Conflict makes me sick to my stomach, but Cynthia enjoys it—gets her juices flowing. She'll be great."

Raj smiled again, and this time the sadness was replaced by something more mischievous. "There's a bottle of Pepto-Bismol and a bottle of Scotch in the bottom drawer of the desk. I'd advise either or both."

I walked up the stairs and watched from above as the pink-haired sprite unlocked and opened the entrance doors and the literati of St. Louis flowed in. Evenly split between men and women, there were college students and retirees, professor-types and precocious-looking teens. Many looked unfashionable, some bordered on unkempt, as though being a fan of Cynthia Harmon's poetry required a level of devotion to high literary aesthetics at a cost to mundane self-care. Her groupies were so unlike Cynthia herself, who took inordinate pride in her appearance, that under different circumstances, I would have laughed. I unlocked the door to Raj's office, stepped in, and closed it firmly behind me.

The room was spartan, trending toward monastic. Along one wall was a nondescript beige sofa with a low coffee table in front of it, St. Louis tourism magazines, and museum exhibit catalogs carefully arrayed on the surface like in a dentist's office. The only decoration on the walls was a canvas print of the Gateway of India, tastefully if blandly framed in the same hues as the couch. I sat and then stretched out, trying to calm my frayed nerves. The fury had passed, but the after-effects of the confrontation lingered.

I pulled out my cell and FaceTimed Penny. She answered, holding the phone in one hand and a vacuum with the other. The sound was deafening. It looked like I'd caught her in full domestic mode. Wearing her Queens College sweatshirt, she had her hair pulled back, her contacts replaced by her thick glasses.

I yelled to be heard. "I'm coming back to New York."

She turned off the Hoover. "What did you say?"

I told her again, at a more normal decibel level.

"What do you mean? You have four more weeks."

"Cynthia and I had a big fight."

Penny frowned into the phone. "What kind of fight?"

"It was awful. She was awful. She's a witch."

Penny sat in a chair and balanced the phone on her knee. "Tell me what happened."

I replayed the scene in the auditorium in my head, shuddering when I remembered Cynthia saying that if I participated in the reading it would be "nepotism of the worst kind." Like she could think of nothing more despicable than bestowing some benefit on me because I was her daughter. It stung more the second time around.

"Jess? I couldn't hear you. Do we have a bad connection?" I knew the social worker in Penny loved to dissect a fraught interpersonal conflict, but I couldn't stomach relating all the gruesome details.

"You were right. There was no possibility of this trip turning into anything other than a disaster. Cynthia's not capable of a normal relationship, at least not with me." I felt a pre-crying tingle in my nose and paused the video until I got myself under control.

"Well, I'm not surprised, but I am sorry."

I wiped away a couple of tears on the sleeve of my sweater and considered taking Raj up on a shot of Scotch. "She says she has some big reveal for me, but she's hinted at that many times before and then clammed up. I don't know whether I'd believe anything she told me anyway."

Penny was warming up to the subject just as I was ready to put my relationship with Cynthia back in the box where I stowed it. "Hmm. Maybe it's about your father? I think of all those years we tried to figure out who the real Vincent Galway was and what happened to him. Cynthia might feel like it's time for you to know."

"I guess. But seriously, if Cynthia lied and he didn't die in a freak accident before I was born, then she should have told me a long time ago when I needed a father. And if my father is still alive, where the hell has he been for the past thirty years?"

"Good question. Besides, maybe the scaffolding did fall on the poor guy's head. Who knows. There are other things she could be ashamed of from her past. Or maybe her own mother screwed her up."

I yawned, not bothering to cover my mouth. "I don't know. She had an idyllic Midwestern childhood, and she's been sitting at Hunter College since she was eighteen years old. What could have happened to her that I wouldn't have already heard about?"

"Are you falling asleep? What time is it there?"

"It's a little after 5:00. Fighting with my mother saps me."

"All I'm saying, Jess, is that everyone has formative events that make them who they are. Your mother's must be pretty whacked."

"Yeah. I told Cynthia that was your theory."

Penny clapped her hand over her mouth. "You didn't!"

I nodded. "I did. Don't worry, she was unimpressed. Okay—new game. You'll never guess where I am." I kicked off my boots and put my feet up on the armrest.

"According to the tour schedule on my refrigerator," she paused and walked across her kitchen, "you're in St. Louis."

I watched in silence as Penny threw kale, half a banana, almond butter, and kefir into a blender. "Hang on," she said and hit the button. "Sorry, that was loud. Would have been worse with ice."

"I'm in St. Louis, and I'm lying on Raj's couch."

"Raj who?"

"Raj Chakrabarty. The grad student from my sophomore year at Hunter."

Penny was quiet for a moment. Then a huge smile crossed her face. "Hot Raj? The guy from the lit magazine with the ripped pecs and the skin as smooth as a baby's butt?"

"Glad to see motherhood hasn't entirely addled your brain. And I think the expression is as smooth as a baby's bottom."

"What are you doing on his couch? Or should I use my imagination?"

"He's the Program Director at the venue where Cynthia is reading today. I'm using his office to cool off. I'm going to catch a flight to New York tonight. I'll call you tomorrow."

I pictured myself alone in my apartment in Astoria, with no job, no boyfriend, and now more cut off from Cynthia than ever.

"Penny?"

"What, Jess?"

I felt the catch in my voice before I heard it. "I'm going to need your help. To start all over again."

Penny pressed her free hand to her heart. "You don't have to ask."

I put my cell on the coffee table and wandered over to Raj's desk. It was a large, modern piece, a slab of thick tempered glass resting atop a polished nickel base. Furniture worthy of an art gallery. Raj's computer monitor sat in the center with neat piles of papers surrounding it. The whole impression was restrained and orderly, a grown-up and tamped-down version of the Raj I'd known when I was in college. Did that guy who'd lit up my short stories and lifted up my short skirts still exist underneath this subdued corporate persona? He'd been playful talking about the body parts in the gallery—there was hope.

Sitting in Raj's desk chair, I spun around to check out the view from the windows facing the street. There wasn't much to look at—brick buildings and car traffic and bedraggled pedestrians heading home from work—nothing more inspiring than the vista from my apartment in Queens. Still, his set-up was a whole lot more professional than the makeshift and clandestine writing space I had at home, or that I'd had at my old cubicle at Canyon Press. It was hard to believe I'd left behind my former life, Tyler and Clark and Larry and all of that, only a couple of weeks earlier. I'd burned my bridges. When I told Penny I'd be starting from square one, I wasn't exaggerating.

I absentmindedly pressed one of the keys on Raj's computer keyboard. The screen lit up and filled with page seventy-four of a Google doc, a long paragraph that ended mid-sentence. It was a trick Raj had taught me back in the day—leaving a thought unfinished provided a way back in when you returned.

I was sucked into the story after a few lines, the writing unpolished but edgy and powerful. A wave of heat passed over my body, and I pulled off my cardigan and tossed it onto the couch. Jumping to the top of the document, I read all seventy-four pages of the manuscript from the beginning. I knew reading Raj's work in progress was a disgusting violation. But I didn't stop. I devoured his pages. Here was the fiercely talented and passionate man who'd gotten under my skin all those years ago.

When I looked at my watch, an hour and a half had passed. Cynthia's reading must have ended. She'd be signing books now. I'd screwed up my original plan to leave early and avoid another confrontation with her at the hotel. Now it was inevitable. Still, Raj had been right. I'd cooled off, and now I would be able to pack and head to the airport with my wits about me. I leaned back in his chair, closed my eyes, and let the images he'd painted with his words play over in my head. I felt amped up by his writing even as his certain future success highlighted my continuing failure.

Raj sauntered into the office and placed a few programs from the event and a copy of Cynthia's book on the coffee table, startling me. "Sorry! Were you sleeping?"

"Just relaxing. Did you get your book signed?"

"No. I was afraid of how she might inscribe it." Raj came over to the desk, reached out for my hand, and pulled me up from the chair. "Are you hungry? There's a fantastic Vietnamese place a couple of blocks from here."

"Is Cynthia still here?"

"No. One of the interns took her back to the hotel in a taxi. I hope that's okay."

"How was she?" I asked, although I already knew the answer.

"She was spectacular. They ate her up. But they would have loved you too."

"I read your manuscript," I blurted out.

Raj let go of my hand and backed away a few steps. "Oh, wow."

I sank back into his chair and put my head in my hands. "I'm sorry. I'm a terrible person."

Raj sat on the couch and shook his head slowly. "It's just that it's a first draft. I'm not ready for anyone to read it."

"I don't know what came over me. But it's wonderful, Raj.

It's vibrant and original. I'd follow your characters to the end of the earth, and I'm only seventy-four pages in."

"*I'm* only seventy-four pages in. But thank you. That means a lot to me. You always were a careful reader."

My praise seemed to revive him, and I was emboldened to say more. I rushed to the couch and sat next to him. "The Joseph character is fantastic. So bleak. Basically, his whole life is a shit show. I totally relate."

Raj inched closer on the couch. "Hey, your whole life is not a shit show."

"I'm envious of you."

"You're crazy. I'm sure you're living the life in New York. St. Louis is a second-tier city, a backwater. Nothing happens here."

"I'm not jealous of St. Louis. I'm jealous of that manuscript, Raj. I'd sell my soul to have the courage to write like that."

"I don't know. I don't remember you as a shrinking violet when we were at Hunter." Raj ran a finger slowly up my leg from my knee to my hip, and thoughts about my mother and my failed writing career flew out of my head. When he leaned in to kiss me, I stopped thinking altogether.

"Hmm, exactly. Baby's butt," I murmured, my hands underneath his shirt. His chest was as smooth and muscular as I remembered it, though less boyish.

"What?"

"I was checking on something." Penny would be pleased to hear Hot Raj had aged well.

The couch was technically a love seat, and our limbs intertwined to accommodate the limited space. We explored each other cautiously at first, and then with abandon. In Raj's arms, I was twenty years old, lithe, hungry, and full of hope.

We were interrupted by the ping of an incoming text message. I reached for my cell, but in one quick motion, Raj scooped it off the coffee table and stuffed it behind the cushions of the sofa.

"I should check. What if it's Cynthia?"

"And if it is?" Raj lifted his sweater over his head and began to unbutton my shirt. Cynthia would have to wait.

Raj reclined on the couch with his arms behind his head. "I think you just used me to turn your mood around. Should I feel dirty?"

"Up to you. I feel pretty good. But I need to get back to the hotel." I retrieved my cell and stepped into my skirt, smoothing out my top before putting it on.

"You know we can still get dinner. I'm starving. It doesn't have to be Vietnamese." Raj scrambled to catch up to me getting dressed.

"Next time, okay?" The sweet throwback to our earlier selves was over. We were adults now, and I was going back to New York. I couldn't hope for a next time.

"At least let me drive you back to the hotel." Raj took his wallet and car keys from the desk. "And I forgive you for reading my manuscript."

CHAPTER NINE

We drove in silence, the highs and lows of the day crashing in on me and rendering small talk impossible. When we reached the hotel, Raj pulled over and killed the motor.

"What's next?"

I took a deep breath. "I'm going to go to my room, throw my stuff into my bag, and tell Cynthia I'm leaving. No apologies, no explanations."

"That's definitely what you want to do? Because once you go down that road, there's probably no going back."

I heard where Raj was coming from, but he hadn't grown up with Cynthia, and he had no right to judge me. I couldn't act the part of the good daughter this time, even if it offended Raj's sensibilities. I opened the door and stepped out onto the sidewalk. Then I leaned into the car and gave Raj an awkward wave. "Thanks for letting me hang out in your office."

"Go grab your things. I'll drive you to the airport."

"I can't let you do that."

"You can let me do what we did on that couch, but you can't let me give you a lift to the airport?" Raj grinned. "I'm teasing. It's no big deal. Take your time."

I stood with my hands on my hips and gave the elevator doors my best threatening stare.

"Oh, sweet Jesus," I said, pressing the call button again. This was taking forever, and I was afraid I'd lose my nerve if I didn't confront Cynthia soon. It was only 8:30 p.m., but the lobby was nearly abandoned. A prematurely stooped-over man silently mopped the floor around the couches and coffee tables, and the same pasty-faced woman who'd been working the front desk when Cynthia and I had left the hotel earlier was still on duty. The hotel lobby looked as depleted as I felt.

I knew I should be rehearsing what I would say to Cynthia, but I couldn't focus. I'd have to wing it. And really, what was the difference? She'd hear what she wanted to hear. The trick was to get in and out quickly before she could work some mind game on me and guilt me into staying.

When the elevator doors opened, I practically bowled over a kid holding an empty ice bucket and looking lost. I pressed the button for the fourth floor. As the elevator ascended, I forced myself to think of Raj waiting patiently in the car. Ready to whisk me off to the airport and back to Queens.

As I walked down the hall, I rummaged through my backpack for my card key, checking the zippered compartments. Then I searched my wallet, taking out the cash, spilling the coins into my hand, and leafing through the receipts and bits of paper where I scrawled ideas. I didn't remember taking the key out while I was in Raj's office, so it had to be somewhere, but I couldn't find it. After a few minutes, I gave up and knocked on the door. When there was no response, I knocked more insistently.

"Cynthia? Cynthia!"

When she didn't answer, I felt like I'd won the lottery.

Could this be as easy as getting a new key and escaping without confronting her? I didn't get lucky too often, and this would be twice in one day.

I hurried back to the lobby, taking the stairs to avoid the pokey elevator, and approached the desk. The clerk, whose name tag read "Donna," had her head resting on the desk and her eyes closed.

I cleared my throat. "Sorry to disturb you.".

She sat up abruptly, giving her head a quick shake. "Forgive me. I've had a doozy of a day."

I forced a smile. "You and me both."

"How can I help you?"

"I forgot my key in the room. Can you please make me a new one?"

"Yes, sure. What room are you in?"

"413."

"ID please?"

I handed over my non-driver's ID card. Donna looked at it for an extra beat, brow furrowed. "A lot of people in New York City don't drive," I said. "But I swear, it's me."

"No, of course. You're here with Professor Harmon, right? I had a nice chat with her when she returned this evening. She recommended I check out the new Arts center downtown. She seemed to have enjoyed herself." Donna pressed a few buttons on the computer and put the new card key on the counter.

"Yes, I heard she had the audience enthralled. Maybe she could stay in town for a while." Donna looked away, and I immediately regretted my remark. It wasn't this woman's fault my mother was who she was. "I'm sorry. I'm glad she enjoyed St. Louis. I guess she must have gone out for dinner with someone who came to the event. Thanks for the key." I turned to go back to the elevator.

Donna called after me. "I've been at the desk the whole time since she came in, and I didn't see her leave. Maybe she's in the shower or turned in early."

But Cynthia was a creature of habit. She showered in the morning, not at night, and there was no way she was asleep at this early hour. I made my way quickly to the stairwell and took the stairs two at a time, reaching the fourth floor landing breathless. At the door, I swiped the key card and the light flashed red.

"Damn it!" I swiped again. On the third try, it turned green. I pushed the door open and burst into the room. The lights were on, and I heard Anderson Cooper dissecting Trump's chances of being impeached, but there was no sign of Cynthia. I raced toward the bathroom, my heartbeat pounding in my ears.

"Cynthia? Cynthia!"

I narrowly missed stepping on her glasses, which lay on the floor, the horn-rimmed frames camouflaged by the beige carpet.

She lay on her back on the bathroom floor, a white terrycloth hotel bathrobe open around her naked body and her hair loose on the tiles around her head. "Oh my God! What happened? Are you okay?" Cynthia fixed me with a watery, unfocused gaze but didn't respond. A wave of nausea washed over me. I knelt down and leaned over her, taking her hand. It felt limp.

"You must have slipped on something. Come, let's get up—" I tried to lift her from underneath her arms, but she wasn't helping, and her dead weight stopped me. I didn't realize I was crying until I heard myself speak.

"Alright—everything will be okay. Stay here. Don't go anywhere. I'll get help." I raced into the bedroom and picked up the phone.

Donna answered on the third ring. "I need an ambulance to room 413."

I hung up and propped the door to the room open with the desk chair. Praying EMS would come quickly, I went back to the bathroom and pulled Cynthia's robe together, tying the belt loosely. "Let's fix this here a little," I babbled. "No need to cause any extra excitement! Were you going to take a shower? That's not like you. What happened? Did you bang your head?"

Now tears were rolling down Cynthia's cheeks too, and she still hadn't said a word.

"Don't cry. Please don't cry. Why aren't you speaking, Mom? Say something. Please."

Minutes later, I was following the paramedics carrying the stretcher, grateful that someone, probably Donna, had thought to stop the elevator on our floor. They'd given Cynthia oxygen, and her color had returned a little.

When we got outside, someone with a clipboard spoke to me. "You the daughter?"

"Yes."

"You riding in the wagon?"

"If that's allowed." I'd never been in an ambulance before. He motioned to me to get in, and I was fastening my seatbelt in the jump seat near Cynthia's feet when I heard Raj talking to the EMS guy.

"Which hospital are you taking her to?"

"Barnes Jewish," the paramedic barked.

"Raj—what—why—" My confusion must have been written all over my face.

"I was waiting to take you to the airport, remember? I'll meet you at the hospital."

I tried to jump up, but the seatbelt held me firm. "No! Don't come!"

The guy checking the straps on my mother's bed gave a short whistle through his teeth. "Hey, try to keep it down. It's better if everyone stays calm."

Raj appeared unfazed by my outburst. "I won't get in the way. I'll be there in case you need anything."

"Please, don't."

The EMS guy closed the second door of the back of the ambulance. The driver took off, sirens wailing, lights flashing. I watched Raj's fading figure through the tiny square windows on the rear doors.

It took me a moment to realize the EMS guy was still speaking to me. "Don't worry, she's stable. The hospital is really close, and it's a good one."

I glanced back at Cynthia, and she looked too peaceful. "Why are her eyes closed?"

"She's resting. Emergencies are exhausting."

I followed my mother's gurney through the hospital doors

as the EMTs moved swiftly from the ambulance bay into the triage area. The ER was jammed, a cacophonous hodgepodge of misery, fear, and pain. I tried to focus while different hospital staff—first the triage nurse, then a timid young man with sweaty palms who introduced himself as a resident, then another nurse, then an over-eager medical student who stood too close—each asked me what had happened. As I explained, their eyes bore into me, questioning, judging: *Where were you when your mother collapsed?*

An IV inserted, an EKG taken, a heart monitor hooked up. Question after question about Cynthia's health, prior surgeries, allergies, her daily medications.

I told them what I knew, which wasn't much. An emergency appendectomy when I was a child. High cholesterol. Allergic to penicillin. Mostly, I said I didn't know. "She's afraid to fly," I told a nurse with a kind face.

"I'm sure it's been a long day for you too," she said to me. "We're going to take your mother for brain imaging. Why don't you go sit in the waiting room? We'll come and find you when we know more."

My legs grew weak. If I didn't sit down soon, they might buckle. "Really? It's okay for me to leave her?"

"You can't come into radiology, honey, so you might as well take a break. It will be a little while."

I didn't murmur any encouragement to Cynthia or kiss her forehead, although I thought about doing both. Instead, I squeezed her foot. Then I turned away and walked out into the waiting room to sit by myself.

The place was packed with people less critical than Cynthia waiting to be helped. I sat on a gray plastic chair and used the toe of my shoe to push someone's half-eaten apple underneath. On my right, a middle-aged guy with long hair and an intricate Spider-Man tattoo on his biceps was clutching his stomach and moaning. On my left, a pregnant woman was taking up her seat and encroaching on mine as she balanced a toddler on her lap with a makeshift bandage on his thumb nearly soaked through with blood. His eyes were red from crying, but he must have wailed himself out because he was eerily calm.

I took some deep breaths and focused my eyes, if not my brain, on a television showing a rebroadcast of the evening's St. Louis Cardinals game. Sirens screamed into the ambulance bay outside. "GSW! GSW!" the paramedic yelled as he and his partners raced by the open doors of the waiting room, just out of my line of sight. I imagined a teenage boy writhing on the gurney, blood seeping through the white tourniquet near his shoulder.

Spider-Man dude leaned closer, speaking near my ear. "It's a tough town." I winced but managed a nod.

In the hush that followed, I moved to the corner of the waiting room and pulled out my cell.

When Penny answered, my throat closed, and my voice sounded as mangled as my nerves.

I could hear Carlos in the background asking who was on the phone, and Penny shushing him. She sounded groggy; I must have woken her. "Jess? Jess, what's wrong? Are you crying? It's after midnight."

"I think I killed her."

"Who? What are you talking about?"

"Cynthia."

"Cynthia's dead? How could she be dead?"

I paced, following in the tracks of a guy wearing an orange sanitation jumpsuit and clutching his left elbow, cursing at top volume. "She's not dead, but something's happened to her. I let loose on her this afternoon—I told you—and then when I got back to the hotel, I found her lying on the bathroom floor. They're taking her for a CT scan. They said she might have had a stroke. I did it to her. I got Cynthia so upset that something exploded in her brain."

Penny turned on her calm and capable social worker voice that usually pissed me off but now I craved. "Okay. Try to slow down, Jess. I can barely understand you. You're at the hospital now?"

"Yes. The nurse said someone would come get me when I could see her. Or when they knew more. I can't remember exactly. This place is a nightmare."

"Was she awake when you found her?" When I didn't answer, Penny tried again. "Did she know where she was?"

I pictured my mother, eyes wide and helpless, half undressed on the hard white tiles. And silent.

"She was awake." The room tilted and I sank onto the nearest free chair. A woman sitting nearby with wiry gray hair stopped wheezing for a second and stared at me.

"I hate that you're there alone. I wish I could fly out and be with you, but Carlos has regional meetings all week and he can't help with the kids on such short notice—"

I looked across the room to where Raj sat, his head resting against the wall but his eyes trained on me, his hands folded in his lap. "It's okay. I'm not alone."

CHAPTER TEN

When I shifted my body, a throbbing ache traveled from my knees through my lower back and lodged between my shoulder blades. My legs were tucked beneath me at bizarre angles, my neck contorted so my head rested on the arm of the chair next to me. I opened my eyes. In the dim light, I could see Raj, still sitting at a respectful distance, but not as far away as before.

I stretched my arms carefully, groaning with the effort. Sometime before midnight, the ER doc had taken my written consent to give Cynthia a clot-busting drug and then told me I could move to the neuro ICU waiting room. I must have fallen asleep after that.

"What time is it?" I needed to brush my teeth, and a hollow echo in my stomach reminded me I hadn't eaten since some toast and jam for breakfast at the hotel. There were a few other people scattered around, but compared to the other waiting room, this place was a morgue.

Raj tilted his head toward a chair closer to me. "May I?"

"Sure."

Raj sat next to me and handed me a coffee in a disposable paper cup. "Drink it while it's hot."

"Oh my God. You're the best."

"And you are fickle, my friend." He looked like he wanted to smile, but wasn't sure he should risk it.

I took a sip, letting the steam rise from the cup and warm

123

my face. A wave of embarrassment washed over me as I remembered my behavior earlier in the evening when Raj had tried to help. "I'm sorry for yelling at you."

Raj smiled, radiating a sweetness that I remembered from our younger days. "It's okay, Jessica. There was a lot going on. And to answer your question, it's three in the morning."

When I heard the time, I stood as quickly as my cramped limbs would allow, sloshing coffee over the top of the cup and onto the chair. I started toward the double doors leading to the ICU. "Shit! It's been a long time. Do you think I should go ask the doctors what's going on?"

Raj shook his head. "I would wait. Someone from the team came out about an hour ago. They were running blood tests. He said your mother was stable and resting—that they'd know more after they reviewed the scans and the neurologist examined her."

"Why didn't you wake me? And shouldn't that HIPAA thing have prevented him from talking to you since you're not related?" Somehow, I didn't think Cynthia would appreciate Raj being briefed on her medical condition.

"We tried, but you were dead to the world. It wasn't much of an update. Besides, maybe he thought I was your brother from another mother."

I smiled despite myself. "That's the best you've got?"

"Hey, I'm not working on a lot of sleep myself."

When I sat back down, I noticed how rumpled Raj looked. His shirt, so crisp before the event, was now a maze of wrinkles, and his thick black hair was going in ten different directions.

"I appreciate your waiting with me. Now it's time for you to go home and for me to take over here. The coffee was above and beyond."

Raj took out his cell and slowly jabbed at the keys with his index finger. "I'll go if you promise to let me know what's happening. Give me your phone number."

"Is that how you type? No wonder that manuscript is taking you so long. Hand me that," I said, reaching out for his phone. I put my name and number into his contacts and passed it back.

"Jessica—I thought of something else when I was watching you sleep—"

I braced myself for some awkward reference to our afternoon together.

"You should probably let someone from the Committee know what's going on with your mother."

I let out the breath I was holding. I'd almost forgotten Cynthia was on tour, and I'd been on the verge of leaving her. "I barely know what's going on."

"They're going to want to put out a press release. Even if Cynthia's okay in a few days, which I hope she is, they'll need to postpone the next leg."

I opened my wallet and took out the card Monica had given me in New Haven, offering it to Raj. "Can you let this woman know?"

He stood up and put his cell into his back pocket. "If you're up to it, I think it's better coming from you."

I put the card back. "Right. Of course. This is my responsibility. Please, go get some sleep."

Raj leaned toward me. I turned my face away at the last second, and his kiss landed near my ear. He bowed his head and walked to the elevators.

A few minutes later, my phone pinged.

Trying to find my car. No idea where I parked
last night. ;)

I was typing a reply to Raj when I saw the text I'd ignored
while he and I were horizontal on his couch in his office. It
was, of course, from Cynthia. The words were gibberish, a
jumble of random keystrokes. The only word I could make out
was "you."

At 3:30 a.m., I took Monica's card from my wallet a second
time and dialed. I assumed the call would go to voicemail, so I
was caught off guard when she answered.

"Oh. Hi," I said.

"Who is this?"

"Sorry. It's Jessica Harmon. Cynthia's daughter." I walked
across the waiting room to a vending machine I hadn't noticed
earlier. I pulled a single from my pocket and pressed B6 for a
packet of peanut M&Ms. No candy came out. "Damn."

"Jessica? Is everything okay?"

"A candy machine just swallowed my dollar."

"That's why you're calling me at this hour?"

"No—I'm sorry. I haven't eaten in a long time, and I was
hoping for the sugar boost. Wow—and my back kills from
sleeping in a chair."

"Is something going on?" Monica's question sounded
simple, but the answer was anything but. It had been a horrible
day. I'd finally been emboldened to tell Cynthia what I really
thought of her, and then she'd been struck down. And though

I'd meant every word I'd said about her and her screwed-up parenting, she was still my mother.

I took a deep breath. "Cynthia is in the hospital. She had a stroke."

"Oh no! Is she okay?" Monica sounded discombobulated but genuinely concerned. I remembered I hadn't called some random clerk at the Bollingen Committee office, but Cynthia's friend.

I leaned into the machine with my shoulder and tried to jostle the M&Ms loose. A harder shove and a packet of Twizzlers slid down into the tray.

"I don't know. I haven't seen her since she was moved to the stroke unit. But she's a fighter." And for the first time in my life, I was grateful for that.

An hour later, a woman emerged from the ICU into the waiting room, looking more like she was off to an exclusive art gallery opening on Madison Avenue than signing in for her shift in a St. Louis critical care unit. She wore stiletto heels and a skirt so short that at first glance I thought she might be naked underneath her white coat. Her auburn hair was thick and lustrous, and her make-up was a little overdone for my taste but flawless. She surveyed the handful of people in the waiting room and then made a beeline for me.

"Are you Ms. Harmon?"

"Yes." I ran my fingers through my hair and clumsily tried to cover up the remaining Twizzlers in my lap.

"I'm Dr. DiFulvio. I'm the neurologist on call. Why don't you come this way, and I can explain to you and your mother what we know so far." I could tell she was all business, which was reassuring. I also thought I detected a little submerged Brooklyn in her accent. I followed her silently through the double doors.

The stroke unit was divided into four separate areas, each with three or four beds. In the middle was a large nurses' station where scrubs-clad women and men milled about, checking monitors and charts, chatting and laughing, as they spun off with medications or blood pressure cuffs toward the patients. The place had the feel of a living organism where all but the patients were full of energy and good humor.

I followed the doctor into the quadrant where my mother lay in her bed, an IV in her arm and monitors overhead, beeping and assessing. Cynthia was propped up on pillows and her eyes fluttered open when we came closer. Although her color was better than it had been when I found her, she looked so diminished I swallowed back a gasp.

I was grateful the doctor covered my reaction by addressing Cynthia in a voice louder than necessary for my mother's excellent hearing.

Referring to Cynthia as Mrs. Harmon, the doctor introduced herself and asked if it would be okay to speak in front of me. She didn't give my mother time to object, but of course, she didn't know that, if given the option, it was a real possibility. The doctor motioned me to sit near my mother's bed while she pulled up a chair for herself.

"Poems... teacher." Cynthia's words came out haltingly, but emphatically. Dr. DiFulvio looked from my mother to me. I was relieved to hear her speak, but the obvious effort was heartbreaking.

"I think she wants you to know she's not a 'Mrs.' She

prefers to be addressed as Professor Harmon. And she's a poet."

"Of course. I misspoke. I'm sorry." Dr. DiFulvio seemed flustered. She looked at the chart, as though Cynthia's resume was attached. I thought it was a good sign my mother had asserted herself. But I also sensed that in the realm of the hospital, professor or not, Cynthia was just another patient with a dire issue in her brain.

"Can you explain to us what happened?" I asked.

"I'll do my best. But first, it would be helpful if you can tell me how long Professor Harmon might have been incapacitated before you reached her. The timeline is helpful in our assessment."

"I don't think it was very long." But when I ran through the evening in my head, I knew that was my guilt speaking. The reading was over by 6:30, Cynthia had sent me the indecipherable text at 7:15, and I was back at the hotel at 8:30. She might have been lying there on the bathroom floor waiting for help, waiting for me, for an hour or more. "Maybe an hour, at most an hour and a half."

"Okay. Professor Harmon. I know you've had a long night and this is a lot to take in. We'll take you for another CT scan and an MRI later this morning, but the initial scans confirm you had a stroke caused by a blood clot and not a bleed in your brain. When you were brought into the ER, there was still time to administer a clot-busting medicine to restore blood flow. So that's excellent news."

I pictured myself in Raj's office, our clothes in disarray and bodies in unhurried exploration as the time bomb ticked away in Cynthia's brain. I tried to understand whether what this doctor was saying was that my delay hadn't made a difference.

With any luck, Cynthia wouldn't remember my betrayal.

I was so lost in thought that Dr. DiFulvio's question to Cynthia startled me. "Have you ever been treated for atrial fibrillation—an irregular or rapid heartbeat?"

When Cynthia didn't answer, the doctor turned to me, eyebrows raised. "I don't believe so," I said.

Dr. DiFulvio paused. "Is there someone else who might be more familiar with your mother's medical history? Just for now, when she's having some trouble relating the information herself?"

I was searching for an answer that wouldn't reveal more of my ineptitude when Cynthia muttered "tart" under her breath. I was going to apologize on my mother's behalf but decided to let the moment pass. The doctor didn't miss a beat.

"We've put you on a blood thinner, Professor Harmon, and we're monitoring your heart now to get a better sense of how to treat the a-fib going forward."

She was flipping through Cynthia's chart, making it impossible for me to catch her eye. When she finally looked up, I spoke urgently but quietly.

"So you're saying the rapid heartbeat caused the clot, and the clot caused the stroke?"

"Yes, that's our understanding of what happened."

"And the rapid heartbeat—that's a condition my mother may have had for a while?" I was out of my depth, but I needed to know.

Cynthia's expression was blank, and I couldn't gauge how much she was following. I turned away from the bed and spoke quietly, directly to the doctor.

"We had an argument earlier in the day. We were both very

emotional. I thought I might have done something to give her the stroke."

If she'd been my kindergarten teacher and I was a traumatized five-year-old, Dr. DiFulvio could not have looked at me with any more kindness in her heavily made-up eyes than at that moment. "You didn't cause this, Ms. Harmon."

Cynthia had dropped off. Asleep, she looked unharmed and harmless.

"The stroke caused some damage to the left frontal lobe of her brain. As a result, she's weak on the right side of her body, and it's also affecting her ability to communicate. But these are early days; there's no way to tell yet how this will shake out."

I swallowed hard, willing myself to act like a responsible adult and not a frightened child. To ask the important questions. "What do you mean affecting her ability to communicate?"

Dr. DiFulvio put the chart on the tray table and looked at me steadily. "Remember, this is my best guess at this point. The condition is called Broca's aphasia or non-fluent aphasia. Your mother understands what's being said to her, but she may not be able to express herself, even though she'll feel like the words are on the tip of her tongue. She may speak in incomplete sentences or a few words at a time. Like earlier, she understood I had called her Mrs. instead of Professor, but her response—what did she say?"

"Poems teacher," I said, cringing.

"Right. That probably wasn't exactly what she wanted to say, and sometimes deciphering her meaning may be harder. She'll likely have difficulty reading and writing as well. It can be very frustrating. But a good PT and speech therapist will help her—and you—get through it."

I closed my eyes, and my own words came out in a painful frenzy. "You don't understand. This can't be happening. Words are my mother's life. It would be like consigning her to hell."

CHAPTER ELEVEN

Dr. DiFulvio and her team strongly recommended that Cynthia do her inpatient rehab in St. Louis rather than traveling to New York, so I settled myself in at the hotel. Although the Bollingen Committee had offered to pick up the tab for my room, I knew even before I asked her that my mother would have none of that. Cynthia Harmon was not a charity case.

Now, three weeks later, the hotel had come to feel like a second home. Today, like every morning, I made a beeline from the elevator to my favorite chair, the threadbare blue one closest to the breakfast room. The Everton was designed for the business traveler, and it did the job. The accommodations were adequate, not more—who came to St. Louis and stayed for three weeks? There was no need for me to race to claim my usual place; the lobby was nearly empty at 6:30 in the morning. I was wide awake, another day at the rehab awaiting me. The last day.

I sat down and opened my laptop. I hadn't checked my emails since the beginning of the week, figuring anyone who needed me would text or call. There were two messages from girls I knew in high school—both had heard from Penny that Cynthia was sick. We weren't really friends back in the day, and I hadn't talked to them in ages. Their good wishes felt a little forced, but I decided to give them the benefit of the doubt, emailing each a simple "thanks." There was an email from Judy, Cynthia's long-time secretary at the college.

"Hi, Jessica. Wondering if you know yet what I should do about Professor Harmon's teaching obligations for the spring semester? Also, there's a junior faculty member asking about using your mother's office while she's out this term. Not sure what to tell him."

I had no idea what Cynthia would be well enough to do when she returned to work, if she returned to work, so I told Judy to hold off on talking to the registrar as long as possible. As for the young colleague using my mother's office, I told Judy it was a hard no. I knew from my own recent experience of shamelessly snooping around Raj's computer that the temptation to invade someone's privacy was just too great.

There were all sorts of spam emails, advertisements for products I didn't buy or need. At the bottom of the screen was an email from Clark.

I could hear Clark's voice, twangy and teasing. "Hey, Jessica. Saw the press release about Cynthia. What a drag! Seriously, I'm sorry you got stuck in that, I know you weren't that down for going with your mother to begin with. Maybe it would have been better to stay here at Canyon—although the job sucks just as much as you remember it. Anyway, when you come back to New York, we should get together. You can buy me a cup of coffee."

I smiled and closed my laptop as Donna approached me with a Danish.

"I can't believe you're leaving today."

What I couldn't believe was the unlikely friendship that had developed between me, a diehard New Yorker whose default wardrobe was all black and who could go weeks without uttering a pleasantry to a stranger, and a woman twice my age who favored pastels and matching lipstick, who manned the desk in a business hotel and greeted every guest with a melodic, "How are you today, Sugar?" But ever since Donna had called 911, she'd kept her eye on me. She worked crazy hours and as far as I could tell was basically always around. She also seemed to know when I needed a candy bar and when I needed to be left alone. And now she sat across from me at the end of this leg of the journey.

"Don't you think it's about time I got out of here?"

Donna fluffed the pillows on the couch, picking up yesterday's newspaper from the coffee table where someone had left it. "I don't know. I think it was smart you stayed and your mother did the rehab here. It would have been too hard to take her to New York right away."

"Well, that's what the doctors advised. But now she's well enough to go home, and I think she'll improve faster in familiar surroundings." Although truthfully, I wasn't sure. I pictured Cynthia in her apartment, unable to negotiate the shower or the coffee maker on her own, or trying to make herself understood with the stream of visitors who would flock to her as soon as word got out she was back in New York.

Donna pulled off a piece of my Danish and popped it in her mouth. "Do you think she'll be alright?"

"Hard to say."

Cynthia was better than she had been in the immediate aftermath of the stroke, but the improvements were incremental. I'd spent every day of the last three weeks at the rehab with her. Despite its excellent reputation, it wasn't a state-of-the-art facility. The staff was underpaid and unmotivated, often missing scheduled sessions for physical therapy or speech therapy. Sometimes, Cynthia's meals came an hour or two late. But that was all window dressing. The doctors said by far the most critical aspect of her recovery at this point was for Cynthia to walk, to regain her strength. Up and down the long hallways we paced, Cynthia leaning into her walker, slowly navigating around the other patients as they did the same.

One day a nurse pulled me aside.

"It will help your mother improve if you talk to her while you walk. It doesn't matter what you say. It's like when you're talking to a baby—the sound of the words and the structure of the language is what sinks in. Tell her old family stories or talk about what you read in the morning newspaper."

I thanked her and returned to my mother's side. We resumed our silent procession.

Donna's voice brought me back to the hotel lobby. "You know," she said, leaning toward me and speaking quietly even though there was no one around, "your young man stopped by again yesterday to see you. But you weren't back from the rehab yet."

For a second, I drew a blank, until I realized that, compared to Donna, Raj was a young man. And I was a young woman. I was surprised she didn't call him my gentleman caller. That would have made me laugh.

"Raj was here?" He'd texted me every day to see how I was doing and ask what about Cynthia. I'd kept him updated, although I hadn't seen him in person since that night at the hospital. It felt too overwhelming to add Raj into the mix of my messed-up existence. But hearing from Donna that he'd come to find me made me question my resolve to keep him at a distance.

"He's come a few times, usually around lunch. Once in

the early evening. He's a catch, that one." Donna slipped her shoes off, wiggled her toes, examined a bunion on her left foot, and put her shoes back on. "Okay, I better get back to work. You never know what notables might want to check into the Everton Hotel early on a Thursday morning in October. Hope you enjoy what's left of the Danish. And don't leave without saying goodbye." She reached down and squeezed my shoulder.

I watched Donna as she made her rounds checking on the various plants positioned around the lobby, pruning leaves and feeling the soil with her fingers, watering the ones that needed refreshing from a plastic watering can she kept behind her desk.

I was so lost in thought about the logistics of getting Cynthia to the airport and on the plane that when Donna spoke, I jumped a little. "Oh, he's here again. Clever to try early in the morning!"

I turned and saw Raj coming in the front entrance. His hair was wet, and he had his car keys in his hand, as though he expected Donna to send him on his way. Instead, she waved him over.

"You caught her. I stalled her with pastry," her tone triumphant.

I stood and shook the crumbs from the front of my shirt.

"Hey," I said.

"Hey." He stepped a little closer, and we hugged, briefly but long enough for me to breathe in the woody scent of his cologne. "Can we talk?" he said.

"Sure." I looked over at Donna, whose fingers were now on her computer keyboard, unmoving. She winked at me, and

I shook my head. "Let's sit outside. There are some benches out front."

Raj followed me out through the glass doors, and we sat facing the street. A steady stream of people passed on the sidewalk in front of us, walking with purpose but seemingly not in a rush. My nostalgia for the summers I'd spent with my grandparents probably colored my perceptions, but this was the St. Louis I remembered from my childhood. Friendly, wholesome, a little bland. The men in functional but unfashionable suits, toting brown leather briefcases. The women walking in twos and threes, lost in conversation, the commute to work somehow more social than in New York. I could have sat and people-watched all morning. Avoiding the rehab, avoiding Cynthia. Avoiding Raj's body so close to mine.

"How is she?" Raj asked.

"Not great. She has a lot of hard work ahead of her. But she's stable. It's time for us to go back to New York."

"When are you leaving?"

"Today, if I can pull it off."

"You must be happy to get out of St. Louis."

I chose to ignore the edge in his voice. "New York is home. My happiness seems a little bit beside the point right now."

Raj shifted away from me on the bench. "Maybe there's someone in New York waiting for you."

Tyler and the spurned engagement flashed through my mind, and I shook my head. It all felt like it was a million years ago. "No, there isn't anyone. That's not it."

Raj looked down at his hands. "So, I'm right that you're actually avoiding me?"

I shook my head. Raj deserved an explanation, but it

wasn't that easy to put into words. "It's not about you. I don't have the bandwidth right now for anything more than getting through each day."

"I hear you. I guess I'm just not sure how to interpret what happened here. There was some intense reconnection, segueing into an overnight in the ER, and then what? See you when I see you?"

"Look, that afternoon was special. Not exactly something I do every day."

"Well, that's good to hear."

"And I won't forget how you saw me through that night at the hospital, even when I begged you to go away."

I looked down the block, my eyes finding a young couple holding hands as they walked toward the corner. "You've been a good friend. But you don't want to get tied up with me. I don't know if I'm capable of anything more."

Raj stood, put his hands lightly on my shoulders, leaning in close. "I don't think you have any clue what you're capable of."

I turned back toward the entrance to the hotel, moving out of his reach. "I need to go. We've got a flight to catch."

Raj made a show of standing, taking his keys out of his pocket, and walking a few steps toward his car. "Right. Maybe that's for the best."

"If you're in New York, will you call?" I asked.

"Have a safe trip, Jessica."

• • •

I walked around Cynthia's spacious living room, methodically opening each of the heavy windows, letting in the autumn breeze and the sounds of Central Park West. I knew it was futile. The suffocation was inside. No amount of fresh air would free me.

The buzz of the intercom startled me.

"Penny is here to see you, Ms. Harmon."

"Thanks, Alberto. Please send her up."

When I opened the door to the apartment, Penny swept in, did a little pirouette in the foyer, and gave me as big a hug as her small body would allow.

"I can't believe you're finally back! I was beginning to think you were relocating to St. Louis."

"Haha. Very funny." I hugged her again, squeezing so hard I lifted her a few inches off the floor.

"How was the trip home?" Penny asked.

"It was okay. I think one of the side effects of the stroke is that Cynthia forgot she was afraid of flying. She downed a vodka tonic and passed out."

Penny looked around the living room. "I haven't been in this apartment since high school."

"*I've* barely been in this apartment since high school."

Penny's eyes widened. "Jess—you can't stay here. It's crazy. Why don't you go home to Astoria? I mean, I don't have to tell you it isn't healthy for you to live here, do I?" She put her hand over her mouth. "Oh, shit! Your mother didn't hear that, did she?"

"No, don't worry. She's lying down in her room. She gets wiped out from the therapy sessions. And it isn't permanent, me being here. I just don't feel right walking out on Cynthia now. This is a whole new reality for her."

As we talked, the backside of a wide-bottomed woman passed the entrance to the living room on her way slowly down the hallway.

"Is that?—" Penny asked.

"Vera," I confirmed. "I needed someone to help, and my mother trusts her. And Vera still makes the best snacks. Remember her strawberry jam and marshmallow fluff on Triscuit sandwiches?"

"This place is like a time warp."

"You haven't seen the best part. This way, M'lady." I took Penny's hand and led her to my childhood bedroom. I opened the door with a flourish, revealing a twin bed with a girlish pink comforter and white frilly pillows. The wallpaper was festooned with tiny roses, and the ceiling was painted with silver stars. I lay on the bed, pulling Penny down next to me.

"Oh my god, Jessie—your room is exactly the same as when we were kids! Cynthia didn't touch a thing."

"I know. I thought for sure she would have erased me, turned this room into something more useful. A library. Or a shoe closet."

"So why didn't she? Have you asked her?"

I sighed. "You haven't seen her yet. I can't ask her complicated questions like that. When she can't express herself, it upsets her."

"That must suck for her. Does it upset you?"

I thought about the question for a moment, running my fingers over the silk border on the baby blanket my grandmother had knit me when I was born. "There were so many times when Cynthia used her words to hurt me, or maybe worse, used her silence to hurt me. But this is unnatural. Like a soundtrack has been screwed with or turned off. Except eerily, sometimes, when she seems to find the exact words she wants."

Penny squeezed my hand and pointed to the ceiling. "This was the only place I could ever find the Big Dipper."

"Me too. My bedroom made me feel like there was some part of Cynthia for some period of time that wanted me to be happy."

Penny pointed to a Red Hot Chili Peppers poster on the wall next to the bed.

"Remember how we listened to that album over and over, *Californication*? We were so excited to say that word."

"Yes. And look, there's the poster from *The Texas Chainsaw Massacre*. That was one fucked-up flick. It was the first R-rated movie we saw without sneaking in."

We looked around, laughing and pointing out moments from our shared history. Moments even Cynthia hadn't managed to spoil for me.

"There's our prom photo," I said. "I can't believe you went with smelly Kevin Escobar. He still hadn't discovered deodorant by the twelfth grade."

"I wore enough of my mother's perfume for both of us. Besides, he was tall and had his own car. And look who's talking!"

"What do you mean? My date was hot," I protested.

Penny was laughing so hard her face turned bright red. I got the giggles just watching her. "Hot? You could barely see Freddy Nelson's face behind that big calculator he toted around. He brought the damn thing to the prom. What equations was he solving for on the dance floor? Or maybe you two were working out some angles in the back seat of the limo."

"At least Freddy was smart. And he smelled fresh, like wintergreen."

Penny rolled over on her side and put her hand on the top of a wooden box on my bedside table. "What's in here?"

"Nothing."

She playfully shoved my shoulder. "Condoms? Diaphragm? Tell me."

"Hey! This is my *childhood* bedroom, remember? Open it if you must know."

Penny lifted the cover and put her hand into the box. "What are these?"

"Gumballs. The kind you get from the machine in the supermarket."

"Yuck!" Penny dropped the ones she'd been holding, and several rolled under the bed. "Are these like twenty-five-year-old gumballs?"

I closed my eyes. "When I was six, my grandparents gave me a Barbie doll for my birthday. I loved everything about her: her tiny waist, her pointy boobs, her platinum blond hair. And the clothes!"

"Let me guess. Cynthia was not a fan," Penny said.

"'They limit the imagination and reinforce gender stereotypes.' She took away my Barbie and put it on the highest shelf of my closet. She's probably still there."

Penny inched closer to me and put a reassuring hand on my shoulder. "And the gumballs?"

"An ingenious substitute. I would take nickels from home and hit the gumball machines on the way out of D'Agostino's with Vera. Then I'd hide the candy in my pocket until I got home and put them in the wooden box I'd salvaged from

Cynthia's perfume. I gave the gumballs names and prayed they wouldn't attract roaches. I used to lie on my stomach on the floor and play with them. They had elaborate lives— they rolled around, fell in love, married, had kids, fought and divorced, died. I'd hear conversations and noises coming from Cynthia's bedroom on the other side of the wall, and those would be part of the game too."

Penny sat up suddenly and took my hands.

"Listen, Jessica. I've worked with enough sick people and old people to know one thing for certain. People don't change when they get sick and old. They become more themselves. You've got to get out of here."

"I can't. For the first time in my life, Cynthia needs me."

144

CHAPTER TWELVE

A stranger might have thought the somber mood lighting was intentional. The sunlight that streamed in through the large windows in the living room during the late afternoon didn't reach the dining room, and the crystal chandelier that hung over the table hadn't been dusted in ages. Vera used to take care of that, back in the day, but now she took care of Cynthia instead.

Vera brought a bowl of tomato soup from the kitchen, placing it in front of my mother and tucking a cloth napkin over her sweater. I sat next to Cynthia and picked up her spoon to help, but she pushed my hand away, and the spoon clattered onto the table.

"It's okay, Jessica. I can do it," Vera said.

I went into the kitchen and ladled soup into a bowl for myself, my hands shaking as badly as my mother's did.

This time, I sat across the wide table, focused on eating my soup and trying not to stare when Vera lifted the spoon to Cynthia's lips. Vera was patient with Cynthia, as she'd been with me when I was a child. And neither my mother nor I were easy people.

Cynthia was improving, but incrementally. The weakness on her right side had lessened, and she was getting around mostly with a cane now rather than the walker. Her word retrieval and the clarity of her speech were getting better. Her sentences were short and stilted, and there were times no matter how she frowned or stamped her foot, the wrong word came out. But she could often make herself understood.

Still, she was silent more often than not. I tried not to take it personally, figuring she was probably self-conscious about the aphasia. Against my better judgment, I tried to make conversation.

"We hardly ever ate in the dining room when I was a kid," I said.

Cynthia looked up.

"Always," she said. Confused, I turned to Vera.

Vera looked down at the table. "*You* didn't eat here, Jessica. I gave you dinner in the kitchen when you finished your homework. Professor Harmon ate here, in the dining room, later in the evening. Sometimes with colleagues or friends. Sometimes alone."

"So we never ate dinner together?" How had I blocked that out?

Cynthia took the spoon from Vera and carefully fed herself several spoonfuls of tomato soup. Then she pushed away from the mahogany table and sidled out of her chair, the way the therapist had shown her. She took several steps toward her bedroom.

"Don't you want to finish dinner? You've hardly eaten anything," I said.

Her eyes swept across my face, as if she didn't recognize me. "Enough," she said.

I focused back on my soup, listening to the sound of her cane as it struck the wood floors. When she was gone, I forced down some of the roast Vera had made and then helped her clear the dishes to the kitchen.

"Don't take it to heart. She's still not herself," Vera said.

"I'm not sure how much more of herself I can take."

I took refuge in my room and lay on my bed. I pulled a worn stuffed animal close to my chest. It was only 7:00 p.m., but I was tempted to go to sleep. I stared at the ceiling. When I was a little girl, I loved the painted stars above my head. They made me feel like my world was infinite, that I could fall asleep on Central Park West and wake up anywhere in the universe. Now the false stars were another trap, the painted ceiling a dream threatening to cave in on me.

I'd only been home with Cynthia for a few weeks, and it felt like forever. I'd given up complaining to Penny, whose constant refrain was to point out my situation was self-imposed—that I could leave at any time. She wasn't wrong, but it didn't help. That same inexplicable need that had compelled me to go on the tour in the first place now compelled me to stick it out during my mother's convalescence. It was getting more difficult each day.

I had an urge to reach out to Raj. Although we'd texted, I'd held back from calling him and having a real conversation. I didn't know if he was frustrated or angry about how I'd left things when we said goodbye in St. Louis. Maybe he didn't care enough to have any feelings one way or another. I pulled my cell from my pocket.

"Hey," I said.

"Hey, back," Raj answered.

"Is this an okay time?"

"Perfect. Let me shut my office door. Okay. I'm lying on

the couch. Do you want to know what I'm wearing?" he teased.

"This is not that kind of call." I hoped he could hear the smile in my voice.

"Don't get excited. I'm fully clothed. I'm even wearing a tie for a dinner meeting with a donor. But it's not until later."

I threw my stuffed ducky into the air and caught it—once, twice, three times—listening to Raj's breathing on the other end of the line.

"You okay?" Raj said.

"Depends on how you define okay."

Raj was quiet for a moment. "There are so many ways to measure okay-ness and not okay-ness."

"Is that even a word?"

We were both quiet for a moment.

"When was the last time you laughed?" Raj said.

"There's not a lot of funny going on. Unless you count me walking in on Vera practicing Blanche's soliloquy from *Streetcar* in the kitchen for her drama club. She wasn't half bad, and it did make me smile."

"See?"

"Can I be honest with you, Raj? I know I'm a downer, but you have no idea what it's like here. I'm living with my mother, who didn't like having me around much when I was a kid. And as soon as I walked in the front door, I became that unlovable kid again."

"Don't be so hard on yourself, Jessica. You're trying to help her, and she's not ready to be helped. If you're determined to stay there—"

"Do I have a choice? My mother is sick, and her world has fallen apart. And I'm her only child."

148

"You always have a choice. You can choose to change the dynamics of this relationship."

I looked at the constellations above me. "I'm the product of thirty years of Cynthia's special brand of mothering. It would take something awfully dramatic to realign our stars."

Raj sounded resigned. "You know best."

I kicked the duck onto the floor and turned onto my stomach. "I'm lying on my bed, also fully clothed. Can you picture that?"

"I'd rather plan when I'm coming to visit you." When I didn't answer, he said, "I'm figuring your silence means you're not ready for that."

I wiped at my eyes with the pillowcase. "It's not that simple."

"Look, it's your life, Jess, and maybe one or both of us will decide I don't belong in it. But this is crazy. You're a grown woman, and you're letting your mother call the shots."

"Well, if you have the answers, what would you suggest?"

"For starters, get out of that apartment. You're in New York City, for Christ's sake. There's life all around you. Go *do* something."

I pulled the blankets over my head and lay as still as possible, trying to quiet the voices in my head. But Raj's advice kept coming back to me: Get out of the apartment. Grow up. Save yourself.

When word initially got out that Cynthia was ill, I'd had a flurry of contacts from friends checking in on me and asking how my mother was doing—former colleagues from my first job, the women from my CrossFit class at the no-frills gym I belonged to, the Hunter high school yearbook crowd that met for lunch twice a year, a couple of old boyfriends who still spoke to me even after I'd broken things off. But that had died down as people returned to their regular lives. I'd barely been in touch with anyone since we'd gotten back to New York. When I pictured who I could reach out to on little notice, the list was short.

I texted Clark.

Meet me at the Met at 7:30? Admission is free on Tuesday nights. Will buy you coffee.

Half an hour later, I was sitting on the steps of the Metropolitan Museum of Art when I spotted Clark loping toward me, his old red backpack slung over his shoulder and his glasses slightly askew. When he reached me, I climbed a couple of stairs to even out our height differential and gave him a quick hug. A look of disapproval crossed his face.

"I'm still mad at you, you know," he said.

"For what?"

"It was unforgivable the way you abandoned me like that at work. Just walked out one day. Who does that?" Clark sat on the steps, his backpack between his long legs. I sat beside him.

"I quit a nanosecond before Larry fired me, Clark. Was I supposed to hang around our cubicle drinking tea?"

Clark cracked his knuckles. "I guess not. It all seemed kind of haphazard—poorly planned and executed if you know what I mean."

I sighed. "No argument there."

A charter bus pulled up and unloaded a group on Fifth Avenue, the tourists strolling past us. I caught a snippet of French here and there. Then Clark pulled a white tissue paper package that looked like it'd been wrapped by a five-year-old out of his backpack. "I bought you a present. Be careful, don't break it."

Inside was an oversized coffee mug inscribed with the words, "There, They're, Their. It'll be okay."

I smiled and put my arm around Clark's shoulders. "Thanks. I love it. And we'll both be okay, eventually."

"It's lonely at work without you."

I nodded and quickly changed the subject to Clark's favorite, his love life. "Hey, how's Sven?"

"Sven? Yesterday's news. There've been several prospects in between, but now I'm all about François. He makes a mean café au lait, by the way. A far cry from cheapskate Larry's Keurig." Clark turned to watch the people streaming through the doors. Free Tuesdays drew a crowd. "Listen, do we have to go in? I know I'm a Neanderthal, but looking at art gives me hives."

I laughed. The Met was one of my favorite places in New York, and I wondered if sitting with Clark *outside* on the steps of the museum qualified as grabbing hold of life in the city. But I was glad to be out and away from Cynthia. "Sure. I can come back another time. So, how's work otherwise? Does Larry miss me as much as you do? Have you taken over Meteor's manuscript?"

"Canyon Press sucks. If Larry misses you, he has a funny way of showing it. He barely mentions your name, unless he can't find something in the kitchen and he's accusing you of stealing it. He dumped all your loser manuscripts on me. Now I'm so overwhelmed I have no time to give proper short shrift to anything."

"What does he think I took from the kitchen?"

"And I was sorry to hear about Cynthia. I'd barely had the chance to savor the discovery that one of my favorite poets was your mother when she was stricken by the cruel whim of a blood clot. Is she functioning at all? My Twitter feed says no."

I thought of Cynthia storming off after dinner earlier that evening, or at least what passed for storming off in her condition. Not only was she functioning, but she'd managed to make me feel like I wasn't. I needed to do something to set myself right.

"Listen, do you think Larry would let me come back to work? I mean, I didn't take his stupid can opener or anything else from the kitchen. And I know it would be humiliating to beg for my job back, but—" I stopped talking when I saw the horror on Clark's face and the way he was violently shaking his head.

"Don't do it, Harmon. You walked out of that shithole a hero. Don't come back on your knees."

I turned away and fiddled with my hair, twisting it into a knot as I tried to ignore the tears blurring my vision and threatening to fall. When I felt I could speak normally, I looked back at Clark. "Okay. I hear you. I have a better idea. What about the two of us going into business together?"

"Wow, we'd be partners."

"Yes! 50/50," I said. I sat on my hands so I wouldn't clap.

"Like opening a coffee shop? But do you know what hard work that is? Hey—weren't you supposed to buy me a coffee?"

"No, not a coffee shop you halfwit, an editing service. We could get clients through referrals from writers we know. We can do the developmental edits, better and more professionally than we did for Larry, and then the clients can self-publish or—"

Clark held out his hand in front of him like he was directing traffic. "Stop. I was kidding. I can't afford to go into any kind of business with you. I need this job."

"Well maybe you could keep your job at Canyon and we could start out slowly. I could take on one or two clients as we build it up, and then when we had enough to make a go of it—"

"Jessica, you working on other people's manuscripts isn't the answer. You're a writer, and you have talent. What you need to be doing is writing."

I could feel Cynthia's disapproval closing in around me, holding me down. "You don't understand."

"I think I do. Don't write to please your mother. Write in spite of her."

It was after ten when I got back from seeing Clark. The apartment was quiet. In the foyer, Cynthia's mail was stacked in a neat pile on the front table, get-well cards on top, literary magazines and bills underneath. The smell of Vera's tomato soup lingered in the air.

While I was out, Vera would have given Cynthia a shower, another task like helping my mother eat her dinner that I'd offered to take on but had been rejected from. I imagined Vera adjusting the water to the near-scalding temperature my mother preferred, then turning away slightly to preserve her dignity while keeping a watchful eye on her. After handing her a white, fluffy towel, Vera would have helped Cynthia into her nightgown and administered the medications she now took to thin her blood, control her hypertension, and help her sleep. All the while, Vera would have murmured, "There you go, Professor," and "That's right, just so, Professor." I knew how it felt to be taken care of like that; long ago, Vera had been there for me too.

Both women were probably asleep, but I tiptoed down the hallway anyway, first past my mother's bedroom and then past the small bedroom off the kitchen where Vera stayed. I could have easily gone to sleep myself, as emotionally spent as I was. But Clark's advice had shamed me. I needed to get some words on the page before I talked myself out of trying.

I went into my bedroom and removed the laptop from my backpack. I hadn't used my computer for anything more than checking emails in months. I opened it and placed it on the desk where I'd written school term papers and college application essays. There were flyers tacked up on the bulletin board on the wall above the desk from the last weeks of high school—senior ditch day at the beach on Coney Island, a notice of where to pick up our yearbooks, an invitation to Drew Callahan's graduation party where I'd gotten wasted and, in a mortifying moment, fooled around with a freshman. I closed the laptop. This was no place for a writer.

I walked further down the hallway, remembering with each step how I tried to wipe away the footprints I made in the plush pile carpet when I snuck into Cynthia's office as a kid. There was no lock on the door, but she said the room was for adults only, meaning Cynthia and whomever she invited in.

Lord knows, her friends and colleagues and students sprang up like weeds in every room of the apartment, even in my bed sometimes. Often drunk on Cynthia's alcohol or half-naked. No, it wasn't the office as off-limits inner sanctum that pulled me. It was the poetry. And the poet.

Although there were books all over the apartment, in tall bookcases and makeshift ones, piled on side tables and in corners on the floor, all the poetry books were housed in walnut bookcases in Cynthia's office. Alphabetized, the collection read like a who's who of Cynthia's universe, both literary and personal. I ran my fingers over the spines of the books, letting myself feel the energy and the beauty they emitted. There were volumes by poets my mother had studied and volumes by poets she'd written about, volumes by poets from other eras and collections by poets who wrote in languages she could only read in translation, which frustrated her enormously. And then there were the ones by poets Cynthia knew personally. Her colleagues, or those she'd mentored, or people she'd met because she was Cynthia Harmon and she was one of them. These were the books I loved most, the ones that contained a personal inscription to my mother, not a pro forma scrawling "thanks for coming" like the ones Cynthia signed for strangers at readings. These fellow poets, many of whom I'd never met, expressed admiration and gratitude and love for the woman who was out of my reach.

The aura of Cynthia's creativity filled every crevice of the space, grand and bold and all-encompassing, and I knew this was where I had to push back against all that she had done over the years to squelch my aspirations. Tonight, the forbidden room was mine. I switched on the Tiffany lamp on the desk, casting a warm glow. I was surprised when I sat in Cynthia's swivel chair; I felt it embrace me, the soft leather molding to my contours. I closed my eyes for a moment, breathing in the smell of the books. I put my laptop in the center of Cynthia's desk and opened it.

My computer lit up, icons of word processing documents covering the screen. Beginnings of stories, some more promising than others, some shorter, some longer, none finished. Hours of effort and hope that I'd poured into the work, none of which had seen the light of day. I thought of Raj and his discipline, the novels in the drawer leading to the one I'd read on his computer, coming alive from the depths of his being and destined for great things. And then I pictured myself, my words crippled by a profound insecurity that I'd battled but that so far had defeated me. I needed tonight to be a new beginning. The words came slowly at first, and then in a rush. I rode the waves of description and dialogue, reveling in the joy of putting sentences together. The feeling of creating was intoxicating, and I wondered how I'd ever tried to live without it.

I was so focused I didn't hear my mother pad in, slippers and cane silenced by the carpeted floor. When I looked up, she was a few feet away from me, across the desk. We locked eyes. Cynthia's flashed with a vitality I hadn't seen since the stroke, and her voice was sure and strong.

"Get out!" She reached back with her good arm and threw a book at me, missing my head by only an inch. It landed on the floor next to me, splayed open. *The Collected Works of Cynthia Harmon.*

CHAPTER THIRTEEN

Hey Clark-I picked the wrong place to stage my comeback as a writer.

Harmon, it's 3 a.m.

I know. I'm so sorry. Insomnia.

It's 3 a.m.

The early bird catches the worm?

There was a long pause, and I figured he'd gone back to sleep.

Don't you need to have succeeded at something previously to make a comeback?

You always were a stickler for vocabulary.

In the morning, I stayed in my room with the door locked and lay in my bed watching reruns of *Will and Grace* on my laptop until I was numb. I ventured out around noon when I heard Vera leave the apartment with Cynthia for one of her therapy appointments, and then only to use the bathroom and grab some leftover meatballs from the fridge. In my head, I'd already taken to calling what had happened Bookgate, but it wasn't accurate. What Cynthia had done wasn't just scandalous. It was an attack. Whatever I labeled it, it was among the lowest moments I'd ever had with my mother. It said a lot that it wasn't definitively the worst.

At least I felt safe in my bedroom. The lock on my door was an addition I'd made on my own when I was a freshman in high school. Twenty bucks and what passed for a sultry look got Tomasz, the Super, to install it without alerting Cynthia. I hadn't used it much back then, but now it felt like a lifesaver.

Over the course of the day, Vera knocked to check on me several times.

"You okay, Jessica?"

"Flu," I responded each time.

Cynthia didn't knock.

By late afternoon, I realized that I shouldn't be the one hiding, and I got out of bed and showered. I needed to move. I hadn't been back to my apartment in Astoria since our return from St. Louis, and the clothes I had with me from the tour were for warmer weather. In the bottom drawer of my dresser, I found an old pair of jeans I could still squeeze into and a heavy sweatshirt from a college prep program I'd done at Brown the summer after my junior year in high school. I looked like an overgrown teenager home for fall break.

I caught sight of Cynthia sitting in her favorite chair in the living room, a book open on her lap but her eyes seemingly fixed on a credenza across the room. I wondered what it must be like for her to struggle to read, much less to write. Was it this frustration that propelled her to lash out when she found me in her office, the place where she had been all-powerful? I felt a pang of sadness for her, struggling to counter the simmering anger. I walked out of the apartment, closing the door noisily behind me, my mother's unasked question, "Are you leaving me?" hanging in the air.

It was a cold November day, the kind that's so clear and fresh it forces you to think about the end of the year approaching and how screwed up your life is. I entered Central Park at 79th Street and was immediately overcome by twin smells. Weed emanating from a guy sitting on a nearby bench and roasting chestnuts from a cart parked on the south side of the path. It wasn't a bad combination.

Although a contact high was tempting, I bypassed the bench and approached the nut vendor. There were customers at the other carts—hot dogs, pretzels, and sodas weren't seasonal. Even the novelty ice cream lady was doing okay. But no one was buying chestnuts. "It's too early in the season for those. It needs to be closer to Christmas."

"Who made up that stupid rule?" The chestnut guy raked the nuts over the grates. "You want some or what? You're the boss."

I sat on a bench further from the guy smoking weed, the paper bag warm in my lap. I peeled the skins off slowly, small pieces breaking off in my fingertips and getting under my fingernails. I willed myself to focus only on the sweet taste and the spongy texture as the nuts crumbled in my mouth. When I finished the whole bag, I looked up. The vendor winked at me.

In my rush to escape from the apartment, I hadn't taken a jacket. And without the warmth of standing by the chestnut cart, I was getting cold. I decided to walk to the East Side to keep moving. I got to Park Drive and took a step off the curb to cross, misjudging the speed of an oncoming cyclist. As a blur of yellow and black spandex whizzed toward me, I jumped back one second before he rode into me.

"What the fuck, lady? You got a death wish?" he screamed at me.

I flipped him off as he rode away and then weaved my way more carefully through the oncoming bicycles and joggers to reach the path on the other side.

I was walking at a clip when the sweet sound of a woman singing and playing the guitar made me stop. She was typical of the legions of street performers that dotted the grassy areas in different parts of the park during the day. She could have been thirty or fifty. Her skin was pock-marked, and her hair was long and lank, a streak of cobalt blue running down one side. She wore an ankle-length flowing skirt, a Mexican-looking woolen poncho with beads on the fringes, and Birkenstocks with white tube socks. Her smile was sad, and her eyes begged the small group that had gathered to connect with her. A yellow lab with rheumy eyes lay sleepily by her open guitar case where a bunch of coins and small bills had collected.

I tossed in a dollar and asked the woman to play *Moondance*, the song that would have been the first dance at the wedding with Tyler that wasn't to be. I didn't stay to listen.

By the time I got to the East Side it was close to 7. There was no way I was going back to the apartment for dinner with Cynthia, so I decided to walk the fifteen blocks uptown to Penny's. It was a little rude to arrive at mealtime without calling first, but what were best friends for?

The doorman who greeted me was one of the older guys Penny liked. She'd nicknamed him Shorty because he stood about six-foot-five, and he wore a terrible hairpiece that was often in danger of falling from that great height. Shorty kept strawberry lollipops in the jacket pocket of his doorman's uniform that he handed out to the kids. The Beresford, where

Cynthia lived, wouldn't have tolerated that.

Although Shorty never remembered my name, I was a frequent visitor to Penny's building, and he gave me a warm hello.

"Let me ring up and tell them you're on your way—"

"Jessica," I filled in.

"Right. Big day is coming up. I'll sure miss those kids."

I was about to ask Shorty where he was going, if he had plans for his retirement, but then the elevator came. I pressed 11, accidentally catching a glimpse of myself in the mirror. I looked pale and unkempt. My hair had grown out longer than I usually wore it and was now a shaggy mess. I couldn't face trying to get my contacts in, so I was wearing what Clark liked to call my demented owl glasses, and I hadn't put on make-up in weeks. As I reached to press the button to return to the lobby, the elevator doors opened. Avia and Kyle were waiting for me in the hallway.

"Aunt Jessica!" Avia squealed. "Come with me." Her hand felt warm and squishy in mine as she pulled me down the hallway. Kyle, the little one and the more reserved of my two godchildren, followed behind.

"Are your parents angry that I showed up without calling?"

"They're busy. They won't notice," Avia answered.

I followed them through the small foyer into the living room.

There were cardboard boxes everywhere, filled or half-filled with books and clothes and knickknacks and kitchen utensils. Rolls of packing tape and black permanent markers were strewn across the floor. Penny was dressed in sweatpants and a T-shirt, her hair up in a ponytail, "Candyland" and

"Junior Monopoly," last year's Christmas gifts from me, in her arms.

"What's going on? Spring cleaning in November?" But as soon as the words left my mouth, I remembered Shorty saying he'd miss the kids.

Penny averted her eyes. "We're moving."

"Why? Do you need a bigger apartment?" I smiled tightly as a thought dawned on me. "Are you having another baby?"

Penny's nose twitched like it did when she was about to sneeze or cry. Or both. "No, we're not having a baby."

I wanted to sit, but there were linens and towels and toys piled on all of the furniture. I chose the nearest armchair and tossed some tablecloths onto the floor.

"I don't get it. You love this apartment. And why are you sneaking out?"

"We're not sneaking out, Jess. I was going to tell you the other day at your mother's. But you've been so preoccupied; I mean, understandably, and you have so much on your plate. I was afraid to pile on."

I rubbed my face where I felt a sting as though Penny had slapped me. "Where are you going? Wait, don't tell me. Let me guess. New Jersey. A suburb with good values and excellent public schools. Montclair?"

"Don't be like that." Tears were running down Penny's face, like she'd been the one who'd been left in the dark. I did my best to keep my tone conversational so I wouldn't frighten the children, although they must have sensed the tension, and I could see them already cowering by Carlos on the other side of the room.

"Look, I'm happy for you, okay? But you haven't answered

me. Where are you moving, Pen? Where are you taking my godchildren?"

Penny spoke so softly I had to lean forward in my chair to hear her. "Silicon Valley. Carlos accepted a really great job with a tech start-up in Palo Alto. We bought a house where the kids will each have their own bedroom, and it's close to the elementary school—"

I took a couple of deep breaths to calm myself, but my head was reeling. "You've already bought a house in California? When did you go house shopping? Where was I?"

"St. Louis." Penny's face flushed, and I knew she felt ashamed.

I got up from the chair and walked over to her, putting my hand on her arm. "Were you planning to tell me? Twenty years we've been like sisters, and this is how much you care about my feelings?"

Penny carefully put the board games onto the nearest surface and wiped away the tears that continued to fall. She called out to Carlos to take the kids out for pizza. Carlos looked over at me and opened his mouth like he wanted to say something but decided against it. He ushered the kids out the door.

"Of course, I was going to tell you, Jess. It all happened so fast."

I gestured toward the piles and the boxes. "Too fast to give me a heads up before I came here and saw all of this? Maybe you were going to disappear, not say anything until the movers had finished the job."

Penny turned away from me and walked into the kitchen, washing her hands at the sink and drying them slowly on a dishtowel before she spoke again. "You're turning this into something it isn't. I hadn't found the right time."

"I'm turning this into something it isn't? You're moving to California, and you weren't going to tell me because you know my life is spiraling out of control. Better to cut me loose and move with your perfect little family to sunny California. That's the bottom line, isn't it?" I could hear the venom spilling out of me, but I couldn't control it.

My hysteria seemed to trigger the opposite reaction in Penny. I watched as she calmly walked past me back into the living room and gathered the tablecloths from where I'd dropped them, refolding them neatly and adding them to an open box. Her tears had dried, and her face was serene once more. I watched as this woman whom I knew so well collected herself, deciding how to handle me. When she spoke, her voice was steady and sure.

"I was wrong not to tell you earlier, Jess, and I'm so, so sorry. But this isn't about you. We're not children anymore. Moving on is normal. This isn't the third grade, and your best friend moves away, and your whole world falls apart. We're not passing notes in class about the cute boys anymore, and we don't stay up late on sleepovers eating banana splits. I've been your support system forever. And not only me; my parents, too. But we're both adults now, with adult lives."

If only.

I knew I was making a mistake as soon as I hailed the cab and sputtered out the address downtown, but I did it anyway. Fifteen minutes later, I was outside Tyler's door. It had been close to two months since I'd turned down his proposal. For all I knew, he'd left New York without telling me, like Penny was about to do, or maybe a new girlfriend would answer the door. In the wake of the blowout with Penny, I felt the urgent need to make sure Tyler knew I was sorry for what I'd done to him.

Tyler didn't smile when he saw me. He seemed to take in my strange clothes and my disheveled look with an appraising eye and then stepped aside to let me into the front hallway. He stood with his feet planted and his arms crossed over his chest, and I understood that I wasn't supposed to go in any further. A football game was playing on the television in the living room. I could smell burgers cooking on the range.

"What are you doing here, Jessica?" He didn't sound angry. He sounded like he'd had enough of me. Like everyone else.

"Did you hear my mother had a stroke?"

"Yes. I ran into Penny at a movie a few weeks ago, and she told me. I'm sorry."

"Penny's moving to California. Did she tell you that a few weeks ago, too?"

"She mentioned something."

"Everything's falling apart, Ty. I'm so alone." I wanted to come in, to sit on the couch where we used to watch Saturday Night Live, to look in the fridge for leftover Thai noodles, to lie in the bed where we'd made love.

Tyler glanced over at his food on the stove. "What do you want, Jessica?"

That question, again. "I wanted to apologize for what I did to you. I want to make sure we're okay with each other."

Tyler shook his head. "I think you should worry about whether you're okay, Jess. And how you can make things better for yourself. You don't need to worry about me."

I tried to smile. "I'm looking for a friend."

"I don't want to be your friend."

"Right. Of course." I took a last look at Tyler, holding myself back from touching his worn blue sweatpants, so soft from years of use and laundering. Then I turned around and walked out the door. He didn't try to stop me.

It had started to rain, a cold November downpour. I went out into the night.

CHAPTER FOURTEEN

When I got back to the apartment, I was drenched, my clothes soaked through in the short few blocks I'd run from Tyler's to the subway. I stripped down to my panties and camisole, leaving the old sweatshirt and jeans in a soggy pile next to the door. The apartment was overheated, as usual, but I was chilled. The lights were off, and I assumed Cynthia and Vera were sleeping.

I walked to the sideboard in the dining room and checked what was on offer. Gin, rum, vodka, tequila, Triple Sec, and my vice of choice, Scotch. Cynthia was a social drinker, but she was social most of the time. She'd never been one to hide the alcohol in a cabinet. "In France, they give the children wine at the dinner table," she'd say. "And the French don't become alcoholics."

I didn't know if that was true, but I did know my mother's liberal views had made our apartment a popular destination when I was a teenager. I'd gone from "the girl whose father died in a freak accident" to "the girl whose mother lets her friends drink." A step up. Even Penny, a good girl, had her first Vodka tonic from my mother's supply.

I took the Balvenie and a shot glass and sat in my mother's place at the dining room table. I poured and drank a toast to Clark and his allergy to art. I poured and drank a toast to Larry and his pretend literary integrity. I poured and drank a toast to Penny and her move to sunny California. I poured and drank a toast to Vera and her blind loyalty. I poured and drank a toast to Tyler and his broken heart. When I couldn't think of an appropriate toast for Cynthia, when I could barely think at all, I put down the glass and stood up from the table.

I swayed from side to side, holding on to the back of the dining room chair, watching the crystals on the chandelier dancing above my head. As I felt my knees buckle, I reached for Cynthia's walker, no longer in use and tucked safely into the corner of the room. I did a lap around the room, whooping and hooting like a kid at a rodeo.

Then I made my way to the piano, the baby grand standing in the center of the living room. I sat on the bench. It had been eighteen years.

"Do you remember, Cynthia?" I yelled out. "Can you picture that day?"

I placed my hands on the keyboard, feeling the coolness of the keys beneath my fingertips. I raised my arms, smashed my hands down, and banged. Harsh and loud and dissonant. Then I leaned over the keyboard and vomited on the soundboard, the strings faintly humming, the taste of warm chestnuts again in my mouth.

I woke up in my bed. I was dressed in clean pajamas, and my hair had been pulled back from my face into a neat ponytail. My head was pounding and my tongue felt huge and useless in my mouth. I squinted at the clock on my bedside table. Four a.m. I lay back carefully, my skull crying out to be treated gently.

I couldn't remember how much I'd had to drink, but I knew

I'd made a big dent in the bottle, and on a virtually empty stomach. I didn't regret it. I'd obliterated Penny and Tyler in one shot. Or a bunch of shots. But erasing Cynthia would take something more potent than alcohol.

I must have dozed. When I woke again, a weak light was coming in through the windows and Cynthia was sitting on a chair next to my bed. I thought I was dreaming. I reached out my hand to touch her arm to see if she was real. She put her hand over mine. Her skin felt papery and cool. I wanted her to put her hand on my forehead.

"Finished?" Cynthia said. I thought she was asking if I was better, and I shook my head.

"Not by a long shot."

She withdrew her hand from mine and gave me two Advil and a tall glass of cold water. I swallowed the pills, sensing Vera's hand in this kindness. Yet, it was my mother at my bedside.

When I tried to lift my head off the pillow, a wave of nausea crashed over me. It was then I remembered what I'd done.

"Did I destroy the piano?" I asked.

She shook her head.

"Too bad." I rolled over onto my side, away from Cynthia, and pulled the blankets close around me. She stayed in the chair for what seemed like a long while, and then I heard her cane as she made her way out of my room.

The third time I opened my eyes, a plate of dry toast was on my bedside table, and a cup of black coffee. The smells of breakfast made my stomach turn, but I was also ravenously hungry. I was debating whether to heave or eat when I saw Cynthia standing at the foot of my bed, leaning on her cane, looking down at me. My headache still raged and my limbs were heavy. I kicked the blankets off and sat up as best I could to even the playing field.

"What do you want from me?" I demanded.

Cynthia shook her head. "Opposite."

I searched my Scotch-soaked mind for Cynthia's meaning. "What do *I* want from *you*?"

There was so much, and there was nothing. The woman who had been larger than life was now physically weak but still wielded power over me. I looked at her standing in my bedroom, surrounded by my childhood memories. She was at the center of them all, and yet nowhere to be found.

"I don't know."

Lying on the wall-to-wall carpeting on my bedroom floor, I had no idea what time it was or when I had gotten out of my bed. I was hardly able to think past the pain boring into the back of my eyeballs. I felt like a caricature of a pathetic loser in a third-rate novel. A vacuum whirred outside in the hallway, and I was alarmed at how reassured I felt knowing Vera was close by and I wasn't completely alone. I desperately needed to connect with someone after the previous night's debacle, and I was too embarrassed to go back to Clark. I reached for my phone and flipped through my contacts.

Liam, my colleague from my first publishing job? He'd become a successful literary agent, and I'd probably reach him in the middle of meeting with one of his authors in some chic restaurant. Hannah, my yoga instructor? She'd try to persuade me to come back to the studio, which, although downward dog was a fitting description of my state of being, I couldn't bear. Patricia, from my book group? No way. She thought Cynthia walked on water.

I'd have to take my chances on a less obvious choice.

"Good morning, Everton Hotel, Donna speaking. How may I help?"

It was such a profound question. I opened my mouth to speak, but nothing came out.

"Hello? Can I assist you?"

I cleared my throat.

"Yes? Are you there?" she said, a little louder.

I could tell I was trying Donna's patience, which, in the brief time I'd known her, had seemed nearly infinite. "Hello? Can you hear me? It's hectic here. I'm going to hang up in a second if you don't state your business—"

"Donna, it's me. Jessica." Silence. "Harmon."

A pause, and my heart sank. Maybe she had already forgotten me.

"Jessica! I'm so happy to hear from you! A little surprised, I admit, but happy."

I groaned as I pulled myself up and sat cross-legged on the rug. For a second, I was eleven years old, playing jacks with Penny and scrubbing at a spot where we'd spilled chocolate milk before Vera found out and ratted us out to Cynthia. And then Penny faded out and there was only the sound of Donna on the other end of the line.

"Jessica, are you still there? I think there's something wrong with this connection. I can barely hear you."

I coughed to give myself a minute. I could hear the dinging of the pokey elevator in the background and the muffled

JESSICA HARMON HAS STEPPED AWAY

sounds of people talking in the lobby near Donna's desk. "Yes, I'm here. What's the weather like there?"

"It's raining and raw."

"Sounds about right for St. Louis at this time of year."

Donna played along. "Probably colder in New York, am I right? But I'm going to guess you didn't call to talk about the weather."

"I'm not sure why I called."

"Well, maybe you felt like checking in with a friendly face. Nothing wrong with that, sugar. How's the job search going? Have you had any leads?"

"Not to speak of."

"Are you okay, Jessica? You don't sound right."

"Not really."

"Oh, hon. Is it the Professor? Has she suffered a setback in her recovery?"

"I wish."

"No, you don't. Don't say that."

I put Donna on speaker and pressed my fingertips into my temples. "She's doing alright, all things considered. It's me."

"I'm sorry to hear that. You're in a tough spot. You know, I always felt badly for only children. When your parents get old, the responsibility all lands on you. I'm one of five, the only girl. I still bore most of the burden—my brothers were useless—but I knew they'd be around if I needed help."

Donna couldn't tell me anything about the pros and cons of being an only child that I didn't know, although I hadn't experienced a whole lot of the upsides. It was true that I'd had a lot more freedom growing up than Penny; Cynthia was on one end of the involved parent spectrum, and Penny's parents were on the other. But Penny was also an only who'd been doted upon, spoiled, and worried over, the recipient of all the love and attention her parents had to give.

I reached for a sweatshirt that someone—Vera?—had laid over the back of a chair and pulled it over my head. I caught Donna mid-sentence.

" ——The American Actuarial Association is having its convention in St. Louis this week. Boring crowd, but at least they don't trash the place. One of the guys asked me for a paper map—can you imagine? Hasn't anyone told him about Google?"

And then I was on hold, listening to a repeating loop of Judy Garland singing "Meet Me in St. Louis." I thought about hanging up, but I knew Donna would call me back.

"Sorry that took me so long, love. Some of these guys wanted restaurant recommendations. I find these actuaries creepy. Like when they talk to you, they're silently calculating when you are likely to die. Anyway, I suggested a couple of heart attack–inducing barbecue joints to see how they'd react."

I smiled. "And what did they say?"

"They were thrilled. I don't think they get out much."

"I can relate to that."

"I don't believe you. You must have lots of friends in New York. I was thinking how wonderful it was that you were back in your happy place."

The notion Donna had been thinking about me at all was so comforting that I no longer felt like telling her what was going on.

"Everything's okay. Just a bit at loose ends."

"Hmm. I hear that in your voice."

I lay back on the floor and covered my eyes with my arm. "I'm home with my mother, and it's as bad as I remember. But it's also bad in completely new ways. It's hard to explain. And I know it's irrational, but I feel paralyzed, like I can't escape."

I could hear Donna breathing on the other end of the phone, punctuated by an occasional "Mmm."

"I'm proud of you," Donna said out of nowhere.

"You're crazy."

Donna laughed. "I've been called worse."

I stared up at my starry ceiling until the sting of tears forced me to close my eyes again. I whispered into the phone. "Why are you proud of me?"

"Because you're trying, hon. That's all we can do; all anyone can do. You'll make a change when you can, when you see a way forward. And I'm glad you called. Nothing's worse than being lonely."

"What makes you think I'm lonely? Maybe I called you by accident."

"What do you young people call that? A butt dial? Good one. Oh—sorry, Jessica. I have to go. Call me later if you'd like. A bunch of these suits got stuck in the revolving glass doors. I guess smarts and number-crunching don't necessarily go together. Think about what I said. It's easier to face the world with someone by your side. Call him."

And then the call disconnected.

Sometime midmorning, I was drawn out of my bedroom to the living room by a voice I couldn't place mingled with Cynthia's laughter. I hadn't heard my mother laugh since she'd had the stroke, maybe longer. It was jarring.

A smiling Monica sat across from my mother, a cup of tea in one hand and the Arts section of the New York Times resting in her lap. She'd reached out to me a bunch of times since my mother got sick, but I hadn't spoken to her since I'd called her in the middle of the night from the emergency room to say the tour was off. In another lifetime.

"Jessica," Monica said, standing to give me a perfunctory hug. "What a lovely surprise. I didn't know you'd be here."

In truth, I hadn't added much to my mother's convalescence, but Monica didn't need to know that. "Let me guess, Cynthia didn't tell you I'd been playing Florence Nightingale? Where else would a devoted daughter be?" I looked over at the Steinway. The soundboard had been removed, but the faint smell of vomit lingered.

Monica ignored my sarcasm but added what I took as a touch of her own. "I think it's wonderful you put your life on hold to help your mother."

I glanced at Cynthia, waiting for whatever snarky comment she could muster that would put me in my place. Instead, she was looking down and folding and unfolding a napkin in her lap.

"I'm so pleased to see how well your mother is doing. We're about to go to a reading and get some fresh air on the way. The new Poet Laureate is reading at Symphony Space this afternoon. Would you join us?"

I shook my head. "Thanks for the invitation, but I have some things to take care of."

Standing outside my bedroom at the end of the hallway, I

watched Monica help Cynthia into her navy wool winter coat as Vera handed my mother her cane. Cynthia looked old and frail standing next to Monica's robustly healthy body. They walked slowly to the front entrance, Monica's hand resting lightly on Cynthia's back, supporting her and gently urging her forward. The younger woman maintained a steady stream of light chatter. Cynthia said nothing at all. I retreated into my room.

When I heard the door close behind them, I waited a couple of minutes to give them time to take the elevator down and leave the building. Then I grabbed my wallet and my phone. If Cynthia was taking baby steps toward getting back to her life, it was time for me to pick up the pieces of my own. On my way out, I passed Vera in the hallway. She gave me a thumbs up. I managed a weak smile and kept moving.

In the lobby I breezed past Maurice, the building's only doorman on continuous duty since my childhood. Now in his early seventies, his tufts of hair had gone from black to gray and his hearing was shot. He no longer patrolled in front of the entrance on Central Park West but instead sat on a high stool right inside the door. He tipped his hat and bowed from the waist when he saw me. I blew him a kiss.

Donna might be right. I'd struck out with Penny and Tyler, but there was no reason I had to be alone. Out on the street I texed Raj.

New York too far for dinner? Great Vietnamese take-out place in Astoria.

He didn't respond immediately, three dots appearing and disappearing from my screen. By the time he answered, I had second thoughts about having asked.

Too short notice. Working.

You're right. Sorry. Too crazy.

Then I deleted it. I looked back at the front entrance of the apartment building and pictured myself walking past Maurice as I returned to Cynthia's. I typed a new message.

Know it's last minute. Had to get up the
nerve to ask, given how MIA I've been. Didn't
know if you'd even consider it. I'm sorry.

It's okay.

Maybe another time? This weekend?

This time the silence seemed to go on so long I was afraid Raj had put down the phone.

If you're ready to see where this is going,
then I'm ready to come.

I hesitated, then jumped.

Please, come.

He fired back.

Nothing's too far for pho.

I smiled and texted him my address.

Should be an emoji for 'corny puns will get
you nowhere.' See you whenever.

By the time I got off the subway in Queens, the sun had chased away the morning's freezing opening gambit and the air was cool and fresh. The air in my apartment, on the other hand, was stagnant and smelled faintly tangy. I'd been gone for two months, the longest stint since I'd moved in after high school, and everything looked more decrepit than I remembered. I opened the windows and turned on the standing fan.

An outsider would have guessed that the tenant was an aspiring hoarder or a poverty-stricken undergrad, or a cross between the two. The living room was piled high with books I treasured and ones I hadn't read and likely never would, piles of sheet music for the ukulele I'd left at Penny's house once when I babysat the kids and would probably not see again, and clothes I'd bought secondhand and then realized were outdated or beyond repair. One corner was piled with blank canvases, dried-up paints, and an easel from a hobby I'd forsaken ten years earlier. The couch Penny and I had originally bought on the street was still the centerpiece of the living room, but now every inch was covered with pillows and throw blankets designed to hide the effects of years of spills and wear. The wood surface of the dining table was stripped away, and the tablecloth masking the damage was itself thin and frayed. To add insult to injury, I'd left several half-filled coffee mugs on the kitchen counter, which were now covered with mold. I spilled them out in the sink and ran the water, the greenish-blue flecks swirling lazily in the basin.

How could I possibly let Raj come here in two days?

CHAPTER FIFTEEN

Picturing Raj's office at the High Low, so sleek and modern and *clean*, I was tempted to tell him not to come. I could only imagine what he'd think about me after seeing how I lived. I'd wasted the first day back in my apartment immobilized by the magnitude of the task ahead of me. Saturday, when Raj had said he'd arrive, had crept up on me. I realized he'd already have headed to the airport in St. Louis for his two o'clock flight; it was too late to rescind my rash invitation. I didn't know where to begin to make my apartment look presentable, but I had to try.

First, I took half the pillows off the couch and shoved them onto the top shelf in the hall closet. Then I envisioned Raj hanging up his coat and the pillows falling on his head. I took them out of the hall closet and piled them on the floor in the corner of my bedroom. Then I glanced at my bed. It was the only place in the apartment that looked genuinely appealing. I panicked. What if after Raj had traveled such a distance, I had second thoughts about inviting him in between my 100% organic Egyptian cotton sheets? We were strangers, practically, and I hadn't intended this to be a thousand-mile booty call. At least not definitely. I pulled an extra set of sheets, a blanket, and a pillow from the linen closet and put them on the corner of the living room couch. Better to keep my options open.

When I'd finished straightening up, I started over again. I reshelved the books that had gathered on the coffee table, the ottoman, the floor, occasionally taking a moment to read a few pages. I pulled a bookmark out of the middle of *The Brothers Karamazov*, which I was supposed to read in my Russian Lit class in college but had never finished. I lingered over my well-worn copy of *The Artist's Way*, resisting the pull toward a fruitless attempt at writing some morning pages. I swept old crumbs from the tablecloth into my hand and brushed them into the trash. Then I took out the trash, although the bag was empty save for the crumbs. Moving to the bathroom, I ran the toilet brush on the inside of the bowl and sprayed the shower with Clorox. A vision of Raj in my shower appeared before my eyes, and I felt the same panic I'd had looking at my bed. Then the picture morphed into one of myself and Raj in my shower, and I felt something else entirely.

I glanced at my watch; the afternoon had flown by. It was time to try to fix myself up. I surveyed my wardrobe. There were some more or less presentable work clothes, a few skirts, a bunch of pants, and some sweaters, arranged in no discernible order. I changed out of my jeans and sweatshirt and pulled on the clingy red knit dress I'd worn to my college reunion a few years back. It was more form-fitting than I remembered and no longer clingy in entirely the right places. I took it off and put on sweatpants and a T-shirt, going for an at-home casual look, but I didn't want Raj to feel he'd come all the way from St. Louis and that was the best I could do. I picked up my jeans and sweater from the floor where I'd tossed them and put them back on.

When I couldn't think of anything else to do to prepare for Raj's visit, I sat on the couch and turned on CNN. If things were awkward, I could make small talk about the day's news. But I couldn't concentrate and turned it off. My stomach growled and I wandered into the kitchen and opened the fridge, forgetting I'd emptied it before I left on the tour. All that remained was a bruised Granny Smith apple, an open jar of pimento-stuffed olives, three half-full bottles of XXX hot sauce, and two cans of diet Dr. Brown's. I rinsed off the apple and sat back on the couch.

It was then that I noticed my plant. The Ficus tree stood three feet tall and had been a birthday gift from Penny's parents when I turned twenty-one. I'd begged them not to give her to me. "It's not a good idea. I won't make a good plant parent. I kill everything I come near." But it was love at first sight, the way she stood at attention but her deep green leaves hung down, proud and forlorn in the same moment. I named her Fern, although she wasn't one. The name suited her.

"Don't worry, dear," Dr. Chan had said. "You'll do fine. It's hard to kill a Ficus." And he'd been mostly right. He told me that a Ficus doesn't like to be moved around. I could relate, and once I found a spot for Fern in the corner of the living room, I let her be. She was happy with the bright sunlight that came in through the windows and didn't need a lot of water. It was an uncomplicated relationship, and I'd kept her alive for nine years.

Until now.

I'd meant to bring Fern to my upstairs neighbor, Ruthy, before going away. But in the tumult of quitting my job and giving up my marriage prospects, I hadn't been thinking about my plant. She might not have needed a lot of water, but even Fern couldn't survive on no water for weeks on end. I thought about an immediate water infusion, but I knew it was too late. And now there she was, stooped and without her leaves, which had fallen unceremoniously to the floor and lay in a yellow mass beneath the pot. How had I missed this sad mess when I vacuumed the living room? I hadn't vacuumed, that's how. I took a tissue from the bathroom and blew my nose, carefully avoiding looking at myself in the mirror. Then I pulled out the Hoover.

When I moved Fern's remains, I saw another gift from bygone days, one I'd forgotten about entirely. Tucked in the corner was the eight-by-eleven cover of the prominent literary magazine that had published my short story when I was a senior in college. Penny had spent a small fortune framing it in polished teak wood inlaid with mother-of-pearl and protected by glass. The student artwork on the cover of the magazine looked a little like an oil spill, but the title of my story, "Dog Days and Summer Thrills," was splashed across the front in a friendly font, my name in bold underneath. It was an achievement I hadn't matched in all the years since, rather than a harbinger of the great literary career to come.

"This is so thoughtful, Pen," I'd said when I unwrapped the gift. "But what will I do with it? I don't know where I could hang it where it wouldn't look like shameless self-promotion."

I imagined how Cynthia would react to Penny's gift if she were to see it. Most parents would have been happy to display the magazine cover, a grown-up version of toddler artwork held up by colorful magnets on a kitchen refrigerator. But my mother was not "most parents." There was no way it would occur to Cynthia to proudly hang it up to be admired by people who might take an interest in my writing and be in a position to help me along. And there was no way I was going to ask her.

Penny walked around the room, holding the frame up

and trying it out on different walls. "We'll hang it here in our living room. It's a memento of something wonderful you accomplished." But I couldn't bring myself to do it. Maybe I had a premonition I'd turn out to be a one-hit wonder. I was grateful Penny didn't give me grief when her gift ended up in the corner propped against the wall, hidden from view by Fern's leafy fronds.

Now I held the frame against the wall over my desk. I found a hammer and a stray picture hook in the junk drawer in my kitchen and went to work.

On the fourth swing, I smashed the hammer into the nail. Of my thumb.

"Fuck!" My thumb turned red and began to swell, the cuticle peeling away and bloody. I hurried to the bathroom clutching my hand and ran it under cold water. Back in the kitchen, I put ice in a Ziploc and wrapped a towel around the whole monstrosity.

I looked at the frame where it had landed on the desk. Who was I kidding, hanging up a relic from the past that had heralded creative success that hadn't materialized? That part of me had died long ago. I picked up the framed magazine cover and threw it in the kitchen trash can, shattering the glass. Then I took two expired Tylenol with codeine I'd saved from when I'd had my wisdom teeth out and sat on my couch to wait for Raj to text that his plane had landed at LaGuardia.

The painkillers made me woozy, and I lay on the couch. Half an hour later, the buzzer downstairs rang. Assuming it was the take-out I'd ordered earlier, I grabbed a few dollars from my wallet for the delivery guy and held them out gingerly in my injured hand while I opened the door with the other one.

I saw Raj look at the money and raise his eyebrows. "Why

don't you see how the service is first?"

"Oh! How embarrassing." I took a bouquet of pink tulips from Raj's hand and ushered him into the apartment.

He put his bag on the sofa and reached gently for my towel-wrapped hand. "What happened?"

"My plant died."

"Looks like it put up a fight."

"She. The plant's pronouns are she/her/hers. And it's a long story."

"Hey—are you crying?" Raj asked.

I turned away and wiped my eyes on my sleeve. "Allergies."

"When I hurt myself in some klutzy way as a kid, my mom would say I was punishing myself for something."

I thought of the magazine cover in the trash, my potential squandered. Maybe Raj's mother was onto something.

"Your mother sounds like a wise woman."

"She had her moments."

I carefully unwrapped the towel from around my hand and dumped the plastic bag of melting ice in the trash. "Anyway, are you calling me a klutz?"

Raj walked a slow circle around my tiny apartment, poking his head into the kitchen, taking in the bedroom from the doorway, glancing at the bathroom.

"This is a great place, Jessica."

"It's a dump, but I've lived here forever and it's home. I shared with my friend Penny until she got married a bunch of years ago. She had the bedroom because she had a serious boyfriend who stayed over most nights—Carlos, the guy she married. There was a temporary dividing wall here," I gestured to the middle of the living room, "that partitioned off a bedroom for me."

Raj smiled. "So you could have not-serious boyfriends who stayed over when you felt like it?"

"Something like that. The rent has stayed reasonable, so even when Penny moved out, I could afford it on my own. Nothing works—the faucet drips in the bathroom, the air-conditioning unit only stays on for an hour at a time, the windows in the bedroom are painted shut—but it's mine."

"I think it's wonderful. You've got a little piece of New York City. What else matters?" Raj picked up the tulips from where I'd put them on the kitchen counter. "Vase?"

"In the cabinet over the sink." I watched him stretch his arm overhead, pulling his sweater up a little over the waistline of his jeans, exposing a sliver of smooth brown skin. He found the glass jar I used for flowers and filled it with water, emptied the plant food into it, cut the stems at an angle with a knife he found in the drawer. I walked up behind him and tentatively rested my cheek on his back. His sweater felt scratchy on my face.

"This is pretty weird, isn't it?" he said.

"Yes. But everything in my life is pretty weird these days."

"Then I guess I fit right in." Raj moved away from me and walked into the main room, putting the vase on the table. "Is this good?"

"Sure. We can put the flowers back in the kitchen when the food gets here. There's not a lot of available surface area."

Raj interrupted the awkward silence that had fallen over us. "Show me where you write."

I shook my head. "I told you. I don't write."

"Show me where you don't write."

I shook my head again, but this time I couldn't help smiling a little. I took his hand and led him to the corner of the living room, where the hammer and nails of the frame fiasco still rested next to my laptop. On the wall was a Virginia Woolf quote meant to inspire me, and several harsher quotes of my own authorship meant to shame me. Yellow stickies covered the sides of the computer monitor, the surface of the desk, and the wall—some bearing only a word or two, the glimmer of an idea, others with snippets of dialogue—all in my indecipherable handwriting. A stack of novels by my current favorite authors, Fitzgerald, Faulkner, Strout, Patchett, rested on the printer. Around the perimeter were scattered half-melted candles of various shapes and sizes.

"It looks like a seance."

"I'm trying to make contact with my long-dead talent," I said.

The buzzer downstairs sounded.

Grateful to escape this conversation, I left Raj standing there and moved quickly to the entryway, pressing the button to open the outside door so the delivery guy could come upstairs. "Must be the food."

"Great. Where did you order from? When I was at Hunter, I think I knew all the decent Vietnamese restaurants in every borough and some of the poisonous ones."

The delivery guy knocked on the apartment door, but I didn't reach to answer it.

"Everything okay? Do you want me to get it?"

The knocking became more insistent. "I completely forgot I was supposed to order Vietnamese. I'm so sorry. I was nervous, I mean nervous and excited, about you coming.

I almost forgot to order altogether. I ended up with Indian. Is that okay?"

Raj opened the door and took the large paper bag from the sallow-skinned teenager, pulling some money out of his wallet for a tip. "You got me here on false pretenses. Very crafty. I hope you ordered Vindaloo. I'm not happy when I'm eating unless I'm in physical pain." He brought the bag to the table and took out the different containers, breathing in each one as he opened them. "Aha! My nose says these are nice and hot. Good job."

I took a bottle of Melinda's XXXtra Hot Sauce from the fridge and brought it to the table. "In case you need to supplement. My tolerance is high."

"Impressive."

Half an hour later, we'd demolished everything and, true to his word, the food was so spicy Raj's face was pouring with sweat, while I barely glistened. He mopped himself up with several square paper napkins and let out a slow whistle.

I cleared our dishes to the kitchen, running the curry-stained plates under hot water. "Is it offensive that I ordered Indian food? I mean, just because you're of Indian heritage doesn't necessarily mean you like—"

Raj pushed his chair away from the table. "Hey. Try to relax, Jessica. We're both nervous. It's all good. And, clearly, I love Indian food." He wandered over to the couch and stretched out on his side. I had a flashback to the sofa in his office, and the heat that suffused my body wasn't from the Vindaloo. A wave of anxiety washed over me.

I turned from the sink. "Listen, I'm not sure if we should, you know, whether I'll want to—"

Raj moved his back further into the couch cushions and patted the space alongside him. "Give me a little credit. Why don't we see how things go? Right now, I need to digest."

"I'm okay. I'll sit here." I sat on the other end of the sofa and surreptitiously moved the pile of bedding onto the floor.

"Suit yourself." I couldn't tell if he was annoyed or full.

"When do you have to go back to St. Louis?"

Raj kept his eyes closed but smiled, and I felt myself relax. "You trying to get rid of me already? Feed me and send me on my way?"

"No, I'm pacing myself."

He sat up slowly and scooted closer to me, our legs now just barely touching. "That sounds a little racy—I like it. But to answer your question, I'm afraid I have to leave tomorrow. I have a new show going up in the gallery, and I need to be there for the installation."

"More body parts?"

"No. This artist is sort of like Degas. But instead of ballerinas, she paints pole dancers."

"Wow. That's oddly specific, isn't it?"

When he reached for his wine glass on the coffee table, his shoulder grazed mine. "She's surprisingly popular."

"Will you see your parents in Brooklyn before you leave?"

"My father. And no, not this trip. I'll come in again soon." Something about his tone was off, and my wounded-person radar pinged. I turned so I could look at his face.

"Why would you only see your father? Is your mother—"

Raj shook his head and drained his wine glass. "It's not a pretty story. I don't think you want to hear it."

"I do."

172

He wrapped his arm around my waist, pulling me toward him. "Okay. Settle in."

I reached over to where I'd piled the extra bedding and unfolded the blanket over us.

"The story starts off okay. My father was born in Mumbai. His parents weren't destitute, but not far from it. They believed, rightly or wrongly, that educating their only son would be the ticket out for all of them."

"Were there also daughters? Did they get educated too?"

Raj shook his head. "There were daughters, but that's not the point."

"Sorry. Keep going."

Raj explained to me that when his grandparents saw how intelligent and hardworking his father was, they sacrificed everything to help him win a scholarship to study in the United States. They scraped together the money to move to an area of the city with a better school, they worked more hours to be able to afford tutors, they cultivated relationships with people who could help. Whatever it took for his father to succeed.

"And did it work? Did he get a scholarship?"

"Yes. He wound up at Princeton studying engineering. He did his undergrad degree and then a master's, and he landed a good job in a tech company in New Jersey." Raj paused, his brow furrowed. "This would have been 1974."

"That's the same year Cynthia graduated from college."

Raj shifted a few inches away from me and looked like he was trying to smile, but his eyes weren't cooperating with his

173

mouth. "I know she looms large for you, Jessica, but I'm not sure Cynthia figures into this narrative."

I hugged my knees to my chest. "I'm sorry, Raj, you're right. Anyway, so far this sounds like a classic American success story."

"Wait." Raj told me how lonely his father was, how much he missed his family, how he was too shy to date the American girls he met at the university. After trying to make it on his own here for a few years, his father eventually went home to Mumbai.

"When he came back to India, my grandparents arranged a marriage for him to a girl from a family who lived nearby."

"Wow. Arranged marriages fascinate me. Did your parents get to know each other, like court for a while?"

Raj smiled. "I like the word 'court.' But no, only if you call three weeks a while."

I felt the Indian food churn in my stomach. "What was the problem? They got married and then they didn't get along?"

Raj turned his face away from me and cleared his throat. "You know what? On second thought, I don't think you need to hear all this. It's ancient history. I came all the way from St. Louis to hang with you, to have a good time."

"Please. I know nothing about your family." I caught myself before I added, *or you.* I poured us each more wine. I handed Raj his glass and settled back onto the couch. He put his arm back around my shoulders, and I rested my head on his chest.

"The match could easily have been a disaster. My father was reserved and studious, hated to socialize. My mother was bubbly and gregarious, a great cook and host. Against the odds, they fell in love. They had me in 1985, and then my sister, Anjili, in 1987. They were happy living a few blocks away from both of their families—"

"That's a little hard to believe."

"Right? But there were problems." His father's professional network was in America, and that's where the opportunities were. His parents came back to the U.S. and settled in Brooklyn. It was hard for them, alone in this country with the kids.

"Then my mother got sick."

I swallowed hard and stared straight ahead. "What happened?"

"She had breast cancer, and it had metastasized. My father blamed himself for not catching it sooner, as though a degree in engineering somehow made him an expert in everything. She had every treatment, surgery, chemo, radiation, but none of it helped. It made her sicker. She passed away four months later."

"She must have been very young," I whispered.

"Thirty-seven."

"Oh, Raj."

He drained his wine glass and put it on the floor next to his feet. "This is going to come out wrong, but her dying wasn't the worst part. The worst part was what it did to my father. He was devastated. Inconsolable."

In my mind's eye, I saw the image of my own father, the picture I'd created and refined my whole life, his body lifeless under the scaffolding on the sidewalk. I wanted to believe that Cynthia had been inconsolable.

I felt Raj's chest tense where my cheek rested, his voice coming from deep within him. "It was beyond normal grief."

"What do you mean?"

"He checked out. He managed to keep his job, but otherwise, nothing. He barely spoke. He started drinking."

"He was depressed."

Raj withdrew his arm from around me and gently moved me away. He stood up from the couch and drifted over to the window, looking out at the night, or looking at nothing at all.

"He had two children to take care of. Anjili and I were grieving too. I was fourteen, and I had to be mother and father to myself and my little sister. He took care of us financially, but he abandoned us. He never got any help for himself. He didn't try to live."

I pictured a young Raj making meals for the family, walking his sister to school, helping her with homework, and then staying up late to do his own. I came up behind him, putting my arms around his waist, and kissed the back of his neck.

"But you still see him when you come to New York. You forgave him."

"No," Raj said. "As I got older, I understood better what had happened to him. I came to accept why he is the way he is. I didn't forgive him, Jessica. I did something more important. I forgave myself for hating him."

Later, Raj lay on his back in my bed, his eyes open. "Was that pity sex? Because that's not what I want."

"That's not what it was."

"I like you, Jess, I do."

I failed to keep my voice from trembling. "But?"

"At some point, I decided not to remain a victim of my past. It's so freeing. I hope you get to that place too."

CHAPTER SIXTEEN

Heading back to Manhattan on the subway, I felt like an escaped convict recaptured after several days on the run. I thought a lot about what Raj had said about understanding his father and learning to forgive himself even if he couldn't forgive him. I didn't understand my mother, and my path toward clarity was murky given Cynthia's inability to communicate. I wasn't sure I'd ever learn what had made her who she was, or if I'd ever be able to forgive her or myself for the feelings I had toward her. But if Raj's visit had convinced me of one thing, it was that I didn't have the luxury of waiting for Cynthia to change; it was *my* approach that had to be different.

I tried to distract myself from what lay ahead by reading the ads plastered on the walls of the train. After nearly flunking high school Spanish, I could barely take an educated guess at "¿Quieres estudiar inglés por la noche, gratis?" The ones in Mandarin, and there were many, were indecipherable. I smiled when I spotted my perennial favorite: the ad hawking the services of the dermatologist with the preternaturally clear complexion and the glazed look in his eyes. It had been running since I was a kid with acne in the early 2000s. Was Dr. Z. still alive and kicking? How many teens had he saved from social isolation over the years by clearing the zits from their faces? And was he as stoned in the office as he appeared in his ads?

I turned to see a young woman sitting a few feet away with

beautiful skin and piercings in her ears, eyebrows, nose, and lips, pointing at the ad. "I heard he was a fraud. Running a Ponzi scheme off the dreams of all those pimply kids."

I looked deeply into Dr. Z's glassy gaze and considered defending him but decided to pick my battles. "I believe that."

I let myself into the apartment and found Vera sitting at the dining room table. The *New York Post* was open in front of her, and she was spreading chunky peanut butter on a hard-boiled egg.

I nearly gagged. "That's quite the combination."

"Protein. You should eat better, Jessica. You're too skinny. Ever since you were small, you didn't eat enough protein. Want me to make you one?"

"I'm sure you're right, but no, thanks."

Vera put down her knife and screwed the lid on the Skippy. "You didn't sleep here the last few nights."

I picked up a couple of cashews from a bowl on the table and popped them in my mouth, crunching noisily. "Everyone needs a break sometimes. You could probably use a vacation yourself."

"We're not talking about me. You disappeared."

"I hope you weren't worried."

Vera tilted her head in the direction of my mother's office. "Not *me*."

I smiled. Vera could think what she wanted, but I knew Cynthia's maternal worry gene hadn't expressed itself in recent memory.

I sat across from her, averting my eyes from her plate. "Not to change the subject, but what are your plans, Vera? You were a lifesaver coming here on so little notice when Cynthia and I needed you. Are you going to stay?"

Vera took another bite of her egg, the peanut butter squelching as it stuck to the roof of her mouth when she chewed. "Have you spent much time with your mother lately?"

I shook my head.

Vera made what could have been a clucking sound thwarted by peanut butter. "Putting your head in the sand won't solve the problem, Jessica."

Of course, she was right. I had nothing to say, so I waited for the moment to pass.

Vera pointed at her newspaper. "Kim Kardashian was spotted canoodling at Le Bernardin with a hunky mystery man."

I leaned over to look at the photo. "He can do better."

"I guess. I'd like to eat at that restaurant, though." She held up her peanut butter egg at eye level, turning it this way and that.

"What were you going to say about Cynthia?"

"Your mother is not like she was before she got sick. For a while, she made progress, but then she plateaued. I think she's getting worse now."

Of course, I knew this. I could feel Cynthia's deterioration in my bones. "Getting worse, how?"

"She still has trouble finding words when she talks, and there are times when I understand her less and less as the day goes on and she gets more tired. She sits in her office, and I think she tries to write, but I can't imagine what comes out is poetry. Maybe she's making up some new kind?"

We sat quietly for a moment.

Vera finished her egg and turned back to Page Six, the comings and goings of her favorite celebrities clearly more diverting than Cynthia's recovery. "Who knows if she'll ever be the same? But she's steadier on her feet and she's adjusting to a new way of life. To answer your question, I'll stay until she wants me to go."

I reached over and put my hand over hers. "That means a lot to me."

"Listen, Pumpkin," Vera said, using the nickname she'd had for me when I was a little girl. "I've known your mother for a long, long time. She's an extraordinary woman, strong. Hard to get close to, but she's treated me fairly. I know you haven't had it easy."

I gave her hand a squeeze and pushed my chair back from the table. Raj was right. I was tired of feeling sorry for myself.

Vera's promise to stick around made my decision to go home to my apartment easier. My weekend with Raj had reminded me of how good it felt to be independent, how vital it was, and although I didn't know where my future would take me, I refused to backslide. I pulled my suitcase out of the closet in my bedroom and tossed in everything I'd packed for the aborted tour. There wasn't much, and I was done practically before I'd begun. I sat on the bed and looked around, my eyes drawn to the framed photo on my dresser of Penny and me at our eighth-grade winter concert. Penny looked so small standing next to me. My adolescent growth spurt hadn't made me a shoo-in for the basketball team by any stretch, but at five-foot-five, I was half a foot taller than she was. We had our arms around each other's waists, sticking our tongues out at the camera. I reached over, tucked the photo into my backpack, and shut the lights.

As I wheeled my suitcase into the hallway outside the dining room, Vera looked at me and raised her eyebrows.

"Off again so soon?"

I didn't answer, my voice stuck somewhere near my heart.

Vera picked up her empty plate and took a few steps toward the kitchen. "Your mother is in her office."

If Vera hadn't caught me, I would have left without saying goodbye to my mother—a bold and cowardly move rolled into one. Instead, chastened, I walked down the hall and knocked on the office door.

"Come." Cynthia's voice was strong and confident, not what I'd expected after my conversation with Vera. She was dressed in a black cashmere turtleneck and wore no jewelry or scarf to lessen the severe effect. Her make-up was subtle and carefully applied, Vera's handiwork, no doubt. Her shoulders were thrown back, and she faced her computer straight on, her fingers poised over the keys. She looked completely herself. Only the slight hint of vulnerability around her eyes kept me from losing my resolve altogether.

I slumped in the chair opposite her, hoping not to draw fire.

"Are you working?" I asked.

She shook her head. Cynthia glanced around her office, her eyes not resting on anything for long. Maybe she hoped inspiration might emerge from behind the standing lamp in the corner.

"I'm sure the muse will come back soon. So much material in a near-death experience," I said. "I'm sorry. That came out harsh. I just meant that these past couple of months must have given you a lot to write about."

Cynthia crossed her arms over her chest. "Where?"

I sat up straighter. "Where will you find your ideas? I don't know. No matter how many times I've heard you speak at presentations and answer interviewers' questions about your 'process,' it always seemed like you pulled your poems out of thin air."

Cynthia shook her head again, more violently, and pointed her finger at me. "Where did you sleep?"

Ah. She'd noticed I'd been gone. I tried not to smile, but I couldn't help it; the memory of Raj was too fresh in my mind. "Were you worried about my virtue?"

Cynthia frowned, straightening a pile of papers that didn't need straightening.

"I'm sorry. Again. I was teasing," I said.

"Hmm."

I shook my head. This, from a woman who'd never been known to turn down the attention of any man who might prove useful to her. Cynthia had barely registered the boyfriends I'd had over the years, as if concerning herself with my love life was beneath her. I wondered if she remembered now that Tyler had been on the verge of proposing to me or whether she had sensed the electricity between Raj and me in St. Louis. But it didn't matter.

I stood and walked toward the door, ready to put this chapter of our saga behind me. Then I realized I had something more to say.

"You asked me the other day what I wanted from you. I didn't know. Now I do."

Cynthia sat stock still, her eyes fixed on mine.

I took a deep breath and leaned forward. It was little more than a calculated guess on my part, gleaned from offhand hints and faraway looks, but it was worth a shot. "Something happened to you a long time ago. I want to know what it was while you can still make yourself understood, so I can figure out what's happened to me. How I've turned out. Who I am."

Cynthia furrowed her brow and brought her good hand down hard on the desk, a guttural sound issuing from her mouth where the word she was looking for should have been. "Think so—"

I averted my eyes to let her compose herself.

"Simple?" Cynthia spat out and sat back in her chair, the back of her head hitting the headrest.

"I didn't say it was simple. You have a story. I deserve to know it."

Cynthia looked at me for what seemed like an eternity. As Dr. DiFulvio had explained, my mother's comprehension was far greater than her ability to produce speech. Maybe she couldn't say what she meant to express. Or maybe she thought if she waited it out, I'd give up. Stop trying to get her attention. It wasn't a bad strategy on her part. It had worked in this very office, on a day seared into my memory. But I was no longer a child. I held her gaze.

Eventually, she swiveled her chair around to face the bookcase directly behind her where she kept bound journals of her poetry in progress, written out in longhand, her revisions in the margins. The volumes were labeled chronologically, dating back fifty years when she started to write poetry in college. Cynthia ran her fingers over the spines of the notebooks on the shelf at eye level. She pulled out a worn leather-bound one I'd never noticed in all the years I'd been combing through her collection on the sly. She handed it to me across the desk.

I felt a rush of saliva in my mouth, mixed with a familiar, bitter aftertaste reserved for my mother. I had an urge to spit on her and her journal. Instead, I pushed her hand away hard, sending the book falling to the floor. "I'm done reading your poems. Don't you get it?"

Cynthia rose awkwardly from the chair. Maybe afraid she'd be unable to reach the notebook without toppling over, she used her cane to push it across the floor toward me, the pathetic whoosh of leather sliding on the Persian rug accompanying each step.

"No poems," my mother said.

I picked up the journal, holding it closed between my thumb and forefinger like someone else's soiled underwear.

"Not what you think," Cynthia stammered out.

"You, or this?" I asked. I held the journal away from me and toward her. It felt like a magnetic force field had sprung up between us, as though whatever was in the journal had the power to bring us together or drive us further apart. My fingers brushed over the front cover, the detailed design deeply embossed into the burgundy leather.

"No," Cynthia said.

Now it was my turn to bang my hand on her desk. "No what? Don't touch it? Don't read it? What kind of game are you playing with me?"

She sat heavily in her chair and covered her eyes.

I ignored her and opened the notebook. On the inside front cover was stapled an article from the St. Louis Gazette, a local community newspaper I remembered my grandparents subscribing to when I was a kid. The paper was dated April 30, 1969, and the headline read, "Cynthia Harmon, Budding Writer, To Attend Yale in the Fall."

Underneath was a picture of Cynthia in her private school uniform. Instead of smiling at the camera, she looked off to her right, as though New Haven and her future beckoned. The short article detailed young Cynthia's numerous accomplishments, writing awards, and accolades I had never heard about, culminating in the astonishing publication of a short story in a Sarah Lawrence College literary journal. Cynthia was quoted as saying she was thrilled to be admitted among the first women to attend Yale and was looking forward to studying English literature, "perhaps focusing on poetry."

On the opposite page in an unmistakably more childish, less florid version of Cynthia's adult handwriting was written, "Yale, New Haven, Connecticut—1969." My mother would have been seventeen.

I didn't believe it, despite the incontrovertible evidence I held in my hands. "There's some mistake here. You weren't in New Haven in 1969. You were a freshman at Hunter College in 1970. How could you have been a freshman at Yale in 1969?" But even as the words left my mouth, I remembered the two of us standing by the wooden fence on Old Campus, looking out at the freshman quad at Yale the first night of the tour. How she said she'd been there many years before I was born, how she knew the University had gone co-ed in 1969, how she marveled at how many women there now were on campus.

Cynthia said nothing. Then she rose slowly from her chair, leaned on her cane, and walked out of her office, leaving me alone. Her meaning was clear. There would be no explanations from the infirm old woman. Only the words of a young Cynthia, telling her story.

I closed the journal, breathing to a count of ten to slow myself down. My head was swimming. Cynthia was the poster child for Hunter, the kind of alum they put on the front cover of the college magazine during major fundraising campaigns. I wasn't even allowed to consider any other school when I was applying to college. How could there have been a time before, a time at Yale, a secret time I knew nothing about? In my confusion, I took out my cell to call Penny, to tell her what had happened and get her take on this shocking news. But then I remembered. She'd left for California a week earlier, with barely a goodbye.

I opened the journal.

CHAPTER SEVENTEEN

Cynthia's initial impressions of Yale were decidedly mixed. I winced at her lush, over-the-top descriptions of the campus, the future poet's innate eye for beauty struggling against a schoolgirl's immature expression. *The grassy quads with their verdant green carpeting, awaiting the reckless downfall of autumn's castoffs; the gothic towers penetrating the virginal blue sky; the high-ceilinged nave of Sterling Memorial Library an aspirational cathedral to the Gods of gnosis.* Etcetera, etcetera.

Her assessment of her classmates (230 women, 1,029 men in the freshman class) was more circumspect. She didn't hold out much hope she'd be friends with her roommates in Vanderbilt Hall—wealthy girls from Eastern boarding schools who stuck to their own. Cynthia reserved her harshest evaluation for the Yale boys in their blue blazers and neat haircuts, like children in elementary school who might burst into tears at any moment, crying for their mommies.

Cynthia threw herself into the scene with abandon. She'd missed Woodstock by a few weeks, but she took the train to New York City on the weekends, catching The Kinks at the Fillmore East that October. While she bemoaned how relatively tame the political scene was on Yale's campus, she marched in all the protests and sat-in for whatever was the cause du jour—free speech, racial equality, anti-war. And she could often be found on Saturday nights on Orange Street, getting responsibly stoned at off-campus parties thrown by grad students, munching on potato chips, and eavesdropping on conversations she deemed absurdly inconsequential.

The dating situation frustrated her. An article in the *New York Times Magazine* had called the women of the Yale class of 1973 "female versions of Nietzsche's Ubermensch," rendering them, according to Cynthia, largely untouchable. The boys preferred to date girls bussed in on the weekends from Quinnipiac or Albertus Magnus (derided at Yale as Albertus Mattress). Cynthia resigned herself to being alone.

Love will have to wait, although why the sexual revolution should pass by such a willing recruit is baffling to me.

I skimmed over Cynthia's description of her professors and the classes she was taking—Economics, Art Appreciation, and American History.

Then I reached this:

He wears his thick black hair a little long, and a droopy mustache pulls the eye downward toward his full, red lips. He isn't smooth by any stretch, but he moves around the classroom with confidence. He has no sense of fashion and dresses like someone twice his age—turtleneck sweaters, corduroy slacks, and scruffy loafers—but he's 32. Young for a professor, even a junior one.

And oh, the way the man talks about poetry.

He was Cynthia's professor for her introductory English class on The Great American Poets, whom she identified in her journal only as "M.S.," as though keeping a delicious secret to herself. Cynthia felt an immediate connection. When he looked at her from the podium at the front of the room, it was as if only the two of them existed.

He read to us from Whitman, and his voice was intense and full of yearning. My mouth went dry, and I leaned forward in my seat. The girl next to me shoved my shoulder with hers and said, "Whoa, missy. Keep your pants on."

"Shut up," I whispered. When the class ended, I gathered my notebooks and left as quickly as possible. I felt his eyes on me.

A few weeks later, according to the entries, Cynthia attended a protest organized by SDS. It was peaceful and orderly until the group surged past the campus police, headed for the administrative offices in Wright Hall. In the rush, another protester accidentally stomped on Cynthia's foot, and she cried out in pain. Someone caught her by the arm, and it turned out to be her professor. When he didn't recognize her, she was crestfallen.

A steady stream of people passed by, headed into the building. Cynthia had lost the desire to protest. She turned to go back to her dorm.

Then I felt M.S.'s hand on the small of my back.

"I'm messing with you. I saw how Old Walt turned you on."

Later in the term, Cynthia learned that M.S.'s favorite poet was Emily Dickinson. Despite myself, I smiled. Cynthia Harmon's devotion to Emily Dickinson was legendary. Although her own poetry was not at all similar in style, she'd built her academic career around Dickinson scholarship. Now it made sense. Her love for the poet was tied up in her youthful feelings for her introductory poetry teacher. It was so obvious and so utterly normal, so un-Cynthia, that I was blown away.

One day at the end of a class, her professor asked her which poet she was planning to write about for her term paper. When she answered Dickinson, he suggested she come to his office hours on Thursday at four to discuss some potential topics.

I should have realized something was up when I checked my notes to see where his office was and realized he didn't have office hours on Thursdays. Still, I went.

His office was on the third floor of Linsly-Chittenden Hall, across the quad from Cynthia's dorm. She climbed the stairs, the marble smooth and indented in the center from the footsteps of thousands of students before her. I felt her hesitation as she stood in front of the heavy wooden door, wondering if she should stay or go. Then she heard the Stones' new album playing. She knocked, but no one answered. She banged.

A sweet, cloying odor engulfed me when he opened the door. "I wasn't sure you were coming. I thought you might chicken out."

I tried to keep the tremor out of my voice. "What's to be afraid of?"

He took my hand, pulled me into the room, and locked the door behind me.

I closed my eyes. I couldn't be one hundred percent sure, of course. But in that instant, the image Cynthia had painted of her young poetry professor transformed into the picture from my memory of the elderly gentleman standing patiently in line in Battell Chapel, waiting to speak with my mother or to share a moment's glance while she signed his copy of her book. I thought I understood the nostalgic pull that compelled my mother to dress up more that night and to accentuate the sensuality of her performance. And I also felt Cynthia's urgent need to get away. I'd thought she was being rude, but now I sensed her desperation. Something made an encounter unwanted or impossible. And the roses in the hotel room.

Those must have been from him too.

I turned the page, but the next one was blank. I turned another. Blank. I thumbed through the rest of the journal, but Cynthia hadn't written another word.

I pressed the palms of my hands hard against my eyes where a migraine was taking hold and lay my head on my mother's desk. After a few moments, I sat up carefully so as not to shake up my brain and flipped back to the beginning of the journal. I read through the pages again.

I considered the possibilities. Had Cynthia, at age seventeen, innocent and far from home, lost her virginity to a professor close to twice her age? Maybe. Or perhaps it was nothing that dramatic. Cynthia might have discovered her passion for poetry in this professor's class and shared a steamy kiss or two in his office in a marijuana and Mick Jagger haze and then gone back to her dorm and her regular life as a college freshman. Or her youthful bravado could have failed her altogether and she may have walked back down the grand staircase, untouched and none the worse off.

Then I remembered. Whatever had or hadn't happened between her and M.S. that day in Linsly-Chit or afterwards, Cynthia had not made it past her freshman year at Yale. By the fall of 1970, she was enrolled as a freshman at Hunter College in Manhattan. Nineteen years later, she'd given birth to me, thirty-seven years old and alone in New York City. She'd never married, although countless men vied for her affection. I realized Cynthia had given me the journal to read because it was the beginning of the story of how she'd become the woman, mother, and poet that she was. She wanted me to understand. The time at Yale *mattered*.

Idly thumbing through the pages again, my fingers brushed up against a pocket on the inside back cover of the journal I hadn't noticed before. Inside, there was a thin packet of papers held together with a green ribbon. I untied the parcel and laid the contents out on the desk.

First, I ran my fingers over Cynthia's official Yale transcript from 1969–70. The fall semester might have been acceptable for an average student adjusting to college, especially perhaps for a woman in the confusing world of a newly coed university. But not for Cynthia. She'd gotten Bs and Cs in Economics, Art Appreciation, and American History. The only class she had excelled in was Poetry, where she'd earned an A from Professor Matthew Sheldrake. In the spring semester, Cynthia had received four Fs. My mother, who didn't fail at anything, had flunked out of Yale.

Tucked behind the transcript was a pink sheet of paper folded in thirds. I smoothed it out on the desk. At the top was the Yale logo, *Lux et Veritas*, and below it was written "University Health Services." The body of the flier was an announcement of the availability of counseling services for the newly admitted female students on campus, including provision of "varied methods of birth control." The days and hours of the clinic were listed, and someone, presumably Cynthia, had circled "Tuesdays, 4:00 to 6:00 p.m." I surmised that Matthew Sheldrake or someone else had initiated her into the sexual revolution after all. Stapled to the flier was a piece of paper with an address on East Genesee Street, a date in January 1970, and a time: 10:00 a.m., in Cynthia's handwriting.

Underneath the flier was a letter. I recognized the

Wedgwood-blue stationery immediately. Cynthia's name and a P.O. Box address in New Haven were written in my grandmother's elegant cursive. The return address was St. Louis, postmarked December 14, 1969. I took the letter out carefully, marveling that my mother and her mother, who were cordial at best in later years, had corresponded. The letter began with a description of my grandmother's activities, which included making phone calls to a bunch of her friends regarding a church fundraiser and a visit to the new Zayre's department store that had opened downtown (and which she found "vulgar"). She reported that she'd run into Cynthia's friend Brenda from high school, who was waitressing in a local coffee shop. "She got engaged to Darren when he was on leave. Now he's trying to get out of going back overseas because he's getting married—can you imagine?"

The last lines of the letter held a suggestion, if oblique, of why my mother had held on to the correspondence all these years. "Cynthia," the note read, "your father and I agree with the plan. Really, it's the only way. You'll come home when it's all over, and then you can start afresh. You'll see, you'll put this all behind you. Looking forward to having you home for Christmas."

What exactly had happened? What was Cynthia running away from? I read the words again and again, able to conjure my grandmother's voice, but unable to discern whether the words contained kindness or censure. I wondered how Cynthia had interpreted this veiled communication from her parents. Had she cried?

I had no idea how long I sat in my mother's office. The December morning light that had pierced through the parting of the heavy damask curtains was gone, replaced by the fading glow of a desolate winter afternoon. At some point, Vera came in and placed a grilled cheese sandwich and a tall glass of chocolate milk on the table near me. She stood silently for a moment and then reached out and tucked a strand of my hair behind my ear.

"You look like you've seen a ghost."

I nodded. "That pretty much sums it up."

Vera gestured toward the food. "Eat. There's very little that can't be fixed with grilled cheese and chocolate milk."

"I don't even understand what happened. Fixing it is a whole other story."

Vera walked around to the other side of the desk and retrieved an empty cordial glass from the desk next to the computer. "Your mother likes a little nip after dinner. Sometimes after breakfast, too. I tried to stop her, and then I realized she should drink what she wants. Everything is hard for her now. Who am I to say she should face it all sober?"

I thought about Vera's words. Sure, everything is hard for her now, I thought. But is it possible everything had been hard for her for the last fifty years? And even if the answer was yes, did that excuse everything?

When I walked into her bedroom, Cynthia was curled up on top of her quilt, facing the wall. The clock on her nightstand read 4:15 p.m., and a half-empty glass of water rested beside it. Vera must have brought her afternoon meds to her before she delivered my sandwich. I thought about the Klonopin I'd already decided to take later that night, knowing otherwise sleep would elude me.

I sat on the chair in the corner of her room and spoke softly to the back of Cynthia's head. Her speech was diminished, but her hearing was intact, and I struggled to keep my voice modulated. My words erupted in an uncontrollable rush, pelting my mother with the questions I needed answered.

"Did he hurt you? Did someone else? Why did you fail out of Yale? What happened to you?"

She didn't respond.

In the face of my barrage, Cynthia lay motionless, the only sign she was listening a subtle sagging of her shoulders. I knew it wasn't fair to expect her to answer in words she no longer controlled, but frustration bubbled up in me like a shaken soda can, ready to explode. I repeated my last question, louder this time, "What happened to you?" and watched my mother's body seem to crumple in on itself. I wanted to soothe her long-suppressed pain; she deserved my compassion. But faced with her silence, I also felt rage.

I put my head in my hands, closed my eyes, and willed myself to let the moment pass. I remembered a meditation exercise I'd learned many years earlier and focused on each part of my body, from the top of my head and progressing methodically to the soles of my feet, relaxing every inch of myself. I felt my breathing slow. When I opened my eyes, Cynthia had turned from the wall and was looking at me. Even in the hospital, when she first had the stroke, she hadn't looked this defeated.

I moved my chair closer to the bed and reached out for my mother's hand. "I didn't mean to bark those questions at you. There's just so much I didn't know before, and so much I still don't understand."

Cynthia's chin dipped a bit toward her chest, which I took

as a nod. I pressed on. "What happened between you and that professor?"

Now it was Cynthia who closed her eyes. She cleared her throat. "Ask."

I tried to keep the exasperation out of my voice. "I am asking."

"Ask him." Then she rolled over and faced the wall again.

CHAPTER EIGHTEEN

When I got back to my apartment that night, it took less than a minute of Googling to confirm Matthew Sheldrake was still teaching at Yale. Although now emeritus, he occupied the same office on the third floor of Linsly-Chit, albeit with reduced hours. Sheldrake no longer taught an introductory poetry class for English majors but instead offered a senior seminar on Sylvia Plath and Ted Hughes called "The Doomed Lovers." I wondered if, at eighty-four, he remained the Lothario he'd been when Cynthia was his student.

I studied Sheldrake's photograph in the course catalog, trying to figure out if my suspicion that he was the elderly man who had come to Cynthia's reading in New Haven was right. I couldn't be a hundred percent sure. The photo looked like it had been taken in the 1990s when Sheldrake was middle-aged. In it, he no longer had the long hair, droopy mustache, and full red lips that had so bewitched my mother. Rather, his hair was short and graying, and he wore a neat goatee and round glasses. I couldn't find a more recent photograph on the internet—he'd used the same outdated headshot for the books and scholarly articles he authored. A man trying to evade recognition or the aging process, he had essentially no digital presence.

For close to a week, I stayed in my apartment, considering how to approach the undertaking that lay ahead of me. It was important to get the initial contact right, as I might only have one chance. I'd found an email address for Sheldrake on Yale's website, and I deleted draft after draft message. Each time, I opened with "This is Jessica Harmon, Cynthia Harmon's daughter." Then I hit a wall. There was something obscene about going from "hope you are well" to "what happened between you and my mother in 1969?" in an email. I thought about phoning Sheldrake, at his office or his home numbers, both of which I'd found easily online as well. But if he hung up on me after I identified myself, that would be the end.

Raj was supportive, listening to me talk in a continuous loop about my next steps and my fears. He was endlessly patient, but he also refused to sugarcoat the situation.

"What if he tells me things I don't want to hear?" I asked.

"That's a given."

"Then why put myself through it?"

"I don't know, Jess. Only you can answer that. But remember, whatever you decide, I have your back."

The conclusion was clear. I needed to confront Sheldrake, face to face, and demand that he tell me my mother's story, the one that Cynthia herself was no longer able to relate. The story I needed to know.

I thought I'd left myself plenty of time to get to Grand Central, but I arrived at the station right as the announcement came over the public address system that the train was about to depart. I ran to the platform and winced as the train doors squeezed my foot where I'd shoved it in to keep them from closing. Bracing myself, I counted to three, knowing they had to spring open within a few seconds. When they did, I threw myself into the car and stumbled toward the first empty seat, collapsing into it and sucking in the stale air.

When I looked up, the conductor was standing over me. "You must really want to get wherever you're going. Ticket?"

Forcing a smile, I pulled out my wallet and handed him a twenty. "New Haven, please." After he'd moved down the aisle, I realized he'd charged me the penalty for buying a ticket on the train. As if the trip weren't punishment enough.

When I got my breathing under control, I unzipped my winter jacket. The back of my neck was damp from the mad dash to the train, and my legs ached from the steps I'd taken two at a time to get from the subway level up to the Metro North platform. Pulling out my phone, I checked the time and then opened the calendar app, as if something other than my planned visit with Matthew Sheldrake might appear on my schedule. I put my phone away, leaned my head back, and closed my eyes.

It took me a moment to process the words emanating from the seat behind me. The woman's tone was sultry, a stream of verbiage so salacious I couldn't believe what I was hearing. At first, I thought she was talking to herself, some sort of pornographic rant, but the momentary pauses and "mms" suggested she was on the phone. After uttering several obscene invitations to join in steamy entanglements I could barely picture, I couldn't take it anymore. I lifted myself up in my seat and turned around to put a face to the voice, expecting to see someone who looked the part. Instead, my eyes landed on a mousy woman at least as old as Cynthia, sporting a blue tweed coat buttoned up to her chin and a matching pompom hat fixed securely atop her head.

I pursed my lips to hold back a smirk. You never knew

about people, especially when it came to sex. Or love. Or sex masquerading as love.

"Would you mind texting instead?" I asked.

She smiled sweetly at me. "If you like it better that way, dear."

The train pulled into New Haven's Union Station a little after eleven. The sky was heavy with clouds, and a light rain had snarled the traffic and chased the pedestrians inside. I'd planned to walk, but I hadn't brought an umbrella, so I jumped into one of the taxis waiting outside the station and gave the address on High Street.

The driver ran her fingers through her curly hair and then looked at me in the rear-view mirror. "Thinking about coming to teach here?"

I shook my head and smiled. "No—that ship has sailed. Just doing some research."

"Should I drop you off at the main library? You'll get soaked if you walk to Sterling from High Street." I politely declined her offer and watched our slow progress toward campus. The rain had gone from a drizzle to something just short of a downpour, splashing off the streets and sidewalks like pinballs in a deranged arcade game. I regretted wearing my nice suede boots. I regretted coming altogether.

We pulled up in front of the building, and I tipped the driver more generously than I could afford. She tucked the money into the sun visor. "Good luck." She gave me a little wave, and I waved back.

Inside, I checked the directory in the entryway and confirmed Sheldrake's office was still on the third floor. As I walked up the staircase, I imagined Cynthia climbing up that

Thursday afternoon in 1969. I tried to conjure her emotions. Was she nervous? Excited? Turned on? I wondered if she raced up the stairs or dawdled, contemplating what was ahead.

I dragged my feet.

When I reached the third floor, the door to Sheldrake's office was closed. My watch read just minutes to noon, and the posted office hours ran until 12:30. I sat on a bench a few feet down the hallway, collecting my thoughts for the hundredth time. I hadn't made an appointment because I didn't want to take the chance the Harmon name would make Sheldrake flee. The element of surprise was about all I had going for me. Maybe he was meeting with a student, some black-clad young woman with a nose ring and blue hair, the two of them deep in discussion of "Nick and the Candlestick" as Sheldrake snuck his hand onto her thigh. I put my ear against the door and heard nothing. For all I knew, he'd decided not to brave the rain. But I'd come a long way. I knocked.

Sheldrake's reply was loud and immediate. "Enter!" I jumped back a step.

He sat at his desk, his head bent over some scholarly-looking tome, a large magnifying glass in his right hand. He didn't look up, apparently continuing to examine the page, his bald pate splotchy and red. Even in this posture, there was no question in my mind. Sheldrake was the man who had patiently waited for Cynthia to sign his book that night in Battell Chapel. Now, on his turf, he gestured toward a wooden chair across from the desk, "Lux Et Veritas" stenciled across the top rail. He motioned with his chin. "Please."

I sat, holding my bag in my lap. The room was cramped and dimly lit, Sheldrake's framed Yale diplomas, college and graduate school, the only decorations on the wall. Piles of papers held down with paperweights of polished stone or brass lined the perimeter of his tidy desk. His left hand rested next to a small glass plate with three Fig Newtons on it. I tried to see what Sheldrake was reading, but I couldn't make out the title upside down. His breathing was raspy, as though he had a cold or something more sinister clouding his lungs.

"What can I do for you?" Sheldrake, still looking at his reading material, coughed long and hard after he spoke. He barely covered his mouth.

I fished around the bottom of my bag for a throat lozenge. "Would you like a sucking candy?"

He looked up at me and frowned. "Oh. You aren't one of my students." Without getting up from his chair, he held out his hand, the germy one, to shake mine. "Matthew Sheldrake."

I gave him a feeble salute. "Jessica. And no, I'm not a student. Although I'd love to go back to college."

"Yes, well, who wouldn't? Shortest, gladdest years of life, and all that." He hummed a few bars of what I figured must be a Yale song. He had a sweet voice. "So, if you're not a college student, are you one of those young colleagues who've taken over the English department? I've stopped keeping track of the recent faculty hires. I have trouble understanding their new-fangled literary theories. Although I do try." He lifted up what I could now see was "The Anthology of Modern Literary Criticism." Cynthia read it too. She called it fluff.

"No. I'm not faculty."

Sheldrake seemed to focus on me then, folding his hands on the desk in front of him. "Neither student nor faculty. I'm out of guesses. Should I call security?"

For a split second, I wondered the same thing. But I hadn't

come to hurt him, at least not physically. I needed information. Although there was only so far I'd get playing cat and mouse, I wasn't ready to come clean with him. "I found out recently that my mother spent time as a student at Yale. I'm trying to piece together some of the details."

Sheldrake tilted his head to one side and placed his fingers on his chin in what struck me as a pose of fake thoughtfulness. "And why did you only recently discover this? Most alumni are proud of having studied here, even boastful."

I held his gaze. "I suppose it was a secret of sorts. My mother kept a detailed journal about that time of her life that she chose not to share with me until a few weeks ago."

Sheldrake turned his face away from me and stifled a yawn.

I settled myself back in the hard wooden chair. "I hope I'm not boring you."

"No, it isn't that. Diaries as a literary form don't interest me. But more importantly, I think a lot of people would not want their children to know what they'd gotten up to during college. Those are rightly days of experimentation. Drinking, drugs, sex. Better left unexamined, at least by one's progeny."

"I hear what you're saying, but this is a unique situation."

Sheldrake picked up his magnifying glass and centered his book in front of him. "How so?"

I waited for him to look at me. "My mother wants me to know about that time of her life and isn't physically able to tell me. I learned from reading her journal that she'd been a student at Yale, and she'd taken your introductory poetry course. That class, and you in particular, made a big impression on her. It's why I've come. I'm hoping you'll be able to provide some insights about her time here."

Sheldrake got up from his chair with effort, groaning slightly. He turned his back to me and flipped the switch on an electric kettle I hadn't noticed sitting atop a low bookcase. "Tea?"

"No, thank you."

While the water boiled, he coughed again, this time more uncontrollably. He took a yellowed handkerchief from the pocket of his blazer and spit phlegm into it, and then folded it up and placed it back into his pocket.

"You should see to that cough."

"I've seen to it. Smoking is not as glamorous as it seems in the movies, but I suspect you know that."

The whistle of the kettle sounded. Sheldrake poured water into a Yale mug and let the tea bag steep for a moment. Then he returned to his seat and took a few sips before speaking. "Ah. Well, suit yourself. A cup of tea is the most civilized beverage. It cures all that ails you."

"I'll keep that in mind."

Sheldrake didn't register that I'd spoken. "It may not seem so, Miss, but I have work to do here. Let me be direct with you. I'm as old as Methuselah. I've been teaching here for over fifty years. I'm afraid that with the passage of time, I remember fewer and fewer of the students individually. Lately, I teach one small seminar so I have a fighting chance of learning the students' names and focusing on the topics of their senior projects. But the ones from years ago, they're a blur to me now."

The image of generations of students, and more and more female ones as the decades passed, hit me. I'd been so focused on Cynthia, I'd failed to consider the possibility she was just one of many young women that, if my darkest theory was correct, Sheldrake had preyed upon. Enticing them with beautiful words, then taking advantage of them. Maybe Cynthia had meant nothing to Sheldrake, and he legitimately had no recollection of her.

But then a vision of my mother at eighteen played before my eyes, her beauty and allure exceeded only by her piercing intellect. I'd seen the effect my mother had on men over the years, that she still had before the stroke at nearly seventy. No way this guy had forgotten her. It was time to get down to business.

I cleared my throat and waited for Sheldrake to put down his tea. "I'm Jessica Harmon. My mother is Cynthia Harmon. Perhaps she's one of your former students you remember."

Sheldrake leaned back in his chair. I tried to read his expression, but his eyes were blank. Only the most miniscule tightening of the muscles around his mouth gave any indication of emotion, perhaps a grimace stopped in its tracks. "Ah. I see. Yes, you resemble her. It's quite striking. I'm surprised I didn't notice until now."

"Actually, I don't look like her at all."

"Well, it's usually hardest to see ourselves, isn't it?"

I pressed ahead. "You admit you know Cynthia, then?"

Sheldrake closed the volume on his desk and put the magnifying glass away in its felt case. "Everyone who is serious about poetry knows Cynthia Harmon. She's world-renowned. And her poetry is magical. She just won the Bollingen! She came to campus this year, early in the semester. I was privileged to see her read in the chapel in this courtyard. Marvelous."

I let the reference to that night slide. "What I'm interested in is her time here in 1969."

Sheldrake rolled his eyes. "Ms. Harmon, sometimes I barely remember what I had for breakfast. You expect me to remember your mother's experience at Yale in 1969?"

"I'm betting on your long-term recall, Professor. Perhaps I can jog your memory."

He took another sip of his tea. "If you must."

"My mother was in the class of 1973, the first class of women on campus. She took your class and became enamored with Emily Dickinson. She may have met with you outside of class to discuss her term paper. In fact, I believe she came here to your office."

Sheldrake ran his fingers over his head, as if searching for his lost hair. "Well, again, that's my job, isn't it? Meet with the students, encourage their scholarly pursuits. But yes, even as a freshman, I do remember your mother showed extreme promise. Is there something specific you wanted to discuss with me? Or is this simply a trip down memory lane?"

I felt my jaw tense. How dare he. "My mother is not well."

"Yes, I heard she suffered a stroke. Terrible thing."

I swallowed hard. "It's been a particularly cruel fate for Cynthia. She's still capable, in your words, of a trip down memory lane. But she can't communicate her memories, either verbally or in writing. And her poetry—" My voice cracked, and I stopped speaking, afraid tears would follow.

Sheldrake picked up a smooth onyx egg off a stack of papers and turned it over and over in his hand. "Ms. Harmon, I'm sorry about your mother. Truly. Her condition, I'm sure, is an unfathomable loss for her, for you, for academia, and of course, for Poetry with a capital P as well. But I'm not sure what it has to do with me."

I sat forward on my chair, leaning over the desk toward Sheldrake and waiting to speak until he stopped turning the paperweight. "Why did you stand in line after my mother's presentation in September? You could see there were only a handful of people left and she was trying to leave. Were you hoping to get your book signed?"

Sheldrake moved his chair back a few inches. "Of course. I was disappointed when she ended the program so abruptly. She was a star student of mine. Even here at Yale, one has the privilege of teaching only a limited number of students who use their gifts in truly remarkable ways later on. I was hoping Cynthia might inscribe my book with something meaningful about my mentorship."

I wanted to shove his mentorship down his throat. Instead, I played my last card. "You sent roses to the hotel, too, didn't you?"

"I don't know what you're talking about."

"That was a very personal thing to do. Did you think for some reason my mother wanted to see you after all these years?"

Sheldrake put down the paperweight on the desk so hard that a tiny piece of onyx chipped off and flew an inch or two in the air before landing in front of me. "Hope is the thing with feathers."

I got up from my chair and stood by the side of Sheldrake's desk, ready to pounce. "Did you have a relationship with my mother?"

Sheldrake's face betrayed nothing, and his tone was flat. "She was my student."

I went for broke. "It was more than that. You took her to that hotel when it was the Colony, didn't you? You were a big man. Trying to impress her."

He turned his face away from me, and when he spoke, his voice was high and thin, like the whistle of his tea kettle. "Who said so? Did your mother tell you that?"

"I want to hear it from you."

Sheldrake bowed his head.

I took that as an admission. He'd given up so fast that I was caught off-guard. I exhaled hard and took a moment to gather my thoughts. "You seduced her."

Sheldrake let out an ugly snort. "Seduced? That's such a loaded concept, a word better suited to literature than to real life, Ms. Harmon. It brings to mind rakish men and foolish, weak-willed women. No one ever dared to call your mother foolish or weak-willed. Our relationship was one of equals."

I took a step closer to him. My words sounded strangled when I spoke. "In what world is a relationship between a thirty-two-year-old professor and a seventeen-year-old girl, far away from home for the first time and living on a campus full of men, one of equals?"

Sheldrake shook his head. "Please, Ms. Harmon, sit down." He offered me a cookie and apologized for eating one himself, explaining that he was diabetic and felt faint when his sugar dipped. I figured it was a delay tactic to allow him to compose himself. When he spoke again, his manner was professorial, and his tone was condescending.

"The problem is this, my dear. You're imposing your 2019 values on a 1969 situation. You know nothing about what college was like then. You're a millennial, am I right? The zeitgeist was different in the 1960s. Nowadays, the students are hyper-aware of gender issues and respecting individual expression and the boundaries within relationships. Then, things were looser, more experimental. The framework you take for granted didn't exist on campus in 1969."

I pulled out an article I'd found on the internet from the Yale Daily News archives and laid it on Sheldrake's desk, facing him so he could read it. The newspaper was dated May 12, 1970, and the headline read "University Investigates Rash of Departures of Freshmen Women."

Sheldrake glanced down at his desk. "Ah, the YDN. Bastion of serious, fair-minded journalism written by rich, stoned upperclassmen staying up all night cavorting in their cloistered York Street headquarters, wasting their parents' money to earn degrees they will never have to use."

I ignored his sarcasm. "Seems like a thorough exposé to me."

The article detailed a fact-finding inquiry into five male professors, including Sheldrake, in response to allegations by a dozen women who had dropped out of the class of 1973. The accusations ranged from unwanted attention in the classroom to outright sexual assault. There were also stories of longer-term relationships the women claimed were non-consensual by virtue of the inherent power differential between the parties. None of the accusers were named in the article or anywhere else I could find online. When I'd shown the article to Cynthia, she'd pushed it away and turned her back on me.

Sheldrake shook his head, but something in his tone softened. "Look, integrating women into the educational system at Yale, and I'm sure at other institutions, had its ups and downs. It wasn't a simple process. I was completely vindicated in this investigation—would I be teaching here all these years otherwise?"

"I don't know." I thought of the grad student with the irresistibly pinchable ass; granted, a minor infraction in comparison, but Hunter College had turned a blind eye and let Cynthia get away with it.

"Believe what you will, but Cynthia was not one of the group that accused me or any of the other professors of anything. The situation between your mother and myself was somewhat unconventional."

"Unconventional how?"

Sheldrake's voice was barely a whisper. "I had deep feelings for her."

My mouth fell open. Love was the last thing I'd expected to come up in this conversation. Sheldrake was vulnerable. Now was the time for answers.

"Why did Cynthia leave Yale after her freshman year?"

Sheldrake put his head in his hands and let out a low moan.

"I found a letter to my mother from my grandmother saying she and my grandfather agreed with 'the plan,' that Cynthia could come home to St. Louis when it was all over. What was she talking about?"

Sheldrake looked away. "I don't know."

"Was she pregnant?" The words reverberated in the close space.

He didn't answer. I took that as a yes.

"What was the plan my grandmother was talking about?"

Sheldrake turned his body away from me, facing the lead mullioned window that let in the light from the courtyard outside. He took a deep breath, and I thought I heard a rattle in his chest. I braced myself for more coughing, but this time it didn't come. He spoke slowly and clearly, as if to a child.

"Cynthia was so young. She was gifted. She had her whole life ahead of her. And I had my career to think of—I had secured a tenure-track appointment, which was unheard of at my age. One slip and I would have been out. Getting a student pregnant was an unforgivable sin, even in 1969."

I pulled out the handwritten note Cynthia had clipped to the Health Services flier. "What was located at 1120 East Genesee Street? I looked it up online, but I couldn't find anything in New Haven or any of the surrounding towns."

Sheldrake stood and walked to the window. I think if he could have opened it and jumped out, he would have. "Abortion wasn't legal in Connecticut in 1970. That was the address of Planned Parenthood in Syracuse, New York."

I felt a chill and wrapped my arms around myself. "Did Cynthia want to terminate the pregnancy?"

He bowed his head. "No."

"You claim you loved her. You could have married her."

Sheldrake turned and looked me in the eye. "No, I couldn't have. I was married to someone else."

"You fucking bastard."

I asked the follow-up questions without stopping to consider what a "yes" answer would do to me.

"Did you stay in touch with Cynthia? Could you be my father?"

Sheldrake shook his head. "I never saw or spoke to your mother again after she left New Haven in 1970. Not until the night of the reading in September."

I stormed out of his office, pulling the door closed so

hard behind me the frame shook, relief and disappointment coursing side by side in my veins.

CHAPTER NINETEEN

It was early evening by the time the train pulled into Grand Central, and I went straight to Cynthia's apartment. When I let myself in, I found my mother in the living room sitting in her favorite chair. She was wearing a loose-fitting gray tunic over black leggings, and she looked tiny, her legs tucked under her and her hands folded in her lap. I could hear Brahms playing quietly, and she had her eyes closed.

I closed my eyes too and leaned against the wall. For a moment, I saw myself, a girl of seven or eight, tucked into that same chair beside my mother. Her left arm was loosely around me as she held a book in front of us, reading and slowly turning the pages. In my memory, the book was *The Secret Garden*, but I couldn't be sure. Although I didn't sit on Cynthia's lap, I was close enough to feel the coolness of her silk blouse against my cheek and to smell her Shalimar perfume. Cynthia's voice was soft, but not sentimental—she explained that she read to me because it was important for my success as a reader. I wanted to believe she took pleasure in these tender moments, in the sound and the rhythm of the words, the stories taking shape on the page, how we sat in the chair together.

I shook the memory off, concentrating on why I was here. I cleared my throat. Cynthia opened her eyes, but her gaze was vacant.

I couldn't think of a preamble that wouldn't sound absurd, so I said what I'd come to say. "I talked to Matthew Sheldrake today." She flinched at his name, but otherwise showed no emotion. "He told me about your relationship and about the pregnancy. He told me about the abortion."

Cynthia started to shake, her small body moving so violently the chair seemed to skip sideways a fraction on the hardwood floors. She shook her head and murmured rhythmically, "no, no, no." Her voice got louder and louder until the murmur became a hoarse shout, "NO, NO, NO!" I tried to calm her, but nothing I said made a difference. Over the terrible sound of her yelling, I heard footsteps in the hall and Vera burst into the room. She sat on the ottoman and gathered my mother into her arms.

"It's okay, everything's okay, Professor," she cooed. I didn't understand what was happening. Inside, I was shaking as badly as my mother. I wanted Vera to hold me too, but I stood there, alone. When my mother quieted, I walked out into the hallway, and Vera followed a moment later.

I dabbed at my eyes with the sleeve of my sweater. "I wasn't trying to upset her. I didn't know that after fifty years she'd have that reaction."

Vera put her arm around my shoulders. "I suppose some hurts never go away."

I'd expected to feel relief, a sense of closure, after discovering the secrets that my mother had harbored. Instead, I felt a gnawing emptiness. Although Cynthia, as a woman with a past, stood in sharper relief, her first love and her gut-wrenching loss laid bare before me, Cynthia, as my mother, remained an enigma.

The day after I met with Sheldrake, I sat in my sweats on my couch all morning, watching soap operas in Spanish and fog-eating cheese popcorn. By the afternoon, I had to get outside, even in the freezing cold, and do something physically punishing to block out my ability to think. I dragged my bike up from storage and rode across the Queensboro Bridge to Manhattan. By the time I got home in the early evening, I was sweaty and chilled to the bone and ravenous. I showered and then ate a whole frozen pizza by myself back in front of the television. I stuck to this schedule for several days, sometimes minus the shower.

I couldn't go on this way, not the least because I was strapped for cash. Clark hadn't changed his mind about going into business with me, but he'd kindly referred several writers who couldn't pay Canyon Publishing's exorbitant fees but were willing to fork over a more modest amount for freelance editing and advice on the mechanics of self-publishing. The manuscripts Clark steered my way were as poorly written as before, and the clients as demanding, but my attitude had changed. I was no longer trying to create works of literary art. I did exactly enough to earn my fee.

When my cell rang at 11:00 p.m., I knew it was Raj before I looked at the phone. Neither of us had been in a long-distance relationship before, but we'd both gotten advice from friends that regular communication was critical. That had translated, somewhat unromantically, into Raj calling me every night at the same time. Our conversations followed the same pattern every night, too. Raj would listen to me theorize about how Cynthia's past had affected her as a woman and as a mother. After a while, he'd gently encourage me to try to engage with her again. But I was afraid she was too fragile.

One night, Raj took a different tack.

"Jess, we can keep talking about this as long as you want. But I'm not helping you."

It wasn't his fault, but I didn't disagree.

"Can I make a suggestion?" he said.

"Okay."

I heard him take a deep breath before jumping in. "Either you should make an appointment to speak with a professional—"

I cut him off. "Raj, I don't need to sit on some doctor's couch for months and years and then have him tell me my issues can be traced back to my screwed-up childhood. I already know that. I can sit here on my own couch and save a lot of money I don't have."

"Okay, smartass. I'm not sure that's how therapy works, but fine. Then talk to your best friend."

Raj was onto something. Penny was the only one who would understand the profound effect Cynthia's story had on me, why opening up this chapter of my mother's past had exploded into my present. But she and Carlos were so far away. I figured they were busy getting the new house set up and the kids adjusted and prepared to start school after the Christmas break. I wanted badly to make amends to Penny for overreacting the way I had. But an "I'm sorry," especially over the phone, seemed so inadequate. And there was no way to bypass an apology with a "Hey, you wouldn't believe what I found out about Cynthia!" For now, it would have to be Raj, for as long as he was willing to listen.

The situation would have stayed that way for the foreseeable future if the invitation hadn't arrived for Dr. Chan's seventy-fifth surprise birthday party. I didn't usually check my mailbox in the hallway downstairs; I paid my bills online and hardly anything came by snail mail anymore. Penny hadn't lived in Queens for years, and she got more mail than I did. Half the time I didn't know where my key was. But the envelope was a brazen Kelly green and it was hard to miss through the slats.

I climbed the steps to my apartment, clasping the invitation tightly to my chest like it might disappear and leave me standing out in the cold. The party for Penny's dad was to be held a week later in a neighborhood steakhouse called Ricky's that Penny's parents loved. I'd been there once when they'd taken Penny and me and a bunch of girls for a celebratory dinner for Penny's sixteenth birthday. Cynthia hadn't been invited, and consequently, I'd had a wonderful time. I loved Penny's parents, and I very much wanted to go to Dr. Chan's party, but I didn't know how much they knew about the rift between me and Penny. Maybe Penny hadn't told them anything, and that's why I was still invited, or maybe they knew everything in gruesome detail and were trying to broker a rapprochement. I was mostly worried that Penny didn't want to see me and I'd ruin the evening for her if I showed up.

I didn't RSVP, instead going back and forth in my head until an hour before the party started. Then I got dressed, grabbed the last bottle of champagne Tyler had left behind from the aborted engagement party, and walked out the door.

Ricky's hadn't changed in the twenty years since I'd been there. It seemed entirely possible that the restaurant hadn't changed since it opened in the 1970s. The red awning outside still sagged in the middle and swung precariously, and I imagined how in days gone by it had threatened to sweep the toupee off an unsuspecting dandy as he strolled the carpeted walkway to the double doors, a dyed blonde in fake fur on his arm. These days, the patrons were less flamboyant, early-bird folks like Penny's parents, on a budget and looking for quantity as much as quality.

Inside, the wood bar gleamed unnaturally as though the shellac had been applied with a hose and not a brush, the bottles on the shelves reflecting on its surface. The tables were close together, covered in kitschy picnic-style red and white check, and "I'll Be Seeing You" swelled in all the old familiar places. The room was three-quarters full, and the chatter of the partygoers sounded deafening after days of self-imposed solitary confinement in my apartment.

I inspected the crowd, looking for Penny, my pulse quickening. I'd been to so many Chan family events that I'd met most of the aunts and uncles and a bunch of the cousins. I spotted Aunt Jenny and Uncle Peter in a far corner. They were standing close together, their exaggerated gesticulations suggesting an argument, although I couldn't hear what they were saying over the din. Penny's cousin Angie had come dressed in a magenta spandex outfit more appropriate for a roller derby than her uncle's seventy-fifth birthday party, and I hoped she wouldn't give any of the elderly guests a heart attack. I picked out Pat and Serena, Dr. Chan's long-serving nurse and receptionist, respectively, from his optometry shop where I'd been getting my glasses and later my contact lenses since I was a teenager. But Penny and her parents were nowhere to be seen. I figured she was probably part of the ruse to get her father to the restaurant and they'd arrive shortly.

I decided to hit the bar for a little fortification. The

bartender looked as tired as the décor and almost as dated. He barely glanced in my direction when I sat on the high stool, as though taking an order was above his pay grade. He seemed surprised when I spoke.

"What kind of single malt do you have?"

He refilled a bowl of peanuts and pushed it toward me. "No kind."

"Right. I'll have Chivas and undoubtedly regret it."

He poured. "Beggars can't be choosers."

I finished off my drink and drifted over to the buffet table, smiling and waving awkwardly at more aunts, uncles, and cousins. I hadn't realized how hungry I was until the smell of the food hit me. I piled my plate with chicken wings, stuffed mushrooms, mozzarella sticks, and fried shrimp. No sooner had I taken my first bite of a mini beef shish kabob than Penny's uncle Andrew, of excessive dandruff fame, announced that Dr. Chan would be arriving with Penny and her mother in five minutes.

I reluctantly put down my plate, grabbed a glass of champagne from a passing waiter, and headed to the back. Sandwiched between Aunt Jenny and Uncle Peter, still waving their arms around, I shushed them gently and then watched the front entrance. A minute later, Penny ushered her parents into the restaurant. The aunt and uncle took a break to yell "Surprise!" along with the other guests. I stayed quiet and focused on Penny as she greeted her relatives and her parents' friends. I caught her eye. She didn't smile.

I texted Raj.

This was a mistake.

You don't know that.

I know Penny, and she doesn't want me here.

Don't leave without speaking to her.

Stalling, I ducked into the ladies' room. As I washed my hands, I looked at myself in the mirror. I hadn't slept well in weeks. My eyes were puffy, and I had broken out like a teenager. I pulled my brush out of my bag and ran it through my hair and then put on some lip gloss. I breathed into my hand and grabbed a mini bottle of Listerine from the vanity table, rinsing my mouth until I couldn't bear the sting.

Penny's busybody cousin Margaret sidled up to me at the sink. "Still single? Most of the eligible men here are widowers in their eighties, you know. Not a promising crowd."

I gave her a quick peck on the cheek, confident in my mintiness. "No worries. I have someone much more important to impress."

When I came out of the bathroom, Dr. Chan, flanked on either side by Penny and his wife, was giving his "thank you" speech at the front of the room. He looked dapper and vigorous in a red cashmere sweater and pressed gray slacks, and I felt a surge of love for him. Penny's dad hadn't pretended to be the father I didn't have, but in a myriad of ways—from helping me with algebra, to teaching me to navigate the subway system, to warning me about roofies—he'd played the role. As he talked about Penny, I felt that mixture of happiness for her and jealousy that had accompanied me my whole childhood.

Dr. Chan's voice was warm and embracing. As he spoke, he put his arm around Penny and squeezed her to him. "As most of you know, Amy and I immigrated to this country in the early 1980s not only for economic opportunity, but also to escape the one-child policy that was then in effect in China. We couldn't imagine being limited in that way, especially by the government. And what happened? We came here to New York, and we had one child, Penny. And she, our one child, was our whole world. I'm not saying Penny's perfect, but she was and is perfect for us."

When Dr. Chan was finished speaking, I walked over to where he stood greeting his well-wishers. His face lit up when he saw me, and he gave me a big hug. I'd been a smidge taller than him for years, and I planted a kiss on his forehead.

"Jessica! I'm so glad you're here. You know, I meant what I said about the one-child policy. But the truth is," he said, turning us both toward Penny, "we felt like we had a second daughter in you."

Penny was blurry when I looked at her through the tears that filled my eyes. Maybe it was better. Instead of scrutinizing her face for signs of forgiveness that might not have been there, I allowed her father to pull us all into a group hug, including Mrs. Chan tottering on her high heels. When the embrace broke apart, Penny looked at me and shook her head. "As long as you remember I was and will always be their favorite child."

I smiled. "Only fair."

Penny took my hand and dragged me toward the buffet. "Let's go get some food. I'm starving."

"You always could pack it in for a Lilliputian."

CHAPTER TWENTY

An hour later, the food had been decimated, and the guests, warm inside from too much surf and turf and too many G & Ts, had bundled themselves into winter coats and scarves and rolled out into the Queens night. Penny and I hadn't had much of a chance to catch up, as each time we started to talk, someone pulled her away with urgent family gossip. In bits and pieces, I gathered she'd come in from California by herself, leaving the kids with Carlos and the new babysitter. Although I was disappointed not to see my godchildren, I hoped Penny and I might have some time by ourselves.

I tried to keep the neediness out of my voice, but I wasn't sure I succeeded. "Stay over tonight? It's been so long since you were at the apartment. It'll be fun."

Penny hesitated. "I think my parents might want me to come home. I'll ask." A few minutes later, she came back to where I was licking icing off my fingers and contemplating a second slice of birthday cake.

"Apparently, the house is full of out-of-town relatives, and my mother has given away my bed to Great Uncle Kevin. She said it would be helpful if I stayed with you."

I could hear the ambivalence in her voice, so I moved quickly. "Come on. My feet are killing me. I need to get out of these shoes."

Back at the apartment, I opened the door and turned on the lights. "Welcome home."

Penny took a few tentative steps inside. "Wow. I haven't been here in ages."

I took off my coat and kicked off my heels. Penny hadn't been back since the night before her wedding seven years earlier. But I held my tongue.

She pulled off her hat and shook out her hair. "I guess it seemed easier to meet in Manhattan. Especially once I had the kids."

"I guess." Or Penny was grateful to have moved on with the next phase of her life and didn't have an emotional need to come back to the place where we'd lived together. But she was here now, and that's what mattered.

I hung Penny's coat in the closet and passed into the kitchen. "Tea? I have herbal."

Penny flopped down on the couch, rubbing her hands over its worn surface. "I can't believe you still have this old thing." She looked around the living room. "Something is different here, but I can't pinpoint it."

I handed her a mug of mango tea and sat next to her. "Well, the dividing wall is gone."

Penny pointed at a large cactus Raj had bought me. "It's that. Where's Fern?"

I blew on my tea. "Another casualty of Cynthia's book tour. I told Raj there was no replacing her, but he said the succulent would keep me company when he was in St. Louis."

Penny took a sip of her tea. "Ooh. Too hot! What's happening with Raj? He's also very hot."

I nodded. "He's also very far away. But we're giving it a

try. We've visited a couple of times, but it's expensive. We talk and text a lot." I didn't mention that Raj felt so out of his depth about the whole Cynthia thing that he'd practically begged me to talk to Penny. "Tell me about California. Is it what you expected?"

Penny retrieved her overnight bag from where she'd dropped it near the door and pulled out a pair of pink flannel pajamas. She took off her dress, changed into the PJs, and returned to the couch. "Yes and no."

"Start with the yes."

"The weather is pretty lousy a lot of the time. Still, on sunny days people are outside, exercising, walking, barbequing. But the biggest plus is the space. Our house isn't fancy, but we're not on top of each other. The kids have their own rooms—"

"You said that was important to you before you left."

"It was, and it is. Anyway, the space is great." Penny wrapped her arms around herself. "The heating still sucks in here."

In the bedroom, I grabbed a sweatshirt for Penny and one for me. "I feel like we've reached the 'no' part of 'yes and no.'"

Penny sat up a little straighter, which wasn't easy on the wreck of a couch. "It's nothing big. But you know what it's like when you move to a new place?"

I'd moved exactly once in my life when I was seventeen and fled Cynthia's apartment for Astoria with Penny. It was so long ago I could barely remember thinking anything, except that I'd escaped. I looked at Penny and hoped she'd get my wordless communication. She barreled on.

"When you move somewhere where you don't know

anyone, you suddenly realize what it means not to know *anyone*. I mean, in Manhattan, I might not have known their names, but I knew the cashier in the Gristedes who wouldn't bag the groceries because she didn't want to ruin her manicure, and the guy who sang opera while he sold roses on the corner of 96th and Third, and the dogwalker who got pulled down the block by six standard poodles. I sound like I'm on Sesame Street, but those were the people in my neighborhood. I knew they existed."

I nodded. "And they knew you existed. I get it. But they're like the background noise, or the bit players, in your life. You'll make a new set of them. It takes a little while."

"I know. But Carlos and the kids, they're already adjusting and moving forward. They know people from work and from school—"

I didn't understand what Penny was worried about. She was a friendly, outgoing person. No way was her social life going to be a problem. "And you and Carlos will make friends with his colleagues and their partners, and you'll get to know other social workers, and you'll make friends with the parents of Avia and Kyle's friends."

She shoved my leg with her foot. "You're going to make me say it, aren't you?"

"What?"

"New friends aren't the same."

At midnight, we were hungry again. Penny let out a whoop when she stumbled upon an unexpired box of Duncan Hines fudge brownie mix at the back of one of the cabinets, and astonishingly, I had the oil and eggs needed to make it. After we put it in the oven, we sat at the dining table. I'd forgotten Penny's parents had bought it for us as a housewarming gift.

Penny placed my hand where we'd carved our initials on the underside. "They were so mad at us for doing that. My father said it was juvenile. I remember thinking, 'We're seventeen. What do you expect?'"

"Your parents looked great tonight. They're aging gracefully. I hope they stay that way forever."

Penny shook her head. "That seems unlikely. Speaking of aging parents, what's happening with Cynthia? You haven't mentioned her once all evening. This might be a record."

I moved to the bookcase where I'd shelved Cynthia's journal between Emily Dickinson and T.S. Eliot. It seemed like better real estate than hanging with the H's where she belonged. I pulled it out and placed it in front of Penny on the table.

"What's this?"

"The beginning of the story."

Twenty minutes later, Penny finished reading. "Shit."

"That's fair."

I told her about my mother's reaction and her insistence that I talk to Sheldrake, and I walked her through my whole encounter with him. And I told her about Cynthia's fury when I confronted her with Sheldrake's version of events.

"Well, I think these new facts explain a lot," Penny said.

I collapsed back onto the couch and threw a pillow at Penny. "Do you? I feel like nothing makes sense at all."

"Okay. Explain is a big word. I mean, I think knowing about her first sexual experience and the terrible, even tragic loss she experienced as a result, and then the academic failure on top of that—it sheds light on a lot you didn't understand about your mother."

I'd had all the same thoughts, but it helped to hear Penny spell out her conclusions. "Be specific. What do you mean?"

"Like her screwed-up relationships with all those men over the years. The way she'd flirt and go after them, and then toss them aside when she was tired of them without a second thought. Maybe that's a reaction to how she was treated by Sheldrake when she was a young woman in her first relationship. Thrown out of his bed. You know, the abused becomes the abuser. And pressured to get rid of the baby as well."

"Or maybe she's a hard-hearted bitch. What else?"

Penny paused. "Okay. What about how discouraging she was to you about getting an MFA and about pursuing your writing? Maybe she was afraid for you to go into academia, given her experiences with Sheldrake, and was trying to protect you. And the way she took Hunter by storm could also have been a reaction to her time at Yale, her way of getting back at Sheldrake by becoming more powerful and famous in his world."

The timer buzzed on the brownies, and I went to the kitchen to take them out of the oven. I cut them into squares and put one in my mouth before bringing the rest out to Penny. I burned my tongue, but the sweetness suffused me, and for a moment the sugar rush made it hard to think. When it passed, I turned to Penny.

"None of this explains the one thing that matters. Why doesn't she love me as much as she should?"

In the morning, Penny woke up early to go to the airport. I made her coffee, and we finished the rest of the brownies while she got herself together.

"I'm sorry to leave so soon, but Carlos is kind of hopeless with the kids with all these changes. Avia has an appointment with the new dentist this afternoon, and Kyle is starting soccer club after school."

"You don't have to explain why you need to go home, Pen. I didn't think you were going to stay here with me for good."

She pulled me into a hug. "Listen, Jess. Everything is going to come together for you. You're already on solid ground with Raj—it's obvious he really cares about you, and you're letting down your defenses with him, which is a great start. And that job at Canyon was beneath you. Something better is bound to come along."

Penny hesitated, her pep talk losing steam. "The situation will work out with Cynthia. I mean, one way or the other, you know?"

What I hadn't told Penny was that I'd received a letter from Matthew Sheldrake. It had arrived the same day as the invitation to her father's surprise party, and I hadn't felt up to dealing with both at the time. I considered throwing the letter away, but instead I'd put it in my desk drawer under some unpaid bills. I wanted nothing to do with Sheldrake. I couldn't imagine what more he could have to say to me.

Part of me wished I'd read the letter while Penny was with me, but it was too late for that now. I pulled it out of the drawer. I gave myself a paper cut opening the envelope, and as I sucked on my finger, I thought again about ripping up the letter before I read it. Instead, I unfolded the heavy ivory stationery, leaving a dab of blood where the seal of the University was embossed.

Ms. Harmon,

You called me a bastard. I will add liar and coward. It's beyond shameful that I've chosen to tell you what you have always deserved to know in a letter, rather than in person. I'm an old man, and I'm not well. This is the most I can manage.

I want to correct the misimpression I intentionally gave you when we met in New Haven. Cynthia didn't have an abortion in January 1970, although that was the plan. She spent the Christmas holidays at home in St. Louis. Sometime during her stay, she decided she wasn't going to terminate the pregnancy. She wanted to keep the baby. Your grandparents told Cynthia that if she had the baby, they wouldn't support her or the child.

I told her she was crazy, that she would ruin both of our lives. I couldn't, and wouldn't, force her to have an abortion. But I pressured her not to keep the baby. In the end, Cynthia agreed to stay in New Haven during the term of the pregnancy (so as not to scandalize her parents, was my understanding), and we'd give the baby up for adoption through a private arrangement. A public agency wasn't an option because a background check would have revealed I was on faculty, married, and Cynthia was my student. After a lot of searching, I found a wonderful couple—the wife was my landlord's cousin, and the husband had his own landscaping business— who'd been struggling to have a child. Everything was handled quietly and discreetly. I remained in contact with the family only through my landlord, to help financially, when I could. Cynthia didn't want to know anything. She left New Haven in late September 1970.

I wish I could tell you the existence of your half-sister is the end of the story.

You asked me whether I'm your father, and I told you I hadn't seen Cynthia again after she left campus in 1970. That was a lie.

In 1988, Cynthia returned to Yale as a fellow to teach in the summer session. By that time, she'd made a name for herself as a young poet and a junior professor at Hunter. My marriage had disintegrated some years earlier, and Cynthia was determined that we rekindle our romance. She told me she'd gotten over giving up the baby for adoption, and that she wanted to start a new life with me. My feelings for her hadn't diminished in the least over the intervening years, and I was thrilled to be with her again. She was a different person. Confident and mature and affectionate. It was an idyllic summer.

As Cynthia's fellowship came to a close, I implored her to stay in New Haven. I offered to help her get a position in the English department at Yale or close by or to support her if she preferred to write her poetry full time. I didn't want to lose her again. I asked her to marry me.

One day in September, she decamped back to New York. She left a note that said we'd had a summer fling and I should forget about her.

Slim chance of that.

Two months later, I heard from a colleague in New York that Cynthia was pregnant. The math was inconclusive, and when I demanded to know if the child was mine, she denied it.

She claimed, as you must know, that she'd had a relationship with a visiting professor who'd passed away in a freak accident. I didn't believe her. Cynthia made it clear to me I was not to follow up or seek any access to the baby. She threatened to get a restraining order against me.

I was distraught. Like Cynthia, I was also a different person than I'd been in 1970. I'd gone through a tumultuous marriage and divorce, and at age 52, I had no wife and no children. I wanted to make a life with your mother and you. But I suppose after what I'd done in using my power and position to force her to give up her child the first time, Cynthia wasn't taking any chances. For the first few years of your life, I begged her to let me be your father. When she refused, I vowed to petition for a court-ordered paternity test to establish my rights. She swore that if I took legal action or contacted you in any way, she'd tell Yale that I'd raped her when she was a seventeen-year-old student. It wasn't true, but truth wouldn't matter once the accusation was made.

In time, I concluded that Cynthia was right. I would pay for what I had done in 1970. I owed her my silence.

Am I your father? I don't have proof, but I believe so. I hope so. I respect your courage in confronting me and holding up a candle to my inadequacy. You remind me of someone I used to know.

I'm sure you have questions. I think it's more likely that your mother has the answers you need, and I'm sorry she can't give them to you. What I can tell you is that I have your sister's permission to tell you her name is Grace DiBella and she lives with her family in Nyack, New York. What you do with that information is up to you.

I told you that I loved Cynthia. I've never said anything

more true in my life. I wish we could have been a family.

The rest has been an utter failure.

—Matthew Sheldrake

P.S. In case you were wondering, Cynthia gave me your address.

CHAPTER TWENTY-ONE

I was resigned that, given Cynthia's condition, I would never know her motivations in the summer of 1988 when she returned to Yale and resumed her relationship with Matthew Sheldrake. I wanted to believe that after so many years apart, my mother, like Sheldrake, felt that their love endured and that a future was possible. But Sheldrake's take was compelling: my mother had manipulated him into fathering another child to make up for the one he'd forced her to give up years before, and then she'd cut him out of both of our lives for the sin of loving her. Perhaps the truth lay somewhere in between.

I sat immobilized on the couch, waiting for the tears to come. Crying seemed like the reaction a normal person would have, but I felt numb. I called Penny in California and read Sheldrake's letter to her. She had a more positive spin, pointing out how much Cynthia must have wanted to have me and the lengths to which she had gone to get pregnant a second time with Sheldrake.

I wasn't buying it. My lived experience told me otherwise. Instead of rejoicing in her second chance to be a mother, it felt to me as though Cynthia had never recovered from giving up her first child, that she resented my existence because I was a poor substitute for the daughter she'd lost. And now, in her diminished state, it seemed as though Cynthia wanted me to forgive her. It was a lot to ask, even for my mother.

"So, what are you going to do about Grace?" Penny asked.

"I don't know. You're the only sister I've ever had."

I reached out to Grace on a Saturday about a month later. She answered the phone right away, as if she knew I'd call eventually. She was cordial, but not warm, as if we were total strangers. Which, of course, we were.

We arranged to meet at her house. I didn't invite her to Astoria because I couldn't let her see I lived like an overgrown college student, and meeting in a restaurant or museum seemed awkward. Besides, Grace said she preferred to be around for her kids on the weekends.

"Maybe you'll get to meet Sari and Jack, although I can't make any promises," Grace said. Probably wise; I was a little fragile for that.

Grace called me a couple of days before we were to get together to give me directions. "It's an easy drive. Straight shot up from Manhattan over the Tappan Zee Bridge. I mean the Mario Cuomo Bridge. I can't get used to that. I don't do change well."

Something we shared. I almost told her my whole world had been turned upside down. But she knew that.

"I don't have a car. Actually, I don't have a driver's license."

Grace sounded genuinely shocked. "Really? I can't imagine."

I wondered what she imagined about my life, if anything, this new older sister of mine.

I tried not to sound defensive. "A lot of people who live in

New York City don't know how to drive."

It turned out getting to Grace's house from Astoria by public transportation wasn't simple. I had to take the subway to Grand Central, board a commuter train to Tarrytown, and then switch to a bus to Nyack. I'd been sitting so long I was grateful her house was walking distance from the center of town so I could stretch my legs and get a breath of fresh air. I might not know how to drive, but my ambulatory skills had been honed on the unforgiving streets of New York City. Still, I was unprepared for the suburban hills and was winded when I finally arrived. It was unseasonably warm for March, and a bead of sweat trickled down my temple. That's how Grace found me, standing on the sidewalk looking up at her rambling white Victorian, trying to compose myself.

Watching her walk out onto her front porch was like witnessing time-lapse photography, the years moving forward and backward simultaneously. At forty-nine, Grace was an older version of me—attractive, better groomed, with a more sun-weathered complexion and thicker around the waist. At the same time, she was a younger version of Cynthia—posture proud and unbowed, her hair dirty blonde with a touch of gray at the temples, an aura of competence.

I'd googled Grace, of course, seen photos of her winning a commendation as "ICU Respiratory Therapist of the Month" at Montefiore Nyack Hospital and chairing a community spring fling event at the Old Stone Meeting House. On the computer screen, I'd made out a familiar resemblance, but nothing striking. In person, there was no question we were sisters. We both took after Cynthia in big and small ways; I found myself wondering if Grace's second toe was longer than her first like mine. But we'd also inherited features from the man who had fathered us—characteristics I'd never been able to pin to a genetic source. I'd failed to process the resemblance when I'd met Sheldrake, but now, seeing Grace, it was glaringly obvious. We had the same prominent chin, the same small ears, the same almost non-existent eyebrows as Sheldrake.

"You made it." Grace seemed pleased to see me, and I relaxed a little.

"Yes. I see why people learn how to drive."

She waved me onto the porch and gestured toward a white wicker rocking chair with yellow and purple floral cushions. "Come, sit down. Would you like some iced tea? I can't believe how warm it is today."

I'd hoped she would hug me and was relieved when she didn't. I reminded myself to keep my expectations low. She was on her home turf but seemed anxious, picking up and refolding the napkins she'd put out. Iced tea was probably my least favorite beverage, but I said I'd love some, and Grace retreated into the house. I looked around. The porch was immaculate but gave off a friendly vibe. I craned my neck to see how it wrapped around the house; it was bigger than my whole apartment.

The sound of someone playing the saxophone drifted out through the screen door, sweet and melodic.

"The music is beautiful," I said when Grace came back with my drink. "In the city, your neighbors would've already reported you for noise pollution. It's nice you're not on top of anyone out here."

"That's my wife, Rosa. She used to play more. Now that the kids are older, she's trying to get back into it." Grace handed me a tall rose-colored glass of iced tea, and I took a sip, struggling not to grimace. I put it on the coaster she'd placed on the table next to me, along with a plate of store-bought cookies. Cynthia had a million coasters. Back in the day, she was always mixing drinks for people in the apartment, and she worried a lot about the furniture. I didn't own a coaster.

"Is this kind of a crunchy town? I don't think of the suburbs as being accommodating to non-traditional families. Not like New York City, where everyone's too busy to get into anyone else's underwear. I mean—you know what I mean." I looked around the yard to see if Grace's children were around and had heard my stupid comment, but no one was outside.

"We're actually pretty traditional." Grace forced a smile. I saw neither Cynthia nor Sheldrake in her expression. I asked myself again why I'd come. It wasn't like I thought we'd have some transformational reunion, catch up on a lifetime of experiences we hadn't shared. Perhaps it was idle curiosity. How had she turned out, this daughter my mother had wanted and lost? The one I believed she'd tried to replace with me, who had fallen short.

Grace seemed to be looking intently at me when I came out of my reverie. "Do you have a family?"

I raised my eyebrows. "Well, I have Cynthia, and now I suppose I have Matthew Sheldrake. And you."

She nodded slowly, but her hesitation spoke louder. "I meant a family of your own."

I took another sip of the iced tea and swallowed quickly. "I'm in a relationship with a man I knew briefly in college, but we'd been out of touch, and it only recently became something more. I don't have a great track record with commitment—Cynthia was not an exemplary role model. It's early days. But I'm hopeful."

"Then I'm hopeful for you." It was a nice thing to say. The emotional ups and downs of the conversation were beginning to wear on me, and I had a feeling this was the tip of the iceberg.

We sat in silence for a moment. I added three packets of Sweet'n Low to my drink and took another sip.

I racked my brain for more small talk and then asked what was on my mind. "When did you find out who your biological parents were? How did it happen?"

If Grace was put off by my directness, she didn't let on. "My parents told me I was adopted when I was four. I think every adopted child fantasizes about finding her biological parents at some point. I was no different. When I was a kid, I was convinced my 'real' mother was an anchor on the evening news somewhere and my 'real' father was a Major League Baseball player. But I never actually looked for them, other than watching out for them on television."

She'd learned her father was Matthew Sheldrake when she was a young teen and the family was still living in New Haven. For as long as she could remember, Grace's mother had received letters at irregular intervals and infrequently, hand-delivered by the landlord, with no return address on the envelope. One time, the envelope arrived before her mother got home from work, unsealed. Curious, Grace had found a check for one hundred dollars, signed by Sheldrake, with the note "for the child" in the memo line. She was fourteen, and her mother decided to come clean and tell her what she'd already figured out. "She didn't give me any details, just that Sheldrake had something to do with the university. My mother was clear he wasn't interested in having a relationship with me. Although of course I was disappointed, I wasn't surprised.

Even at that age, I understood that men come and go."

"And Cynthia?" I asked, my voice breaking.

"Ah. That was much more recent." Grace's mother had told her she didn't know who her biological mother was, only that she was seventeen or eighteen at the time, a student living away from home who didn't have a husband or family support and who wanted to give the baby a better life than she could. Grace accepted that explanation, for the most part. After she learned that Sheldrake was her father, Grace realized her mother had likely been a student at Yale or one of the other colleges in New Haven, right in her own backyard, and that was hard. Every now and then she'd press her mother to tell her more, but she claimed that was all she knew.

"When my mother died last year, I was cleaning out her apartment. I knew she'd kept whatever little jewelry she had in her closet in a burlap bag with a yellow dog appliqué I'd made in the sixth grade. She was sentimental like that."

I thought about Cynthia, a Marie Kondo disciple before decluttering was in vogue. I had to ask Vera to hide my art projects if I wanted to keep them.

Grace got up from her chair. "Hang on. I'll show you. I'll be right back."

I was walking around the porch when Grace returned. In one hand she held the burlap bag. In the other, she had five or six thin volumes of my mother's poetry.

"The jewelry was there, but these were at the bottom of the bag. My mother was a hardworking, street-smart woman. She read the local newspaper, and occasionally I saw her open a popular romance. Poetry? No way. I knew something was up."

Grace opened the first volume and picked a poem at random, showing me the page. It was one of my favorites. I could recite it by heart.

She pointed to the pencil markings I hadn't noticed at first. "See? My mother had underlined whatever allusions she picked up to young love, loss, yearning, children forsaken—there were more she'd missed, but I caught them. It was all there in the poetry—not just this poem, but many of the poems. I know it probably sounds crazy, like a huge leap of logic. But there was no doubt in my mind that my mother had saved and annotated these poems because Cynthia Harmon was my birth mother."

It was exactly as Cynthia had always told me. Her story was all there in her poetry. I'd read it all so many times. Foolish me, I'd been looking for Cynthia, looking for myself. I didn't know I should have been looking for Grace.

"Who gave Cynthia's books to your mother? Who told her what to look for in the words?"

Grace put the books carefully back into the burlap bag. "I've wondered that myself. I didn't have the chance to ask her because I didn't find these until after she was gone."

CHAPTER TWENTY-TWO

Grace hadn't done anything wrong, but I felt like my head might explode if I didn't get away from her for a minute. I asked if I could use the bathroom, and she showed me to a small powder room just off the front entrance. I wanted to make a break for it and explore the house, rummage through the kitchen cabinets, peer into the bedrooms to see if the beds were made, run my fingers along the furniture, checking for dust. Instead, I ducked into the bathroom and splashed my face with cold water. When I couldn't stay there any longer without arousing suspicion, I trudged back outside and sat down. I switched to what I hoped would be a safe topic. I asked Grace to tell me about my niece and nephew.

Grace took a sip of her coffee, and I wondered why she hadn't offered me any. "The kids? They're great. They're teenagers. They're sweet and relatively respectful, and they don't want much to do with their parents at this age."

"What do they like to do? What are they into?"

Grace shrugged. "Mostly they seem to be glued to their phones. Otherwise, Sari is a gifted athlete; plays a different sport every season. She gets that from Rosa, not me. And Jack's the total opposite. He doesn't play sports or watch professional sports. He's more of a nerdy computer guy."

"And you're fine with all of it? You let them do what makes them happy?" I failed to keep the edge out of my voice.

"I'm not sure I understand your question. What else would I do?" Grace put down her coffee and shifted her gaze to my almost-full glass of iced tea. "Would you prefer coffee?" Now she seemed to be the one looking for an excuse to escape, but I nodded.

When Grace came back, she seemed more guarded. She barely made eye contact. She scooted her chair a few inches further away from mine. I don't think she meant to do it, would've denied she had. I didn't blame her. My question about what kind of mother she was and her relationship with her children probably got her back up.

"You have no idea what it was like growing up with Cynthia. What it's like now." The statement floated and expanded and sucked the air out of the space between us. I knew Grace could never understand what I'd experienced having Cynthia as a mother. I also knew it was an ugly emotion and unfair to her, but I envied Grace her normal childhood. I needed her to hear what she'd been spared.

Grace closed her eyes for a moment, as if gathering herself, and then her gaze was steady. "Tell me."

"How much do you know about her?"

"Not a lot."

I was astounded Grace had discovered the truth about who her biological parents were and hadn't bothered to learn more. I'd spent my entire life wondering who my father was and wishing my mother was someone else. Yet Grace apparently had gathered only the most basic information about Sheldrake and Cynthia. She must have sensed my disbelief. "I know it probably sounds crazy to you. But I was close to my parents and especially connected to my brother and sister—after my

243

parents adopted me, they had two biological children. I didn't want to hurt them. And I had other identity questions that were much more pressing to me at the time. Coming out to my parents when I was fifteen was more important than hunting down biological parents who had no role in my life. I'm not trying to be unkind. But if you hadn't gone on this journey into your mother's past, that's how things would have stayed for me."

So that's where Grace landed. I wasn't the long-lost sister she was ready to embrace into her family. I was an intruder, stirring up her comfortable life. She'd figured out Cynthia was her mother and hadn't looked for me. That said it all. My legs felt weak, and I wondered if they would cooperate when I got up to leave, her words, "your mother's past," reverberating in my head. Grace was the part of my mother's past I hadn't known existed, the child who stole her heart and hadn't left room for me. Now I was expendable, again.

I could have walked away, let Grace off the hook. Instead, I told her what I hadn't told anyone before.

"When I was a little girl, Cynthia was determined to identify some hobby or interest I would show promise in. That's how she phrased it—'show promise in.' Not something I might enjoy or a talent or a passion I might develop. Talent and passion were reserved for Cynthia. I think she wanted me to be good enough at something so she could justify spending her time on me."

Grace cringed. But the floodgates were open. There was no going back.

"We ran through a bunch of activities—ballet, taekwondo, drawing classes—"

The front screen door squeaked open and slammed shut.

I hadn't noticed the music had stopped, but there was Rosa, standing on the porch.

"Hi." She looked younger than Grace, more exuberant with softer features. Her blonde hair fell in long waves down her back, and she was wearing the kind of denim overalls I'd seen only in 1970s sitcom reruns. She took a few steps toward the empty chair next to Grace, who shook her head almost imperceptibly.

"I think Jessica would prefer we had this conversation privately. Am I right?"

I didn't trust my voice to answer, so I stared straight ahead and waited for Rosa to turn to go back inside the house. It was terribly rude, and I was ashamed, but it was all I could do. Rosa touched Grace's shoulder on the way past. "I'll tell the kids to steer clear for a bit."

I swallowed hard and began again.

"I was nine when she signed me up for piano lessons at the music school down the block from our apartment. Cynthia said it was the perfect age to learn an instrument. I still remember how she put it. 'You're old enough to sit still, intelligent enough to understand no one improves without diligent practice, and impressionable enough to recognize you can achieve beauty when you play.' Quite a mission for a nine-year-old.

"It started out well. I loved the lessons, even when I was learning scales or simple songs. My teacher, Mrs. Gilbert, was ancient, smelled faintly like oatmeal, and wore pants with elastic waistbands Cynthia wouldn't be caught dead in."

At the mention of the fashion faux pas, I pictured Rosa's overalls and felt a flush of embarrassment. Grace didn't seem to notice.

"Go on," she said.

"Mrs. Gilbert was kind and patient, taking a few minutes at the beginning of each lesson to ask me about my day at school and offer me a chocolate chip cookie. I'd wash my hands before touching the Steinway. I knew it was a Steinway because we had one at home, a grander one, although Cynthia didn't play. It was there for show. Or maybe it was there for me.

"The piano lessons, the cookies, and Mrs. Gilbert went on for three years. I knew everyone on the staff of the music school, and I was so comfortable there that sometimes I stayed later and did my homework in the waiting area. I was no prodigy, but I was a conscientious student, and I improved steadily."

My back ached from sitting in the rocking chair, and I got up to stretch.

"We could walk around the block, if you'd like," Grace offered. I was sure she could tell this story was going in a bad direction. I shook my head, sat down.

"When I turned twelve, Cynthia announced I would no longer go to the music school but would instead take piano lessons at home from a man named Sasha. He was a twenty-five-year-old Juilliard student and the son of Sergei Novodkin, the Russian literature department chair at Hunter. In retrospect, I'm sure Cynthia was sleeping with Sergei, and that explains the sudden urgency for me to switch from Mrs. Gilbert to Sasha, but at the time, all I knew was that my happy place had been ripped out from under me.

"On Tuesday afternoons, when Sasha came for my lesson, Cynthia worked from home. She made a show of opening the front door for him and handing him a sealed envelope with his payment for the lesson so she didn't need to reappear later. Then she'd retire to her home office to write. Often while I had my lesson, she'd meet with one of her students, invariably dressed in black and looking desperate for coffee or a shower. Cynthia loved how the students kissed up to her. 'Don't disturb us, please,' my mother would say. Still, I knew she was there, down the hall."

I took a drink of my coffee. It wasn't hot anymore, and it was hazelnut, but it was an improvement over the iced tea. My hands were trembling, and I put the mug down before I spilled or dropped it.

"I missed Mrs. Gilbert of the elastic waistbands, but I thought Sasha was awesome. He was rock-star cool but more refined, with a mop-top of dirty blond hair and the longest, most graceful fingers you've ever seen. There were days when he was withdrawn and days when he seemed about to jump out of his skin. He played the piano as if the music were welling up inside him and needed to be released or he would burst."

"How lovely," Grace said.

"At the start of the lesson, Sasha would sit formally in a dining room chair pulled up near the piano bench. He'd instruct me from there, listening with his head to one side, and then marking my music in pencil with the correct fingering. Sometimes, he'd ask me to stand, and he'd sit on the bench and play passages he wanted me to work on during the week, so I'd know how they were supposed to sound. We rarely engaged in any conversation that didn't directly relate to the lesson. I was twelve years old, and after all the trial and error of trying to find my promise, I believed Cynthia had given me a chance, in the form of Sasha, to nurture a gift."

Grace bit her lip and turned her head toward the street.

A car passed and someone waved from the driver's seat, but Grace didn't move. I kept talking.

"After a few months, the dynamic changed. There were lessons when Sasha didn't stay seated in his chair but instead moved onto the piano bench while I was sitting there, leaning slightly against me, our thighs or knees touching. Sometimes he spoke softly near my ear. 'You're growing up, Jessica,' he said in his accented English. 'You're becoming very pretty.' The back of my throat would seize up, and I couldn't respond. His words and his proximity made me nervous, but it was also thrilling. I would stare at the music in front of me and try to play, but often I'd get stuck, unable to finish a phrase. Sasha would sweep away one of my curls from my face and touch the back of my neck with his fingers, and I would catch myself gasping. Then he'd return to the lesson as though nothing had happened, and I'd think I'd imagined the whole thing."

Grace spoke quietly, her face still turned away from me. "Did you tell your mother?"

"No. I was afraid to interrupt her office hours, afraid she'd say I had invited Sasha's behavior, and more afraid she'd send him away. I tried my best to pour my emotions into my music, to play better."

I stopped talking until Grace made eye contact. I could tell she didn't want to, but I was patient. I hadn't known it, but I'd waited a long time for this moment.

"One Tuesday, Sasha arrived for my lesson, and Cynthia welcomed him at the same time as she let in Astrid, one of her most intelligent but also her most sycophantic grad students. Astrid had boldly declared she intended to write her doctoral thesis on the poetry of Cynthia Harmon, with my mother as her advisor. The conflict of interest didn't bother them; in fact, they both seemed to think the arrangement was advantageous. Cynthia would have the benefit of a devoted and adoring student poring over her every word, and Astrid would pay homage to the woman who could help her achieve greatness in her own right down the line. A win-win.

"That afternoon was to be their first session working together on this project. Astrid arrived in fine form. She'd washed her normally greasy hair and wiped the kohl from around her eyes. She'd changed out of her black pants and black T-shirt and was wearing a rust-colored peasant dress that, if not exactly festive, wasn't morbid. Astrid explained she had a date later that evening with someone outside of academia 'who wears colors.'

"Cynthia nodded, and I wondered whether what I did with Sasha counted as a date. I felt a wave of confusion and took a step toward my mother, but she was gone down the hall and Sasha was sitting on the chair, patting my seat on the bench beside him.

"I remember it was an oppressively hot day. Cynthia didn't believe in air conditioning. Usually in the living room we kept a standing fan running, but when I had my lessons, it would blow the music around, so my mother turned it off. I was wearing my favorite pair of pink shorts and a lavender tank top with tiny flowers on it, and I had my hair pulled back in a ponytail. I had practiced well that week, and I was excited to show Sasha my progress. I sat down, and he immediately moved from the chair to the bench. He sat so close to me I could smell his cologne, which was pungent and reminded me of the newly cut grass in Riverside Park. Sasha touched my shoulder and leaned in so his lips were near the base of my neck.

'You're so beautiful, Jessica,' he whispered. 'You're very grown up. We can be good friends.' I felt paralyzed by his words. I wanted to believe him, even as he frightened me. Then he took my hand as he had many times before to show me the fingering on the piano and the correct position for my wrist when I played. But instead of placing it on the piano keyboard, he put it on his inner thigh, shifting the way he was seated so my hand landed where he wanted it.

'Yes, right there, golden one,' he murmured, his eyes closed, his wonderful hair falling on his brow as he bent his head forward.

"I jumped up and ran without thinking down the hallway to my mother's office. As I banged on the door, I could hear the scrape of the piano bench and the front door closing behind Sasha as he left.

'What is it, Jessica? Why have you stopped your lesson in the middle? Go back to Sasha this instant.' Cynthia's voice was shrill, and I could feel the heat coming off of her face. Astrid leaned back in her chair and looked me up and down. Something made her smile. I wanted to strangle her.

"And then my mother smiled too, although her eyes remained hard. I couldn't understand how Cynthia had sided with Astrid over me. I wanted to yell that something disgusting had happened and she needed to help me. But she kept smiling with Astrid, and I stood there, staring at the floor. I got confused, began to doubt Sasha had done anything wrong. Maybe nothing had happened.

'Let's go finish your lesson. I'll walk you back to the piano,' Cynthia said, her voice cold and even.

'Sasha's gone.'

'What do you mean?'

"I looked up at my mother, forcing myself to hold my eyes on hers. 'He quit. He said I didn't have any talent for piano after all. He was wasting his time and your money.'

"I wanted Cynthia to tell Astrid to leave her office, to ask me in private what had really happened. If that was too much, I wanted her to be furious with Sasha, to say that of course I had talent and she'd find me another teacher, a better one. Instead, it was like the truth was out. I'd finally exhausted all the possibilities, and her defeat was complete. I'd proven I showed no promise, had nothing to hold her interest. The music was over. She turned back to Astrid, and they went back to discussing Cynthia's poem.

"I left the two of them in Cynthia's office, closing the door quietly behind me. I never touched the piano again."

Grace wrapped her arms around her waist and rocked gently in her chair. She looked like she might be sick. "I'm so sorry you had to go through that, Jessica. I don't know what to say."

"I don't want your pity."

Grace shook her head. "I reserve pity for people who can't stand on their own two feet. Your mother is a broken woman, and you've borne the brunt of it. That's a terrible shame. But you're a survivor."

Grace stood and picked up her coffee cup and mine. She retreated into the house, letting the screen door slam shut behind her. My compulsion to unburden myself had been doused, as surely as if she'd poured a bucket of ice water over my head. I had no idea where it all left me.

As I sat watching the front door, uncertain whether she'd return, a teenage girl came around from the backyard and up the front stairs onto the porch. Sari was wearing cleats and a soccer uniform, a black and white ball in her hands, and for a second, I had a vision of myself as the devoted aunt, traveling hours to cheer her on at her game. Then I remembered.

"Oh, hi," Sari said. "My moms are inside. Do you want me to tell them you're here?"

"No, I'm good. Thanks. I'm Jessica."

Grace came out onto the porch and stopped short. I wondered if she was afraid of what I might say to her daughter.

"Don't forget, we need to leave in ten minutes, okay?" Sari said.

"I know. Jessica and I were just finishing up."

"Nice to meet you," Sari said and disappeared into the house before I could respond.

"She's lovely."

Grace nodded.

I'm sure my smile didn't fool her, but I painted one on my face anyway. "I grew up trying to figure out how to reach my mother, how to please her, how to make her love me. What I didn't know until I discovered you was that I was in a competition I couldn't possibly win. You were the fantasy, and I was the consolation prize. I don't think Cynthia ever recovered from losing you."

Grace looked away. When she turned back to me, I read a sisterly compassion in her gaze. "Sometimes the only thing you can do is to step away from someone else's grief. Step away and live your life, Jessica."

On the train from Tarrytown back to the city, my phone buzzed incessantly with news alerts and tweets. A lawyer in a Westchester suburb had gone from healthy to being hooked up to a ventilator in a matter of a day or two, fighting for his life against a virus no one had ever heard of.

CHAPTER TWENTY-THREE

I stretched my arms over my head and leaned back, trying to release the kinks in my back from sitting so long at the computer in my decidedly non-ergonomic chair. My desk was in a state of ordered chaos. Spread across the surface were Cynthia's journal and her other notebooks, *Broken Wings* and selected volumes of poetry by her contemporaries, correspondence, materials from the courses Cynthia had taught at Hunter over the years, and photographs. And scattered throughout, my own diaries, letters, photographs, and short stories.

The book had been my mother's friend Monica's idea. She convinced me that at some point, either before or after Cynthia's death, there would be people vying to write her story. My mother couldn't contribute much herself or decide who to grant access to her papers, as her condition had deteriorated, leaving her largely unable to communicate. Monica's advice was straightforward.

"If you want to control the narrative, you should write the definitive work. I know you write fiction, and there will be plenty of time for that. But you have the unique ability to provide insight into your mother's personal life and relationships, and you have the knowledge to analyze her work as well. No one else has that combination. And of course, you have your own story to tell."

I didn't have a good fix on what Monica knew about Sheldrake, Grace, or me for that matter, but she clearly knew enough about Cynthia and the publishing world to know that a tell-all, even a sensitive, nuanced, literary one, would sell. My mother's popularity had not waned in the aftermath of the stroke. To the contrary, her readership seemed ever more devoted and was growing by the day. *Broken Wings* was moving online and in bookstores, with Cynthia's fans showing their love for a poet whose ability to write was fast slipping away.

After a few weeks of weighing the pros and cons, I wrote the first two chapters and put together a proposal with Monica's help. By June of 2020, I had a book deal with an academic imprint affiliated with Hunter College, which was an impressive feat for the beginning of the pandemic.

Pitched as part semi-authorized biography, part a daughter's memoir, and part literary exploration, the project was taking shape. The most difficult aspect was deciding how much to disclose. I had to differentiate between legitimate privacy concerns—my mother's and my own, chiefly, but Sheldrake's and Grace's too—and my tendency to keep secrets because I was afraid to expose them to the light of day. In the end, I shared what I believed was mine to share, and asked permission, when I could, to tell the rest. My truth didn't match up with Cynthia's all the time, but we'd both laid a lot of cards on the table. Distancing myself from my mother by writing about her was liberating.

The sound of fingers clicking furiously on computer keys interrupted my thoughts, and I looked across the room to the dining table where Raj had set himself up. Even though I'd worked for years in a cubicle so close to Clark that his breathing fogged my computer screen, I found it nearly impossible to write with Raj in the same room. I came behind his chair and mussed his hair, leaning over to speak quietly near his ear.

"There is not enough space for two of us in this apartment."

He tilted his head quizzically. "What do you mean? You lived here with Penny for years and didn't have a problem."

"That was different."

"Well, you weren't sleeping together. So maybe the separate bedrooms gave you the illusion you had more space."

My ability to focus was sorely tested as Raj held me close and slid his hands up the front of my shirt. "Penny and I weren't trying to *write*. I mean, a novel is different; you don't have to worry about getting the facts right. I need to concentrate."

"I'll ignore that inane remark because you know better. Anyway, there are some advantages to working from home," he said.

It had been four months, the longest I'd ever officially lived with a boyfriend. In April 2020, when the pandemic was crushing everything and showing no signs of retreat, Raj moved into my apartment. We were part of a worldwide phenomenon: couples who weren't at a point in their relationships to make the leap to living together but couldn't face lockdown alone. Raj had been the one to suggest it.

"We'd make a rad pod," he'd insisted, although I could tell he wasn't at all confident either. The way everything had shut down in the city without warning, especially the restaurants and the public transportation, had left me anxious and on edge. Not to mention the nightly newscasts of the number of dead, the footage of body bags, and the fact that Queens, with its extensive immigrant population, was the hardest hit of the five boroughs. But until Raj raised the notion of sheltering in place in my apartment, I hadn't realized how freaked out I was to be by myself all the time. When I said I was willing to give it a shot, Raj got in his car and drove the seventeen hours from St. Louis to New York, sleeping in the only motel he could find in Ohio that hadn't shut down. So far, things were going smoothly for two people who were still getting to know one another, trapped in a small space. We tried to work, and when we couldn't, we watched Austin Powers movies, played Bananagrams, and baked sourdough bread we didn't like because everyone else was doing it.

As Raj pulled me onto his lap and kissed me, my phone pinged.

It was a text from Clark. I assumed he was checking on my progress with the manuscripts he'd steered my way, and I was behind. It was hard to get excited about marking up other people's pages when I had writing deadlines of my own. Still, the truth was I needed the money. The advance for "Mommy and Me," as I jokingly referred to the book, was just shy of laughable. I reluctantly read his text.

I did it.

That can't be good.

I got ordained by the Universal Life Church.
I'll be able to officiate at your wedding.

Here we go again.

Listen, you'll be restricted to ten guests
for a Covid wedding. If I officiate, you won't
have to use up one of your spots on me.

You're crazy.

It'll be the two of you, Penny, Carlos,
the kids, Cynthia, and Raj's dad. Doesn't
that sound cozy? That leaves you two more,
and I won't ask to bring a date. Outdoors,
of course. Masks. And no food. Or maybe
individually wrapped peanut butter and cheese
crackers.

You're a freak. Go away.

A wedding was the last thing on my mind. Still, I wondered
whether Grace and Rosa would come.

I tossed my cell on the couch and took Raj's hand, leading
him to the bedroom. He was right. There were some advantages
to working from home.

When my cell rang an hour later, I coaxed Raj out of bed to
bring it to me from the other room.

He came back and held the phone out to me. "Vera." When
I didn't move from under the covers, Raj said, "Jess, you have
to pick up."

Vera had been loyal beyond measure. When the city plunged
into lockdown, she had saved me when she'd agreed to stay
with Cynthia and take care of her. Although she was stoic,
being trapped in the apartment 24/7 with my mother had to
have been a nightmare even for her. The situation was getting
more precarious by the day as Cynthia became frailer and less
able to get across her basic needs. And I could tell Vera was
lonely from hints she dropped when she spoke with me and
the greater frequency of her calls. While the generous salary

made up for a lot, it was time for her to go home.

Today I had good news. I'd been looking into assisted living facilities for Cynthia. Everything had been closed to new residents during the height of the pandemic while the disease ravaged the most vulnerable. But the restrictions were loosening up. The night before, I'd received a call out of the blue from Grace. We'd spoken only a handful of times since that day in Nyack, but the news reports were full of stories of the heroic dedication of medical personnel, especially nurses, during the worst days of Covid. I was sure Grace's work had taken a tremendous toll on her and her family. What she said on the phone could not have surprised me more.

"There's a good place for your mother here in Nyack. It's affiliated with the hospital where I work, so I think I can get her in if we move fast while this window is open. I'd be able to keep an eye on her."

I was so stunned that for a moment, I didn't speak.

"Jessica?" Grace said.

"She's not your responsibility."

"I know. But it feels like my turn."

I took the phone from Raj, but before I could tell Vera about Grace's proposal, she said she had something to tell me. She'd taken a phone call for Cynthia from the Chair of the English department at Yale. Vera gave me a quick summary. She hadn't said anything yet to Cynthia.

I picked up my handbag and grabbed a face mask from where we hung them on the key rack in the kitchen.

"Can I go with you?" Raj asked.

I gave him a hug. "No. I think I need to do this alone."

When I came into the apartment, Vera was standing in the foyer. It was hard to read her expression behind her mask, and I wondered how long she'd been waiting for me. It had taken an hour to get an Uber willing to drive me into Manhattan, even with all the windows open on a sultry August day.

Vera gestured toward the living room. "I told her you were coming."

I hadn't seen Cynthia in person since the beginning of April when the warnings about spreading Covid, especially to those with compromised immune systems, had become truly dire. Now, I looked at her from six feet across the room, sitting in her favorite chair, an Afghan over her legs. Where my mother had once been formidable, she now looked diminutive and defeated. Only her eyes above the mask remained clear and penetrating. A reminder of who she had been.

I stood at a safe distance and waited to see if Cynthia would speak. We'd had weekly phone calls after I'd met Grace, but I'd done all the talking. Either my mother's ability to find words had deteriorated even further since then, or she had nothing more to say.

Vera's voice came from behind me, quiet but firm. "I think you may want to tell her now."

I took a step closer, and Cynthia shrank back, her fragile body sinking into the fluffy cushions of the chair.

"Matthew Sheldrake is dead." Cynthia shuddered but remained silent.

"His department chair called this morning. Do you want to know what he said?"

She looked away but nodded.

"He said Sheldrake had suffered from emphysema for many years. When he got COVID, his lungs were already so compromised that there was no way to save him. He was admitted to Yale New Haven last week and was on a ventilator for a few days." I knew from the news reports that hospitals were not allowing any visitors. Maybe Sheldrake would have been alone in the end anyway. Certainly, the two children he had fathered wouldn't have been at his side. In a parallel universe, would Cynthia have been with him to hold his hand and hear his last words?

Cynthia looked at me, but her expression was inscrutable. I wondered for the hundredth time whether Matthew Sheldrake had been the love of her life or a man who'd used her and been used in return. I was so lost in thought that I was surprised at the sound of her voice. Her tone was agitated, but I couldn't make out the words.

"It's very hard to understand her with the mask on," Vera said.

"What did you say, Cynthia?" I tried.

She spoke again, a little louder. "Writing?"

I was baffled by the question. "Am I writing? Yes. You know I am." I'd presented my idea for the book to her and gotten her buy-in as best I could. I was sure Monica had as well. I didn't feel like I needed to interview my mother; the book was my take on her poetry, her life, and how she had affected my life. I didn't want to get sued for defamation, so I'd cleared the major disclosures with her and with Grace. I hadn't gotten permission from Sheldrake to reveal that he was my father, but that was a moot point now.

Cynthia spoke again, possibly the clearest, most complete sentence I'd heard since she had the stroke. "What are you writing about me?"

So that's what she wanted to know. How would she come out in the book? What would people think? Would I exonerate her?

They were the questions I'd been asking myself all along, and the answers were evolving. I told her what I knew.

"I'll write that you tried to love, but you didn't try hard enough. That you reserved your most ferocious and purest passion for your art. That you suffered, but you chose to let your wounds fester and to inflict pain instead of healing. That you were very strong and very weak, and despite your weakness, you have a strong daughter. No. Two strong daughters."

Cynthia put her head in her hands. The muffled sound of her sobs reached me across the room.

I turned to go. As I walked past the piano, it beckoned to me. I sat on the bench and took several deep breaths. Then I played Chopin's prelude No. 4 in E minor, the last piece I'd learned before Sasha, and then Cynthia, had taken music away from me. My fingers fumbled, but my heart remembered.

The End

ACKNOWLEDGMENTS

One of the greatest misconceptions about writing is that it is a solitary pursuit. Although the hard work of putting the words down on paper is something no one else can do for you, everything else necessary to bring a book into the world is a group effort. I would be honored if you would take a few moments and let me share with you the people who made *Jessica Harmon Has Stepped Away* possible. And if I've missed someone, which I'm certain to have, I apologize sincerely.

Thank you to everyone at Orange Hat/Ten16 Press for publishing the novel. The crew there—Michael T. Braun, owner and editor-in-chief; Katie Ramos, editor; Dana Breunig, cover designer; Dionna Hayden, interior designer—are talented, kind, responsive, and patient. I could not have had a better experience. And a special thank you to Michael for giving a second home to my middle grade novel, *My Name Is Layla*, which was published a few years ago but went out of print. I hope readers will open their hearts to both books.

It's wonderful to be working with my publicist Caitlin Hamilton Summie again. Her dedication is unmatched. Thank you to Jane Rosenman for her invaluable advice on the manuscript early on.

Thank you, as always, to my brother-in-law Stephen Friedgood for designing and maintaining my website and for helping me with all things technical. Thanks also for the new author photo; not an easy task to make me look good!

Thank you to Colleen Rowland, the newest member of my team, for her creativity and hard work, and for making the world of Instagram more accessible.

There aren't enough words to thank the talented writers in my writing group. They have pored over every word of this manuscript as it was written over a three-year period, sharing their good humor, insight, and deep knowledge of human nature to bring out the best in the story. Steve Lewis, our fearless and revered leader, and Art Bell, Jerry Brody, Lynn Edelson, Lisa Mayer, Ed McCann, Marshall Messer, Nan Mutnick, and Jessica Rao–you are all the best.

So many in the writing community have helped me reach this day, from those who willingly advised on agents or publishers to those who read the novel before publication and shared their good words on my behalf. Thank you so much to Karen Dukess, Brooke Foster, Jackie Friedland, Robert Gwaltney, Elise Kipness, Annabel Monaghan, Allison Pataki, Amy Poeppel, Marilyn Rothstein, Susie Schnall, and Rochelle Weinstein. Your generosity floors me.

To my husband Pierre and my children, Ariella and Micah— you inspire me every day. I treasure the family we have built together and the love we share.

BOOK GROUP QUESTIONS

1. Do you think Jessica made the right choice to go on the tour with Cynthia?

2. In what ways do you think Jessica changed over the course of the book?

3. Did you see Cynthia changing as well?

4. Was Jessica's transformation dependent on the time she and her mother spent together on the tour and during Cynthia's convalescence? Or were there other factors?

5. How would you describe the dynamics of Jessica and Penny's friendship?

6. How was Jessica affected by growing up without a father?

7. Did discovering the truth about her father provide healing for Jessica, or was it too little, too late?

8. Cynthia's never married, but always had lovers. How did her attitudes and behavior affect Jessica's approach to love?

9. Why do you think Jessica was reluctant to get involved with Raj, despite her physical and intellectual attraction to him?

10. What was the turning point where Jessica began to trust Raj and her feelings for him?

11. Is Cynthia simply a monster? Or is there more to her character?

12. How does Cynthia's illness change the dynamic between mother and daughter?

13. Why does Jessica attempt the role of dutiful daughter, moving in and taking care of Cynthia?

14. Why does Jessica share the story of what happened with her piano teacher with Grace?

15. What does Jessica get out of her relationships with Donna, Vera, and Penny's parents? Is there a theme that ties them together?

16. What do the scenes that take place in Cynthia's office tell us about secrets, control, and the importance of place?

17. Raj says to Jessica: "At some point, I decided not to remain a victim of my past. It's so freeing. I hope you get to that place too." Do you think that Raj diagnosed Jessica's problem correctly?

18. How is Jessica's experience of discovering the truth about her mother's time at Yale in 1969 impacted by Cynthia's inability to tell her own story?

19. Grace advises Jessica to step away from her mother's grief and live her own life. Does Jessica take her counsel?

20. At the end of the novel, Jessica is writing a memoir about herself and Cynthia. What lessons do you think Jessica will draw for her readers? Will the tone of the book be bitter, angry, hopeful?

ABOUT THE AUTHOR

 Reyna Marder Gentin grew up on Long Island and attended Yale College and Yale Law School. A former criminal defense attorney, she is the author of two prior legal romances, *Unreasonable Doubts* and *Both Are True*, as well as a middle grade novel, *My Name Is Layla*. Reyna's personal essays and short stories have been published widely in print and online, and she is currently working on a collection of linked short stories entitled Open Twenty-Four Hours. Reyna lives with her family in Westchester County, New York. Please find out more by visiting reynamardergentin.com.